Spy Tails

002

BarbarianSpy

www.BarbarianSpy.com

This book is copyright © habu 2014
habu asserts his right to be known as the author of this work..
Published by BarbarianSpy in 2014
Cover design © S Bush 2014
Cover image: All Manipulated: man with gun Copyright: gosphotodesign at Depositphotos, snowscene Copyright: mazzzur at Depositphotos.com,
Print ISBN: 978-1-922187-80-2
E-book ISBN 978-1-922187-77-2
All rights reserved

BarbarianSpy
Jindalee St
Toronto, NSW 2283
AUSTRALIA

Spy Tails

002

by

habu

Table of Contents

Introduction

In this second volume of spy tales delving into the use of male-on-male sex in the espionage operations of nations, habu adds seventeen stories focusing on how the vulnerabilities and desires of men to couple with other men lead them—and others—to become embroiled in the world of spying.

The dirty little truth is that the easiest, most assured way of collecting intelligence is not torture. It, rather, is the "giving" to someone who knows what you want to know what they want most, in exchange for the information they know. And it is in being especially prepared to do so if what they want the most is illicit—that is, for instance, connected to male homosexuality. And you can be assured they will give you the most useful information and continue to give it to you if you are continuing to give them what they want to have—but cannot acknowledge they have gotten, or want to have. Having taken them this far, you can hold over their heads the threat of collapsing their whole world if they don't continue to cooperate.

This, easiest and most assured, way of collecting intelligence has been used as such down through the ages. In this second part of his spy stories anthology, habu, takes you, the reader, with him to the underbelly of the world of spying.

This anthology introduces you to a special unit within U.S. intelligence that is informally known as the Candy Store unit, with its five sections: male on female, female on male, male on male, female on female, and anything goes. This anthology concentrates on stories of the male-on-male section.

If you enjoy this collection and wish to read more of how men-on-men sex is used to gather intelligence and carry out espionage operations, be sure to check out the first book in the series as well, habu's *Spy Tails 001*.

* * * *

These seventeen stories show an aspect of intelligence work very much in the vein of Graham Greene and John LeCarré but delving into spy craft operations that go well beyond where either of these authors dared to go. The reality of spying is that it isn't all Agent 007 glamour. There is a nasty, cynical, and even arousingly sexual underbelly to it, and these stories don't shy away from showing that, or from ignoring the difficult questions of the morality of taking advantage of the vulnerability and weakness of men who have a weakness for men in the pursuit of chits in the power games of nations. These stories not only show the substance of spy craft, but they also show how men are suborned to be Candy Store agents and then how they use other men to extract what their handlers want.

As in *Spy Tails 001*, the first volume, *Spy Tails 002* includes stories linked to habu's "fantasization" of a Candy Story unit of the CIA under the management of one Sam Winterberry, and, specifically, the man-on-man section of that unit. Winterberry appears in "The Invisible Man" and "The Refusal." One of the earliest of Winterberry's agents habu has written about, Silas Collins, appears in "The Brigade."

Two stories, "Sword of Zara" and "Thorodian Horses," both set in mystical ancient island kingdoms in the Mediterranean, are included to evidence that spying is the second-oldest human institution. A much more recent historical piece, "Saigon," is set in the waning days of the U.S. presence in Vietnam. "The Message" is set in the Burma—now known as Myanmar—of the oppressive and isolated New Win regime.

Stories can be historical, but history currently being created is also included, such as "The Syrian Rent-Boy," which is as fresh as the Syrian regime's murderous policies toward its own people and today's newspaper headlines. "Nuclear Meltdown" cashes in on North Korean unpredictability and threat in the nuclear arms race.

"The Negotiator" concerns industrial, rather than political, espionage, and "The Refusal" merges industrial and political intrigue. Although all of the stories reveal means and methods of spy operations, "Staying Retired" and "The Golden Question" delve more directly into the research techniques of it, and "Scourged," "The Ambassador's Son," "The Glass Cube," and "The Invisible Man" focus on ground-level operational aspects.

"The Art of It" is a somewhat tongue-in-cheek illustration of how sex agents are suborned as in "The Trouble with Dirk" is in showing how this can be botched up.

If your penchant is to read of far-off lands, *Spy Tails 002* will satisfy you with its round-the-world journey in foreign settings. "Saigon," "The Brigade," and "The Message" are set in Southeast Asia; "The Invisible Man" and "The Refusal" are set in Africa; "The Ambassador's Son" and "The Syrian Rent-Boy" occur in the Middle East; "The Glass Cube" and "The Golden Question" are set on the island of Cyprus, with "Sword of Zara" and "Thorodian Horse" located on mythical Mediterranean islands; and "Nuclear Meltdown," "Scourged," "The Negotiator," and "The Trouble with Dirk" unveil their action in Europe. "Staying Retired" and "The Art of It" play out in the United States.

If you are interested in the intersection of spy craft and man-on-man action, both volumes of habu's *Spy Tails* should be on your "must read" list.

Of course, it's all fiction.

Nuclear Meltdown

It was all happening so fast. I didn't even have time to feel panic. I just felt a dullness and a foreboding—and a creeping sense of being trapped in a web of some sort. No, more like a cocoon, the sticky thread winding around and around me. Smothering me.

"Just a few minutes, Dr. Winthrop, and you can go back to your room. I know this has been a shock to you. We have just a few more questions tonight, but most can wait until tomorrow. I suggest that you try to get some rest tonight."

"I have a lecture . . . a lecture to give tomorrow afternoon," I replied, looking at the police detective, Adolf Stander. He had been very efficient and solicitous—and respectful. He obviously was very good at this. The Swiss, I am sure, have high-level international situations well in hand and quickly, and with the highest level of discretion. The special Einsatzgruppe Tigris arm of the Swiss Federal Criminal Police arrived at the Lucerne Radisson Blu hotel and conference center and took over the investigation within a half hour of the murder.

"You did say that this isn't your room, didn't you? That it was that of the victim, Dr. Pak Jong-hee?"

"Yes, yes, of course. We were conferring on some notes, here in Dr. Pak's room . . . in preparation for delegation talks tomorrow morning before the afternoon lecture sessions.

And . . . and . . . the assailant . . . just burst in. He went right for Pak. It was over in seconds."

I had to concentrate, try not to hyperventilate. I had to be careful not to say too much. I felt like I was spiraling down already—being sucked down into a vortex.

"And Dr. Pak is North Korean, right, not South Korean? And you're American?"

"Yes, yes, that's right. Nuclear physicists. Advisers both. We had met before. We leave the political negotiations to the principals. We just advise on technical issues."

Oh, god, if that only were true, I thought. How did I let myself get involved in this? Where was Frank? Shouldn't he just be sweeping in here and handling everything? They'd told me that it was just about over. That Pak wanted to defect.

"Perhaps I should speak with the respective delegation head," Standler said. "After," he continued, "after they've come for the . . . ah, yes, here they come now."

I'd been sitting, quaking, on the bed all of the time that the detective was hovering around me. And the body was there, right there on the floor. I could have turned away. I should have turned away. But I couldn't. The knife was still inside him, in his gut, the handle protruding, his eyes open, looking at me. With such a look of surprise. Accusing me.

But I'd done nothing. This wasn't anything like I did. I don't know why I'd even been caught up in this. Frank hadn't told me that anything like this could happen. But, yes, I did know why.

It was my damning weakness.

* * * *

It had been those years in the Air Force in Thailand. The Thai men were so nubile, brown as a berry, and willing. Always the winning smile, the readiness to please.

I'd thought I had put all of that behind me. I'd returned to the university when I'd left the Air Force and continued my studies in nuclear physics. A good professorship had led to government contracts, work that went ever deeper into government scientific and defense projects. And as the work had deepened, it had grown more secret, requiring ever higher security clearances.

The bubble had burst one evening in the sauna of a Georgetown men's gym.

I had seen him when I was working out on the exercise floor. All smiles, just like those young men years ago in Bangkok. He was Thai, of course, and small, and brown, bordering on effeminate, but perfectly formed. And he moved like a dancer. He was doing some sort of Oriental slow-movement exercises, showing a fantastically flexible body. And he had his eyes on me, giving me saucy looks. Gazes that took me back to the Patpong tenderloin district of Bangkok—and to all those talented and willing young men.

I left the gym floor and took a long shower. I was aroused. I couldn't deny that. And I was remembering those earlier days. But times had moved on. I even was married now. Although when it came to arousal, my desires went back to earlier days.

I wrapped a towel around my waist and went into the sauna room. A young, muscle-bound man in the club's signature shorts and T-shirt was standing by the door of the sauna when I went in. I hadn't seen him there before, but he gave me a friendly smile as if we had met.

"We were closing early tonight, professor," he said. "But the front desk said you could stay as long as you wanted. Just close the outer door when you leave."

I thought that was nice of them—and trusting, which later gave me a bitter laugh. And I did want the session in the sauna.

He handed me another, large and high-pile towel, and I went into the sauna and laid that out on the top bench, opposite the door, and stretched out full length on my back. The heat of the sauna was soothing, and I was drifting between feeling the tension draining from my body and semiconsciousness.

I didn't hear him enter the sauna. The first indication I had that I wasn't alone was when I felt his hands on my calves, below my knees, gently spreading my legs. I looked down in surprise. It was the berry-brown, nubile Thai, and he was

13

looking up between my legs, under the towel, and he was smiling.

"Umm, so big," he said, fluttering his eyelashes. "Me like. Me like a lot."

He was moving his hands on my legs, gently massaging. I was frozen there, in shock. All, of course, except for my cock, which was engorging.

"I saw you in the exercise room," he whispered. "And I tell myself that one handsome man. I bet he has big cock. I bet I like to fuck with that man. And the look you gave me. I knew you want to fuck with me too. You fuck Thai men before, I bet."

I moaned.

"So I stay behind when they close up up front. I know you still back here. We fuck fuck, OK?"

"Sorry, I think I'd better . . ." I started to say, and I sat up, ready to leave—or at least try to. But he already had the big toe of one of my feet in his mouth, and the palm of a hand high up and inside my thigh.

I tried to gather my strength, knowing I needed to leave. But the hand was tantalizing. My brain was screaming its want, its need for the hand to rise higher. And then it did, encircling my cock, and I laid back with a groan, letting every sensation point inside me race to my penis. His hand worked me for a few minutes while I closed my eyes and covered my face with an arm and fought with my desires. When I felt the wetness of his lips and mouth pull me inside him, I groaned and gave up any struggle, giving myself fully over to the pleasure of the suck.

When I opened my eyes, he had reversed himself on me and his sweet little buttocks and a pert cock and balls were right there at my face, ready for my attention and preparation. I ran a hand between his legs, pulled his cock back through, and moved between licking and sucking on his pulsing hole and on his cock.

He wound up on his tailbone on the top step, legs splayed, and me between those legs and rising and falling on the balls of my feet on the lower bench as I fucked him in a slow, slow, fast, slow, slow rhythm that had him murmuring "fuck me, fuck me, fuck me," in a singsong little voice.

They let me come before the two men—one of them the young man who handed me the towel when I entered the sauna—burst into the room and flashed their federal government badges in my face.

The young Thai man at least had the decency to tell me he was sorry and that he'd thoroughly enjoyed the fucking. He said I had the biggest cock of anyone who had plowed him.

They sweated me for two days on the dire consequences on my career and private life of what I had been caught doing. On the third day, they informed me that there was an out. I was scheduled to attend U.S.-North Korean nuclear proliferation talks in Beijing as a scientific adviser later in the year. I could save my career by helping them convince a North Korean nuclear physicist who had a proclivity for men of my age and physique—and an extra big cock, as I had—to defect to the United States.

"When we approached him, he asked for you by name," one of the interrogators said.

They would arrange the encounters. I wouldn't even have to seduce him. All I would have to do is service his sexual needs and act as a go-between. He would know that I was there to service him when we first met. A piece of cake. Very little to do to save my career. And I'd even enjoy it. He was a well-turned-out small-stature Asian man. And I had already proven my weakness for such men.

I racked my brain trying to figure out who this might be. I had been at a few meetings with the North Koreans—and the last time we'd met in Beijing, any of the men who wanted to could go to a traditional Turkish bath, where we were naked, and there were some North Koreans there. But, again, I don't remember any of them showing particular interest in me—other than that I did get attention for the size of my equipment whenever I was in a communal shower or locker room. I had grown accustomed to that, though.

When we next met in Beijing, I had no trouble picking him out. His name was Pak Jong-hee, and although he was a senior scientist and was shown extra deference by his North

Korean delegation during the meetings, he was young and small, lithe, and brown—and he made my cock harden knowing that I was meant to fuck him.

I don't remember having seen him at an earlier conference—especially at the Beijing session where several of the men were naked together in the Turkish bath. This was surprising, because he was strikingly attractive to me. Of course, until my handlers had forced an encounter in the sauna in Georgetown, I had pretty successfully suppressed my desire for men—even small, boyish ones like Pak.

He obviously had noticed me. As Frank, my handler had promised, it was fairly obvious that arrangements had already been made with him—and most likely that he had picked me. He frequently looked at me and lowered his eyes demurely in a signal from young Oriental men indicating that they wanted to be mastered.

On the third day of the negotiations, which weren't going well and from which the North Korean delegation had absented itself, Frank told me to prepare myself well, which I did. I was conducted to the same steamy, decorative tile-covered Turkish bath chamber that I had been entertained in during a previous Beijing conference.

When I got to the door of the bath, Frank and another U.S. delegation member who was there purely for security purposes were waiting for me. I was wearing only a silk robe and sandals. As I was ushered through the door, my robe was taken off my back.

"Remember, we want him to be very happy and satisfied," Frank murmured as I passed him. "We will handle the discussions with him on where it goes from here. If he wishes to take our offer, you will be assigned together and you will be servicing him as often as he wants it. Remember, your career is on the line here too."

"Protection or not?" I asked. When I had been suborned, there had been no protection; it had been completely impromptu—and frenzied.

"Packets, already slit, on the side of the pool."

Packets, I thought. More than one. Oh, god. Could I stand up to the challenge? I was quite a bit older than I had been in Thailand—when I could take three sweet young men in quick succession.

At first I thought I was the first of several to arrive. But that was not so. I was the second and last to arrive. Pak Jong-hee was already sitting on a subterranean tiled bench in the octagon-shaped pool. He was staring at me—or rather, at what was swinging between my legs—and he was giving me a sultry smile.

I saw the pile of condom packets and a bottle of lubricant in a tray on the pool side beside where he was sitting.

I slipped my sandals off and slowly walked to the pool and down the steps into the pool at the opposite side from where he sat, eyes glued to my midsection and a sloppy grin on his mouth.

I had my balls and the root of my cock cupped in one of my hands as I walked. I was filling out as I saw him lift his hips to the surface of the water and show that he was in full, curved erection.

When I had approached him in the water, which came up to above my knees and would be where the tip of my cock would touch if I was not in erection myself, Pak smiled, placed the palms of his hands on my buttocks, and pulled me on to his swallowing mouth. He was a master of the suck, and I groaned and moaned as he deep-throated me and worried my piss slit with his tongue.

After fifteen minutes or so of his expert attention to my cock, I reached down and lifted him out of the water, laid him on his back, hooked his legs on my hips, and moved my mouth to his cock, balls, and hole.

He was begging for it in nearly flawless English—with a fine grasp of the crudities of gay male sex—when he took the initiative to crown my cock with a condom and stroke that and his entrance with lubricant.

That was as much control as I allowed him, though. I knew the looks he had given me during the conference. He wanted to be mastered.

Still standing, I lifted him up and set him down on my cock. He clung to me—small and lithe and flexible—as I grabbed his buttocks, spread the cheeks, and pulled him up and down on my cock. I was fucking only at half depth, but Pak was moaning to beat the band.

I laid him back down on the side of the pool and started plowing him deep and fast and hard. He writhed under me and cried out—but he was crying for it, not asking for mercy—and dug his fingernails into my shoulders and my chest. He came quickly after that. I pulled the condom off and came on his belly.

We held there for several minutes as he worked my cock back up with his hands. He whimpered for it and I turned him belly down to the tiles, crouched over him, and reached for a condom packet.

"No rubber," he whispered. "I'm clean. I want it all the way."

OK, I thought. I remembered what Frank said: whatever he wants. Pak got it all the way in one long, deep, skin-on-skin thrust. He wailed like a stuck pig for the next twenty minutes, but each time I offered to let up or stop, he commanded me to fuck him harder. I complied as best I could. And from the way he was stretched out, not moving, just moaning, when I put my sandals on and left the bath, I could report to Frank that his pigeon must be well satisfied.

Over the next year, we found ourselves sitting behind the same negotiations table three times. And each time Frank and his crew managed to get us alone for a "negotiations" session of our own.

This is what brought us to the fifth floor room at the Lucerne Radisson Blu conference center. Not Pak's room, really—or mine—but one that Pak had managed to book separately. Frank had made arrangements in the shower of the men's gym in the hotel—where indeed, I entered a shower where Pak already was and fucked him from behind against the wet tiles of the shower. But afterward, Pak had said he had made arrangements of his own.

Only when I got to the room did I realize Frank probably didn't even know about it. Always before he and another member of his team or two was lurking somewhere in the vicinity. He wasn't there this time. But Frank had clearly told me to give Pak what he wanted—saying they were very close to defection day. So, I met Pak in the room.

And I was giving him what he wanted on the bed, when the assailant—another Korean, I don't know whether a South Korean wanting to neutralize a North Korean nuclear expert or a North Korean realizing Pak was about to defect—burst into the room.

Both men had knifes. I don't know how Pak had gotten his so quickly.

Within seconds, I was alone, with one dead Korean on the floor and the other giving me explicit directions and then gone as well.

* * * *

The body was gone. Detective Standler was gone—consulting, no doubt with the heads of both the North Korean and American delegations, working on smoothing this over, making as much of it go away as possible. The lab technicians were gone—for a coffee break. They'd be back.

I had stopped trembling enough to be able to rise up off the bed, dressed but quickly and sloppily so—I'm sure Detective Standler had tuned into that.

I started for the door to leave and go back to my room. But the door to the adjoining room was open. A naked Pak Jong-hee was lounging against the door frame and giving me a shy smile.

"They will find out quickly it isn't you," I mumbled, still in shock.

"We have time. Come into this room. They'll never know. You can go back to your room in a while and pack."

"Pack?" I asked, as I permitted him to reach out and take me by the arm and guide me into an identical room next to the murder room.

"Who was that you killed? We can't just . . . they think it's you." I was burbling, but I'd just seen a man killed. This was way out of my frame of reference.

"This is perfect for the defection," Pak said. "By the time they realize it isn't me, we'll be over the Italian border."

"The Italian border?" I said weakly. This was all moving too fast. But I seemed to be the only one without a program.

"Come over here," Pak said in the seductive voice that my dick had been programmed to jerk erect at.

He pushed me down into a seated position on the side of the bed. His hands went to the waistband of my trousers, and he jerked them off in one long pull. My cock jumped erect, hitting him in the cheek.

"To Italy? Who, what?" I asked, as he pushed my legs apart and knelt between my thighs.

"Oh, gawd. Oh holy, shit," I exclaimed as his mouth lowered over my cock. He was embracing my waist in his arms. I wasn't going anywhere for a while.

But he said we were going to Italy. He must have a car at his disposal. What kind of defection was this? Frank? The Americans? Or . . . "Oh shit, the North Koreans?"

Who fuckin' was defecting here—to whom?

I thought I had cried it out. Challenged Pak with the question.

But I hadn't. I'd fallen back on the bed, my back arched, my hands clawing at the bedspread. He was working my cock and swallowing my balls. All I could do was moan.

I heard the door open, and two men entered the room. They were still in the shadow of the doorway and I was watching closely to see them come into the light. Were they Koreans or Americans?

Saigon

I was nearly ready, very close to coming. Nguyen had already come. I had felt him stiffen, knowing he was about to come, and had put my hands under him, raising his belly off the sheets with the palm of one hand and encasing his hard cock with the other and stroking him until he had spilled his seed. And then I had taken him by the waist and lowered his midsection on the mattress again and resumed my slow, deep stroking inside him. I covered his brown little body with mine, my arms laced up under his arm pits, my legs covering his, with his feet hooked on my lower calves, my lips buried in the hollow of his neck when he wasn't turning his lips to mine.

Mosquitoes buzzed angrily against the protective netting that covered my bed, centered in the room to catch whatever cross breeze could be captured in the hot, humid Vietnamese night. The rain was coming down in sheets outside the bungalow, sounding like the low roar of a train passing by in the distance. Candles flickered in the corner of the room, their light being reflected and scattered by the slowly churning ceiling fan above the foot of the bed. A gecko ran across the top of the headboard, stopping momentarily to watch the fucking and then go its merry way.

I turned my head and looked up into the roof of the canopied bed, at the mirror I'd had installed when I took Nguyen on as my lover—when he had introduced me to the pleasures of man sex in Southeast Asia—so much more sensuous and guilt free than I had known before—and I became besotted with watching my larger, muscled body, working his lithe, little brown one or his succulent mouth working my cock before I took him. Appearing in the mirror to have full control, to be ravishing a small, powerless man, but knowing all along that Nguyen was the experienced one, the one who was in full control.

I concentrated hard as I watched myself in the mirror—me holding every part of him still, with only my butt cheeks expanding and contracting, listening for the moan, watching for the moment that Nguyen's hips began to rotate, when his butt cheeks slowly moved in rhythm with mine, not other parts of our bodies moving, knowing that my cock was buried deep inside him. Watching for the moment of my release and the effect it had on his body, the expression on his face, half turned to where I could see it, his cheek rubbing the fine, moist cotton of the pillow casing.

Nguyen gave a little cry as my flow started, and I thought I heard another sound simultaneously—a rustling or a scraping outside the bedroom window of my Saigon bungalow. Maybe both. There shouldn't be anything stirring out there in the downpour. All of the usual night creatures out there knew to just wait a quarter hour and the rain would stop and they could come out onto the fetid earth of their playground once more.

"Shh, little one," I whispered, and I placed my hand over his mouth to stifle further noise. "I think I heard something."

Nguyen's body stiffened, as aware of the possibilities as I was, and he rolled out from underneath me and over the side of the bed to the floor as I reached under my pillow for my pistol, and he reached, at the same time, as he landed gracefully and noiseless on the teak flooring, for the M-16 I kept there beside the bed.

I rolled to the floor on the other side of the bed, staying inside the netting, to the great disappointment of the night insects. We lay there, on opposite sides of the bed, breathing heavily for several minutes. But the moment passed;

there were no other unexpected night sounds competing with the chirping of the crickets that started up the instant the rain stopped, abruptly, like the closing of a spigot, and I muttered an all clear—at least I thought it was clear—to Nguyen, and we came back up on the bed and embraced. But that moment was lost now too. Reality had struck, even if it was a false reality—for now—and we had been avoiding the inevitable discussion.

The recent weeks in Saigon had been nerve-racking. We knew now it was just a matter of time. Four weeks if the intelligence Nguyen had passed to me was accurate. The sleuthing he'd done in connection with his news reporting job had concluded that there would be an offensive against the Cam Ranh Bay installations and, if that was successful, soldiers would be streaming down to Saigon for the final coup d'état here. This information had become key to our plans for the defense of the South. Forces had been retained at Cam Ranh Bay that we initially planned to move down to Saigon. Increasingly the embassy staff had been pulled into the compound, not to return to their apartments or bungalows before the danger was past—although few even pretended this was anything other than the prelude to the end—in fear of the night and of what lurked there. I was one of the last still sleeping outside of the compound. And it was now obvious even to me, in my blinders-on optimism, that this would be my last night in this bed too.

I had been putting on an act that fooled only me—not wanting it to be over, so pretending that it wouldn't be, against all indications to the contrary.

That was a sad thought. I had found paradise here in this bed—with Nguyen Van Trinh, South Vietnamese journalist by day and my willing sex slave by night. Although that even was a lie; it was I who was Nguyen's sex slave. I never wanted this to end. But the North Vietnamese Army and the Viet Cong insurgents of the South obviously had very different views on that. And increasingly their views were the only ones that counted.

"You've been a major source of information for me, Nguyen," I whispered. "I've had you on the evacuation list for some time now. Come to the embassy with me in the morning.

23

I think this is it. And when I'm taken out, I want you to go with me. I've arranged for you to be on the list. Come away with me; I will take care of you."

"I must be in Thon Lac Nghiep tomorrow," Nguyen said. "My parents. They call and I must be there."

"We've discussed this before, Nguyen," I said. "I don't think you'll be safe when the Americans are gone. You've cooperated. You perhaps don't fully appreciate all you have told me—or who I work for. You must come out with me. I'll keep you with me. I promise."

"Perhaps, Jim," Nguyen answered, although I got the impression he was only humoring me. "You aren't safe here anymore. On that I agree. It is impossible to hide an American anywhere in Saigon now. You must move to the embassy compound, like the rest. I will come when I can—if I can."

"Promise? I love you. I don't want to lose you. You love me, don't you?"

Nguyen showed his feelings for me by pressing me on my back on the mattress and straddling my hips with his thighs and slowly riding my cock to another, mutual ejaculation, as I watched the languid movements of my lithe, brown lover in the mirror overhead.

In the morning, when I awoke, Nguyen was gone, as was the M-16. I didn't begrudge him that, though. If that got him to the sea and the village of Thon Lac Nghiep to the north of Saigon and then safely back to me again, I wanted him to have it.

I moved into the embassy compound that morning, and the next day we began the destruction of files. This went slowly, because all of us in the Station were called away for periodic Country Team meetings on the military situation. The military attaches kept saying that all indications were that North Vietnamese troops were moving toward Saigon, and, only the Station was holding out that they would divert to the coast, toward Cam Ranh Bay, before coming further south. They did that on the strength of my good source for the information—Nguyen.

Saigon, however, was in a panic. Helicopters were already shuttling back and forth from the embassy roof out to the battleships anchored off the coast with the embassy personnel deemed nonessential—their dependents having evacuated weeks earlier—and a large number of South Vietnamese officials and their families, people who had partnered with the U.S. forces in the futile effort to maintain a South Vietnamese Republic and who now were being evacuated because their loyalty was a death sentence for them, if—no, not if, when—the North Vietnamese took over in the South.

Back at the Station and working the shredders as fast as I could, I took a break when the shredder I was feeding overheated. I went out to the outer corridor to have a cigarette and to wait for the shredder to cool down. I had worked like a zombie all day, worried to death over Nguyen, and for that reason trying to turn my mind off and just sit there and feed sheet after sheet of top-secret paperwork into the shredder. Not for the first time I wondered why we'd created such a mountain of paper out of a losing cause. My hands trembled as I lit my cigarette, and my worries flooded my brain—wondering where he was and whether I should go back to my bungalow in case he was there. I was frantic to see him safely with the other Vietnamese we'd brought into the compound for evacuation.

He was so inscrutable; Nguyen had soldiered along as if the rending apart of his country had little to do with him. I worried that he just did not understand the danger he was in—particularly if the North Vietnamese ever learned how valuable he had been to us.

The windows in the corridor overlooked the front gates of the compound. A mass of humanity pressed at the gates, begging entrance, trying to claim a spot on the helicopters that were landing on the roof, loading, and then lifting up to bank sharply out toward the sea. Each approach and takeoff was different; there was no pattern—all because of the occasional sound of a rifle shot of a sniper taking a march on the arrival of the North Vietnamese and vying for a medal for shooting down a U.S. helicopter. And at each approach of a helicopter, the arms of those pressing the gate went up in the air, as if they could lift straight up into the copter. And each time an overloaded helicopter rose off the roof of the main embassy building, there was a massive sigh and sob that spread through the whole compound—knowing that one more opportunity for life had passed all still on the ground by.

We had lost a few helicopters—and thus some people, as well—but the pilots by now had become geniuses at avoiding more ambitious fire than this, and the snipers—probably the vanguard of the Viet Cong, composed mostly of young boys—were lousy shots—or were just firing for effect, not begrudging our departure but wanting us to soil our pants in the process.

As I stood at the window, seeing those pressing, five or six deep, on the main gates to the compound, their arms raised in supplication and their voices moaning pleas that I heard at this distance only as a whining cacophony of sound, I forced myself to look at individual faces. I would not see these people as just a mass; I needed to see them as individual people. I felt I owed that to them. They had believed in us, and we had failed them. And when I did this, I saw him. Nguyen. My Nguyen. He was at the outer fringe, too proud to beg and plead, but his eyes were raised to the building, searching, looking worried.

I ran through the building, my eyes already blurry from tears, and down to the beaten-earth outer courtyard inside the main gates. I called out to two of the Marine guards who were guarding the gates, ready, with M-16s raised before them, in case the gates collapsed and rioters had to be prevented from entering the main building. The Marines recognized me—and they knew I worked in the Station.

"One of ours is out there," I cried. "He's on the list. There, there, the young man at the back of the crowd, wearing the tan shorts and plaid shirt. Help me. We must let him in. He's on the list. We've got to let him in."

One of the Marines looked at me, helplessly. "We can't open the gates, Mr. Baxter. That would be disaster."

But the other Marine was whistling, trying to get Nguyen's attention. And he did. And when Nguyen saw the Marine, he also saw me and his eyes lit up and he started pushing his way into the crowd.

He'd gotten close to the gates, with both Marines now yelling for the others to let him through. And the crowd, indeed, was parting as well as it could to let Nguyen near the gate. And they were all pressing in on Nguyen, no doubt thinking that when the gates were opened for him, they'd all rush forward. None of them was thinking any further into the future than just getting through the gates. Once there, surely the Americans would give them sanctuary, would let them on the helicopters.

As Nguyen got to the gates, the Marine who had whistled cupped his hands, lowered them, and pushed them between the bars, yelling for Nguyen to step up into them, that they would somehow hoist him over the iron fencing, that they couldn't open the gates. But they would help boost him over.

Nguyen's eyes were on me, only on me, and he was calling to me. He was ignoring the frantic instructions the Marine was trying to give him. I moved to him at the gates. My face was just inches from him. I too was yelling at him to step up in the Marines cupped hands.

I must still have been crying, because Nguyen put a hand through the bars and gently brushed away my tears, and he said, "This is important Jim. Leave now. You all must leave now. One more day. That's all you have. It's not Cam Ranh Bay. It's here."

And then he was gone, swallowed up by the crowd. I didn't know whether he was on the ground, being trampled, or how he had just disappeared in an instance. Totally.

The Marine stood back from the fence and raised his hands and turned to me. He gave me a sad look and a shrug and, with a heavy heart, I thanked him for trying and trudged back to the main embassy building. I went straight to the chief of station—the COS—though, and told him that the same source who had informed us the assault would first be on the Cam Ranh Bay installations was now saying that the North Vietnamese plans had changed, that the main assault would be launched here, in Saigon. And most of our forces had been kept at Cam Ranh Bay.

The COS was unsure, and it was now impossible to reposition troops, but he could see that, regardless, it would be best to step up the embassy evacuation. We went straight to the ambassador, who pulled together the Country Team for the second time that day, and, after much wrangling, the call went out to the battleships.

Hours later, as we came out of the meeting, various advisers were still arguing over the need to double the helicopter flights, which would quadruple the danger of the flights, putting the helicopters in greater danger of sniper fire and, more significant, of crashing into each other.

But the COS drew our attention to the windows overlooking the front of the compound. Now there wasn't a single person at the front gates. The people of Saigon already knew. They knew it was too late to seek relief through the embassy. They were deserting the city—at least until it had been taken and it was safer to return.

I left on one of the last helicopters. Everyone we'd gathered in the compound had gotten out, but the shredding machines hadn't kept up with the time needed, and my helicopter lifted off from the embassy roof in dense smoke and flying ash from the bonfires we'd set in the courtyards to—we hoped and pretended—destroy as much of our mounds of secret paper as was necessary.

I was evacuated to Bangkok and set to work in the Station there, watching and reporting on the dying agony of Saigon from afar—and mourning my lost lover.

I spent too much time at the bar in the JUSMAG compound, the special forces U.S. military mission to Thai forces, where Major Carl Stevens, a seasoned commando, found me and took me back to his billet and fucked me throughout a weekend until I broke down and told him why I was so morose—how my Vietnamese lover, a valuable asset to U.S. intelligence, had simply slipped through my fingers at the gates of the U.S. embassy in Saigon.

Rough and tough on the outside, Stevens was gentle and caring on the inside. We became almost inseparable, and I gladly took comfort in opening my legs to him and found peace and a numbness to the ghost of Nguyen as he made slow, languid love to me.

One morning over breakfast I turned to him and said, "I know I've been a mess, Carl. I'm grateful for all you've done for me. And you are a great lover . . ."

"But," he said.

"Yes, but," I answered. "I can't get Nguyen out of my mind. I'm not really like this. I've been a burden on you. But . . ."

"But there isn't going to be anything but good, casual fucking between us while we're both here in Bangkok," he finished.

"Yes," I answered in a voice full of regret. "I don't want you to—"

"He's alive, and he's back in his village at Thon Lac Nghiep," Carl said.

"Excuse me?" I asked, confused.

"Nguyen. Nguyen Van Trinh. We still have sources in Vietnam. I traced him for you. We can get him out if you want. I have a team going into Vietnam not far from there anyway—on another Op. Thon Lac Nghiep is right there on the coast. If you go with us and talk him into leaving, we can bring him out this time. Off the books, but my CO knows I'm making the offer. If he was a valuable U.S. asset, he shouldn't be left behind any more than we would one of our Marine buddies."

And that was that. That was why several weeks later, wearing camouflage and smeared with black grease, I was hunched outside a window of a native hut at the edge of Thon Lac Nghiep, watching Nguyen's family closing their activities down for the night, going to their own bungalows, and leaving Nguyen alone in his.

I watched him strip, lay down on his matting, turn down his lamp, arrange the mosquito net around himself, and close his eyes. And I wanted him then more than I'd ever wanted him before.

He started to let out a surprised cry when I came down on his body with mine, but I covered his mouth, first with my hand and then my lips, and he wrapped his arms around me, and we moved slowly into our old familiar embrace and rhythms. He reached down and unbuttoned my fly and fished out my cock. I was possessing his mouth, pushing my tongue in as he opened his legs and hooked his heels on the back of my knees and I slid deep into an old familiar sheathing. And then our pelvises were moving in synch and after many glorious moments of becoming one, precision-timed machine, we came almost simultaneously.

We were still panting our release when Nguyen whispered, "You cannot be here. You must go. It's death for both of us."

"I cannot leave you here, Nguyen." I murmured. "I came back for you. They'll learn you worked with the Americans. You'll be executed."

"No, no, you do not understand," Nguyen muttered insistently. "That's not how it is. I have an honored position here."

"Only until they find out. You must come out with me. I have friends . . . and a boat. And there's a ship—"

"I don't want to hear this," Nguyen said, louder, with anger in his voice. "You don't want to tell me this. You don't understand."

I lifted my head from his and, still holding him close, looked down in his face. I had been so stupid.

"You are one of them, aren't you?" I said in a wounded voice. "You are Viet Cong. You were playing me."

"Yes, I am VC. And I was sent to give you misinformation. To have sex with you and make you trust me and listen to me and make as many of the troops guarding Saigon to stay in Cam Ranh Bay as possible. But that's not all."

"What else is there?" I asked dully. My whole world had collapsed. "What else can there be? I have a knife. I could kill you right here. You know that?"

"Yes, I know that," he answered. But I could discern no fear in his voice. I wanted this to make him scared. I wanted to wound him, as his act of betrayal had wounded me. "But I don't think you will," he said

"Why? Why can you be so sure?"

"For the same reason that I came back to tell you to leave right away. I didn't come back to Saigon to go with you. I came back to send you away in time. And for the same reason that I am going to let you leave here and not report that you have been here. Because, my duty aside, I love you and always will—I'm just from another world, our two worlds now no longer touching. Perhaps someday, but not now."

"And I cannot kill you for the same reason," I said at length. I said it for me, though, not for Nguyen. He was a far wiser man than I was. He already knew. And being wiser than me, he knew I would have to leave him now and not look back. Our worlds were too far apart—perhaps not forever, but, as he wisely said, certainly for now.

Scourged

The heavy steel door clanged shut behind me, and I stood there, trembling, knowing what I faced, holding my stack of two towels, a change of clothes, a tooth brush and tube of toothpaste, and, both inexplicably and ominously, a small stack of condoms in front of me as if they'd shield me. I knew, however, that they wouldn't.

The light was dim at first, although I knew my eyes would soon adjust to it. And when they did I wouldn't be able to go out into the courtyard from my few minutes of blessed sunshine without squinting my watering eyes.

I could sense him—and smell him—the smell of Dentyne that would soon become so familiar to me even before I could see him, hulking there beside the metal bunk beds.

Then it started.

He reached out and grabbed my drab-gray shirt by the lapels and, my stack of precious possessions dashing to the floor, pulled me to him, so that, for a brief moment we were face to face and I could clearly see his cruel smile. And then he turned me and literally threw me into the bottom bunk, causing it to screech in shock and disapproval and for my head to hit the solid concrete-block wall.

Dazed by the blow to the head, I heard him mutter, "Just what the doctor ordered," and I whimpered in fear and frustration as he struggled with my zipper and stripped my trousers off my legs. Then I was screaming and grunting and groaning while he was beating at me with a leather scourge in one hand and stuffing his hard cock into my channel with the other. I spread and lifted my legs, digging the pads of my feet in the metal framing overhead and my fists in the springs below the top bunk as Mir Rhutani, Iranian terrorist mastermind, gave me the first taste of what life in his prison cell was going to be like for weeks to come.

"Scream as loud as you want, Pretty Boy," he growled. "They get paid well to look the other way. You are bought and paid for."

And to think that I had half way volunteered for this.

* * * *

Two weeks before I had been working on personal contact files, reports on meetings with in-place agents and possible intelligence targets, in the embassy in Cairo, when the chief of station had called me into his office. He wasn't alone. Two other men were there, one in a suit and one in a military uniform, dripping with shiny metal and ribbons. All three scrutinized me closely as I walked into the room.

"Yes, yes, just what the doctor ordered," said the military uniform.

"Well, if he's willing, of course," said the suit, looking and sounding a little dubious.

"Come on in, Philip. This is Philip Menlow, gentleman, newly arrived from the States. Part of the special services unit, so that part is certainly covered. When you sent out your message looking for a very particular volunteer, he came immediately to mind. A very capable young man."

All three men were looking at me intently, as if it was my turn to talk.

"You are ready for your first special services assignment, aren't you, Philip?" the chief of station broke the silence and asked.

Only a couple of days later I was on an airplane for Frankfurt, from there to be driven—at night—to a very special

34

location near Heidelberg, where an intelligence service that was particularly close to my own was holding some very special guests of ours.

One guest, in particular, was extra, extra special, and time was of the essence in dealing with him. That's where I now came into the picture.

Mir Rhutani was a senior member of an international terrorist organization—or, at least, had been before we had nabbed him and salted him away in a German prison compound. He himself was Iranian, but the group he worked with was so contrary that it recognized no organized government at all. Its only purpose in life was to wreak terror and chaos on organized society. And Rhutani had been picked up in the latter stages of putting one of his signature big-body-count terrorist events into operation. The head had been cut off and was being held in secret—but not secret enough, as somehow influence from the outside had extended into his special prison enough for the guards to give him deference and to supply him with many of his wants. One of his wants was for fresh, young, boyish, Jewish-looking man flesh he could dominate.

I wasn't Jewish, but I looked close enough to his ideal to pass muster.

Rhutani would be dead now—he was that much a thorn in many governments' sides—except that he had something everyone wanted: the particulars of the special event he had been planning and the names and locations of the operatives he had in place. There had been one flaw in their plan. Rhutani had been insistent that it not be launched, no matter what, until he gave the order.

The danger now, though, was that if he could somehow influence the actions of his guards, he presumably was close to being able to get the activation of his plan out. That he hadn't done so already must, the world's intelligence organizations had reasoned, have meant that he himself had been a key participant in the event, and he could not physically be involved as long as he was being held. It was only a matter of time, however, before the operation was likely to be launched with or without him.

The job I had been volunteered for was to find out where he was hiding the information on the operation and how we could get to it before it was launched.

* * * *

"Come here, Pretty Boy."

"No, no, Mir. Please don't." As I often was in this third week of being incarcerated with Rhutani, I was cowering in the corner farthest away from the bunk. The fuckings I could take, but the scourging was getting a bit tedious. For some reason, the guards had let him keep his black leather scourge, made of strips of leather with knots in the strips at random places. He didn't beat hard with this, but he beat often, and it had worn my back and legs and chest and buttocks almost raw.

"I said come here. Don't make me come get you."

I rose and hobbled over to the bed.

"Strip."

I complied.

"Now, lean over the mattress."

With a sigh, I turned toward the bunk and leaned over it, digging my fist into the rough, green blanket covering the mattress. Mir swished at my thighs with his scourge, and as I widened my stance in anticipation of the inevitable, he lashed my buttocks a couple of times. And then he was crouched over me, his breathing heavy, smelling of the Dentyne gum he incessantly chewed. I jerked and cried out as his cock entered my channel. And then he was fucking me yet again and swishing at my flanks and around on my belly with the tentacles of his black leather scourge. The knots in the strips bit into my skin.

Of late, he'd been more chatty. I could tell by his heavy breathing that he enjoyed me, and he was showing me more favor in the last week—not in fucking or lashing me less, but in talking to me more. And getting him to talk to me was my major immediate purpose in life—the one thing that could take me away from all of this sooner rather than later.

36

He bent over me, and I could feel his hot breath at my ear. "You are the nicest one yet. I could keep you. Yes, I think I'd like that."

"Maybe I'd like it too," I whispered back through clinched teeth. I did all I could to keep the bitterness out of my voice, to egg him on, to make him think I was beginning to enjoy this.

"Soon, I could be getting out very soon. Or so I hear. Would you like to come with me, my little one? Be mine forever? How would you like that?"

"Maybe," I whispered back. "Of course, I wouldn't want to go just anywhere. Where might you take me?"

There was silence for a moment. He had let off lashing at me, which was always a sign that he'd become intent on the fuck. And he, indeed, had taken up a steady rhythm and his high-heat panting was matching that rhythm. I moaned for him and told him he was doing me fine, all to loosen his tongue.

"Zurich. Do you think you'd like Zurich? I think I might just settle in Zurich."

* * * *

The next time we were separated and Rhutani was given his hour in the small, open courtyard outside our lone, barred window, the handlers who were monitoring us from the multiple bugs buried in the walls of the cell and who, presumably, would sweep in and save me if Rhutani went overboard in his beatings, took me off to an interrogation room, away from the regular guards.

I, in fact, was becoming a little worried that Rhutani *would* go too far with his beatings. Isolation seemed to make him progressively more crazy and aggressive, and I was sure he had been far down those roads before he was brought here. I thought he was wound about as tight as he could be—and I told both the suit and the military uniform that when we were alone.

"Has he said anything that would give us a lead?" the military uniform asked, brushing aside my expressed concerns, concentrating on his own. "Some of the tapes are just too faint. You two do a lot of whispering."

"Sorry," I answered. "I'll try to speak up more. I guess I've been taking his lead on that. He did mention going to Zurich from here. Does that ring any sort of bell?"

Both the suit and the military uniform perked right up. "Yes," the suit said. "Our people have been busy. They've isolated several possibilities where Rhutani could be hiding his operation plans and lists of operatives in place. They've found a bank in Zurich where he has a safety deposit box."

"Good," I said. "Can I get out of there pretty soon, then? This is getting really scary."

"A number. We can't get into the box without a number," the military uniform said. "The numbers there are seven digits. That's hard to keep in your mind, but maybe Rhutani has retained it. More likely he has it written down somewhere. We'll step up his outdoor periods, and you should spend that time looking for the number. It will be seven digits."

"OK," I said, supremely disappointed this was dragging on.

"Oh, and Philip," the suit said in conclusion, "time is running out. We're getting pressure from international peace groups. They've found out about these detentions. I don't think we can hold Rhutani for more than a couple of more days. And they know about him being here now. So, he can't just conveniently disappear."

I wasn't fully listening; I was thinking more about Rhutani being gone one way or another within a couple of days. That meant I could be gone and done with this too. I'd done what I could. It would be too bad, of course, if the operation got carried out, but I had done what I could. But then I remembered something Rhutani had said to me.

"I think Rhutani knows about the pressure to get him released," I said. "He said something about being out of here soon."

"Shit," the suit and military uniform said in harmony.

* * * *

38

Look as I might over the next two days while Rhutani was given extended courtyard breaks, I could not find any semblance of a seven-digit number in the cell. It was a small cell, and there wasn't much of anything in it, so it wasn't as if a number could be easily hidden. When I had searched thoroughly enough that I was coming up with bugs we didn't want Rhutani to know about rather than a list of numbers, I gave up on looking in the cell.

The number must be on Rhutani's body, I decided.

That night, when Rhutani had me naked and was lifting his scourge to strike, I turned doe eyes on him and said, "Please. Tonight I'd like to make love to you. I want to show you what you mean to me. Come sit here and let me undress you and make love to you."

Perplexed at the unusual offer, Rhutani returned the scourge to its nail, and I had him sitting on the edge of the bed before he could recover and take charge. I slowly disrobed him, being careful to examine his clothes from every angle while I was doing so in search of that seven-digit number. And then, when he was naked, I covered every inch of his body with my hands and lips and tongue—and more significantly, with my eyes—looking for a number while his breathing got choppier and his panting became heavier. And then I climbed into his lap and lowered my channel on his cock and fucked myself on him while he groaned and moaned and I sighed and let tears fill my eyes—tears of frustration at not finding the number.

As the haze cleared from my eyes, though, I found myself staring at his scourge as it hung on the bunk post next to where we were fucking. The more I looked at the scourge, the more interested I became in it.

I could hardly hold my curiosity—and hope—until we had finished fucking and a surprised, but fully satisfied Mir Rhutani turned his face toward the wall on the lower bunk and began to snore.

Quietly, ever so quietly, I lifted the scourge off its hook. I counted the strands of leather. There were seven of them. I began examining the knots on each strand. They were of varied number and position. The first strand on the right, the longest one, had three knots in it, as did the next one. But the third strand had only one.

I replaced the scourge and climbed up into the top bunk and started counting the minutes until Rhutani's next courtyard session permitted me to talk to the suit and the military uniform.

It was the varied number of knots on the seven strands of the scourge that would permit me to tell them that the number that would open the safety deposit box in the Zurich bank was 3315743.

Staying Retired

My head snapped up and my brain spun through its cycles, checking every corner out. It was silent, much too silent. It always was quiet here in my beach house perched on the cliffs, but this was silence. Something was happening.

My brain came up blank. I sighed and looked at the blinking cursor on the screen. Another false lead in the search, but I was getting closer. Just a few more connections of one with the other, I was sure, and I would establish the link between the Eye of God in Sri Lanka and Al-Qaeda. I knew the connection was there and, somehow, my brain knew the establishment of the connection was close. Then the decision. Publish or contact Cleland?

I stood up and stretched. I'd been working on this for hours. Bates should be back by now. Maybe that was the source of my mind's concern—that Bates wasn't back. Or maybe it was just my mind telling me that I'd gotten too tense, too concentrated on the search.

I pulled my T-shirt over my head and spread it out over the back of the chair by the desk before I padded, just in my athletic shorts, out of my study and down the stairs, two flights, to the basement gym. A thirty-minute routine of weights and squats, pull-ups and sit-ups, later I slipped the shorts off and dropped them on the washer. A quick shower and then a towel rubdown as I padded back up the stairs.

Bedroom first and dressing, even though the day was almost over. But I always dressed for dinner. Even though it was only me. Bates serving me in the dining room and then eating by himself in the kitchen—the divide somewhat silly, since he'd be fucking me in my bed later in the night.

Always at night. Slipping into my room in the dark, rolling me onto my back, and teasing my legs open as he stuffed a pillow under the small of my back. Me sighing as he entered me with a big, black cock. Moaning and groaning in pleasured surrender as he stretched and caressed my channel with the thick staff as I grabbed and dug my nails into his shoulder blades—only to have him melt away when we had both come. Always at night, in the dark. Never spoken of during the day. Both knowing that he's here because Cleland doesn't take chances. That Cleland always wants to be in control—that I can be controlled by a big, black cock.

Bedroom and then back to the study, I decided. So close, almost there on the connection between the Eye of God and Al-Qaeda. And then the most important question of all—publish or contact Cleland?

Something, some movement, caught the corner of my eye through the expanse of glass across the back of the house, out toward the sea, as I reached the first-floor landing. I moved silently over to the corner of the glass. Yes, two of them. Sent by Cleland? Did he sense that I was close to a discovery and was making my decision for me? Back to the front of the house, peeking out of the window in Bates' room. Two more. Two black SUVs out on the road—the road that went no farther along the top of the cliff than to this house, selected because of the privacy it provided. Two SUVs. More than was needed by four. Where were the others? Already in the house? Had I put the computer to sleep, or was what I had been working on there available for anyone to see?

I moved, as silently as I could, to the second floor. The bedroom to the right at the top of the stairs—where I should go to get dressed. Nakedness was vulnerability. The study door to the left. Should I transfer the file to the cloud and delete it from the computer first? Priorities. I turned left and stopped in the doorway to the study.

"Long time, Evan. You're looking good. Keeping in good shape. About got the Eye of God connection established, I see."

Jackson. Sitting at my computer, smiling—no, smirking—at me. I should have known. My mind was trying to tell me that. But something larger than just this, just Jackson finding me. I had to be wary. And I had to control myself. Jackson was Jackson. Always had been; always would be. Must control myself. Mustn't show his hold over me. Very difficult to do in the nude.

"What are you doing here, Jackson?"

"I've come to ask you to come back. We need you in the unit."

"I'm retired, Jackson."

"No one retires at twenty-eight, Evan."

"I do. I am. Cleland retired me." I had to be careful not to reveal that I had been retained as a consultant—not totally retired. Not left out in the cold. That it was just separation from the ops floor Cleland demanded. Not trusting me in the struggle between him and Jackson. But still needing me. Needing me in more ways than one. Being the only one who knew of this house, where I had gone—at least until now. The only one with his own side of the closet in my bedroom, his own choice of pillow on my bed.

"I don't think so. I've seen the files. The work had your touch written all over it. We need you back."

He'd found my links into the Special Terrorist Covert Affairs Team files. His power in the office was growing. No wonder my mind had been on edge, had screamed out in the eerie silence.

"What does Cleland think?"

"It doesn't matter what Cleland thinks."

There was only one reason why Jackson would say that.

"Where's Cleland? What have you done with Cleland?"

"Cleland apparently has taken a runner. Counterops is busy tracing him, determined to get to him before he reaches the dark side."

"I don't believe that. Cleland never would—"

"I'm temporarily in charge—temporary being short-lived, I'm sure. I can staff as I see fit. I need you to return as chief of analysis."

"I repeat, what have you done with Cleland?"

He just smiled and stood up from the desk, from behind the computer. He had unzipped himself, and his huge black cock—the reason Cleland had gotten me out of the office—half erect, had flopped out for me to see. As always, I sucked in my breath.

"I see it's time for us to adjourn to the bedroom," he said.

Shit. He knew the effect he had on me. Something I couldn't hide, standing in the doorway in the nude.

"No, Jackson. Never again." And then, a new, distressing thought. "Bates. You've done something with Bates. What have you done with Bates?"

"Bates is no longer here. I'm here now. You should appreciate that; I'm a lot bigger—a lot more man for you—than Bates is." The sneer again. The look of victory couched in the gaze of lust. He'd never liked Bates—for obvious reasons.

He was right, though. He was a lot bigger than Bates was. Growing bigger even as he stood there. He also knew that made a difference to me. I wondered if he could hear me begin to pant. It didn't matter; his smile told me that he was fully aware of his effect on me.

"No, Jackson. Never again," I repeated, but falteringly, my own body betraying what I wanted, what I wanted despite everything else that was happening around me.

I was moaning when he reached me, gathered me up in his arms, and strode across the hallway into the bedroom.

He "neveragained" me deep, thick—huge!—and hard on my bed, a-bucking me, me on my back with my legs jack knifed over my shoulders, with him deep inside me between my legs, his hands squeezing and separating my butt cheeks, his pelvis rocking on my body, and his mouth possessing mine, as we both always had liked.

Filling me, holding there, throbbing gigantically inside me as I gasped at the possession of him, digging my fingernails into his shoulders, not being able to keep myself from begging him to fuck me. Then, with a guttural laugh of knowing victory, beginning to pump me, his thick lips on mine, pushing mine open for his tongue to fully possess my mouth cavity as well. After he was fully mounted, his fists buried in the mattress on either side of my torso, and his cock—his mammoth black cock—pounding, pounding, pounding.

Black cock, huge black cock. My fetish. What I craved. What drove me crazy. The weapon Jackson had used in the office to separate me off from Cleland. The fetish Cleland hadn't been able to fight. Cleland disadvantaged by not being black, with a huge cock. The reason I'd been forced into retirement—to erase me as a weapon in Jackson's power struggle with Cleland.

Others had been employed by Jackson and had just disappeared, as had some of Cleland's closest assets. But me. I had become the battleground between them, neither wanting to give me up entirely.

Slowly, though, black cock, huge black cock was winning. It still was winning.

"Oh, god, oh, god, oh, god, be good to me," I murmured, arching my back, fully aware of every thick and long inch of the monster black cock inside me. Moving slower now, approaching climax. Then quick, quick, quick, deep plunges. Crying out, "Fuck, fuck, fuck! Fuck ME!" Ejaculating and collapsing under him as, laughing, he stroked on.

"That's it, then," he muttered after he had ejaculated. "You will do as I ask now. You will come back to the organization."

"Yes," I responded in a weak, defeated voice. "Whatever you want."

He rolled off me and to the side and pulled me into his body. His laugh was one of claimed and not challenged victory.

I waited for a moment and then murmured, "I'm thirsty. Aren't you thirsty?" I asked, turning my head to his face where he held me, embraced in his arms, my ass cuddled into his crotch, his huge tool flaccid for the moment, but pressed up the small of my back, almost to my shoulder blades, it seemed. My master.

"Gonna fuck you again first. Fuck you silly until you're begging me for it. You'll live with me when you come back to work, of course."

"I've already begged for it," I said, angry with myself in the truth of that.

"Not enough. Not nearly enough."

Under constant observation and control, I knew. He needed me, but he didn't trust me. Never would. But then had Cleland ever trusted me either?

I sighed and gave him what I hoped was a convincing smile. "A drink first. And, then, yes, I want the cock again." And I did. "Still drinking the same?" I asked, as I pulled out of his beefy arms and moved off the bed. I was moving down the stairs to the kitchen before he could respond. Mixing the drinks, I kept looking around as I mixed his, making sure I wasn't being observed.

Back in the bedroom, I didn't see him in bed. The bathroom door was open too. He wasn't in there. I barely had time to put the drinks down on the bureau, his in a tall glass, mine in a short glass, careful not to spill any of the special liquid in his, before he pounced on me, with a laugh, from the closet.

He had always liked athletic positions. So did I. I liked anything in which he could get good depth with that monster black cock. He took me while standing in a crouch in the center of the bedroom, me crying out in tormented passion as every inch moved up inside me and then with my legs wrapped around his thighs and bent down to and facing the carpet, my hands stiff armed into the rug, as he grabbed my waist and pulled me on and off the huge black cock. The wheelbarrow, he liked to call it.

"I'm more thirsty than ever now," I said afterward. "Here's your drink."

"A toast? A toast to you returning to the office."

"Yes, to me returning to the office," I said. "Drink up." I watched him carefully as he drank it down.

He was on top of me, me bent over the foot of the bed, him holding my arms pulled back, almost painfully, across

46

my back as he mined me deep from behind, when, with a surprised "Ouff," he collapsed on my back.

I carefully extracted myself from under him and pulled him up onto the bed. I'd have several hours. He'd wake up without a headache or anything. I could be back in his arms with him being none the wiser if that was what was needed. If what my mind was pressing on me turned out not to be true.

I quickly dressed in jeans and loafers, taking only enough time to move into the study and do what I had to do with the computer—belatedly—and to pull on the T-shirt I'd draped over the back of a chair there. Then it was down the stairs, silently. Not just the two levels to the basement, but to the hidden panel in the laundry room and into the recess behind that and down, down, down, the subterranean stairs to the short tunnel leading to the dock. The motor might be heard by Jackson's men at the house, but maybe not. The wind was up and the surf was strong. It didn't matter anyway. I'd be away before they could react even if they heard and assessed correctly.

I was punching buttons into the cell phone even as I moved up the coast.

My mind had kept drilling into me where Cleland was even while Jackson was fucking me. That showed the strength of my loyalty to Cleland—that his need could break through to me even while I was getting what I most craved in the world—a big, black cock working me. Bigger than Bates. Much bigger.

Ashamedly I wanted Jackson again, even now. I wanted him to still be there when I returned, him waking up to me holding him on top of me, my legs encasing his waist, and my channel moving—under my control, not his—up and down on that huge, thick, black cock of his. I moaned into the sea breeze the want of it. It only took Jackson finding me and fucking me again to make me recognize that Bates wasn't filling enough.

I shook my head, forcing my attention back into the threat of the present. I knew Jackson. I knew his methods, and how close he had held them to himself. How he interrogated; where he interrogated when he could get the terrorists into the States and into his hands. Cleland had never asked him.

47

Cleland wanted results, not knowledge that could incriminate him too.

Within a half hour, I was sitting in the motorboat, watching the shell of the derelict power station as Cleland's men bustled about in the light of the headlights of the SUVs trained on the door of the building. I saw Cleland being brought out of the building wrapped in a blanket. And then Bates. I left the boat and went to each in turn. Bates' eyes were glazed and he'd been beaten. He gave me what smile he could manage, though. The medics told me it would be a few days before he could return home.

Ashamed, my first thought was that it could never be as satisfactory with Bates again after having Jackson inside me just now.

One of Cleland's eyes was puffy, but he otherwise seemed to be untouched. I wasn't surprised. Jackson would enjoy knowing that he was just hanging there from overhead pipes inside the derelict building, slowly starving to death.

Cleland gave me a hard look as we came face to face. "Jackson?" he said.

I nodded and told him where Jackson was and then watched as he and Bates were put into an ambulance vehicle that wasn't a normal ambulance. It was painted black and had no markings on it.

I puttered slowly back down the coast to my cove, knowing there was no haste, knowing what I'd find.

Nothing. Silence.

There was little evidence that Jackson or his men ever had been there. A few pools of blood in the auto park in front of the house that would wash away in the first rain.

Not even that much evidence in the house itself. Even the drink glasses had been washed and left on the kitchen drain board. The bed had been made, the sheets now blue rather than the white that had been on it before. The only other evidence that Cleland's men had been there was that the computer was gone. That was OK. I had others, and my files were backed up. And I'd already decided I wouldn't be able to publish; that when I made the connection, which would be soon, the data would only go to Cleland.

If nothing else lingered from tonight, what had been brought home to me was that my loyalties lay with Cleland.

I also knew that I never would see Jackson again, never would feel his huge black cock working inside me again. Bates would have to do.

The phone rang. I knew who it would be before I picked it up.

"You can come out of retirement now," Cleland said on the other end.

"Thank you, but I think not," I answered. "I think the current arrangement is best."

"Perhaps you're right. There's still Delmar."

Yes, there was. Delmar was black and built even bigger than Jackson was, if memories from the office gym showers held true. And Delmar was poised to make a run at Cleland. The ambitions in the office were insatiable—the methods brutal.

"I think I should stay retired," I said. "There was no need to take the computer, Cleland. When I crack this one, you'll be the one who gets the data."

"Yes, I know I will." Such confidence. Well, he had shown out to be a survivor.

"Jackson?" I asked, knowing I shouldn't ask but not being able not to.

"You know Jackson would have always been a problem where you are concerned. He was valuable to the office if held in check. But the balance was too delicate, as we both have learned. Do you regret that I chose you?"

"No, I guess not," I answered. Of course I had known the answer to the Jackson question. As soon as I had picked up the telephone receiver and had sat on the edge of the bed, my eyes picked out the two bullet holes in the headboard. They hadn't been there before Jackson tossed me on the bed.

"I will be there Friday night," he said.

"Yes," I answered, wishing, not for the first time, that he was black and had a huge cock. But there still was Bates for that. Big, but not the biggest. My mind went to Delmar.

"And do you know Dante Harrison?" Cleland asked.

"Yes, I think so. That NFL fullback who came on board after a knee-shattering career ender on the field?" And a beefy black stud.

"Yes, the same. I think Bates can use some help around the house. I'll send him right out. Bates won't be out of the hospital for a few days."

I tried to jerk my mind away from Delmar's cock. There was no doubt the room was bugged, but I was beginning to think that something had been implanted in my brain as well.

Sword of Zara

"I think it's wreckage of a ship. From the storm last night. It's not strange to find ship wreckage on the Cefalu beach after a tempest like that."

Two scouts, on their regular patrol along the Adrano coastline while the forces of the Prince of Madness sought to invade the island nation, had stopped on the beach, their attention arrested by shattered ship planking and tangles of shredded sailcloth washing up in the surf.

"Shall we hope that it is a ship of the Fonni, even perhaps the flagship of the old mad prince himself?" said the second of the scouts, as they pulled up their horses on the cliff above the beach.

This particular beach had been scouted constantly over the past few weeks because twice the oracle at Noto had said the invasion would come here. If it spoke the same name the third time, this would be a certainty.

"What ho?" called out the first scout. "I see movement below, in the wreckage."

The two spurred their horses along the cliff front until they came to the winding path that led down the beach.

As they approached, a figure was pulling his way out of a pile of splintered timbers. He was slight, but well formed, and brown as the earth in the fields of Riberia. No, he was browner, a rich chocolate brown. And he had black curly hair and was fair of face and limb. As he stumbled to stand and the two riders drew nearer, they could see that his clothes, typical in style and color of the hated Fonni ruling family, were in tatters.

The first rider unsheathed his short lance, ready to erase one more Fonni from the earth, but the other stayed his hand.

"Nay, brother, can you not see? He is one of the browns, one of those we call the Nubians. Not a real Fonni."

"Yet he wears the vestments of the Fonni and no doubt is part of the invasion fleet. He should be dispatched."

"No, hold," the second scout called out again. "Have you not heard? Have you not heard that the browns are meant for the Sword of Zara? The Sword of Zara hungers for them, and this one appears to be well formed. We will take him back to Enna, to the Sword of Zara. The Sword of Zara will dispatch the lad. This too may be an omen, a favorable omen. We will be rewarded."

The small Nubian youth had come to his senses enough to see the two horsemen bearing down on him, in the livery of Adrano. And in panic he turned from them and stumbled in confusion and exhaustion across the burning sands on naked feet.

It was a futile gesture. The two scouts bore down on him, and the first scout reached down and lifted the small young man easily and slung him, belly down in front of him, on the back of the horse.

They two were cantering back toward the capital of Enna when a large contingent of horseman approached from the central plains at a gallop.

The first scout, recognizing the horsemen of the king, raised himself up in the saddle and waved his lance back and forth, signaling that they had news, and by the time the larger force had drawn up before them, the two scouts were off their horses and on their knees, heads bowed.

From out of the pack of horseman emerged a man taller and bulkier and more majestic than all of the rest. He strode to where the two scouts were kneeling, their eyes cast to the ground, their shoulders trembling as all men in the kingdom trembled in the presence of their king.

"Why do you impede my progress?" the king growled. "Are you not supposed to be on coastal watch? What have you seen? And it better not be a trifle."

"No, my lord, it is no trifling matter," the first scout replied in a shaky voice. "We have seen wreckage, the wreckage of a ship, perhaps a Fonni warship, on the beach at Cefalu. As the oracle said—"

"I know what the oracle said," thundered the king. "I speak to the oracle. Only I. I do not expect my scouts to speculate on what they do not know. The storm of last night was mighty. It may have been one of our ships."

"Beg your mercy, lord," the second scout ventured, "But there is evidence."

"Evidence? What evidence?"

"We have found a survivor. The tatters of his clothes are in Fonni style and color. And, you will be pleased to know—"

"Don't tell me what will please me. Did you leave the body on the beach?"

"No, sire," offered the first scout. "He is here, on my horse. We spared him because we understand the likes of him are for the Sword of Zara."

"The Sword?" The king was suddenly interested. "Let me see this one?"

The first scout popped up and dragged the Nubian youth off his horse and set him on the ground, but so weak was the survivor of the shipwreck that he sank to the ground on his knees.

The eyes of the king lit up, and he smiled broadly and stood his full stature. The muscles on his chest seemed to expand, and he became a god of men, a man of huge and divinely sculpted countenance.

"A sign. Another sign that we are to look to the Cefalu beach for invasion," the king announced in a voice that rung out over the gathered contingent.

"Yes, this is one for the Sword." the king declared. "To be dispatched by the Sword of Zara. And on the altar. We are near the hill of the altar to the sea. Come bring him to me there."

The scouts took up the trembling Nubian youth and slung him on the horse's back once more, and then they merged their steeds in with those of the king's contingent, and the force moved up to the top of a hill overlooking the sea. Here there was a small, low-lying altar of smooth stone, flat, with horns at the corners.

At the king's direction, the Nubian youth was pulled off the horse, and his tattered clothing was stripped completely away. He was laid on his back on the altar, and his wrists were tied with a leather thong and forced over his head and attached loosely to the horns at corners above his head.

His eyes were wide in fright, and he was mumbling his fear and begging for mercy in the universal language of the kingly classes. All the men gathered around him in awe. A Nubian knowing the universal language and one of such delicate but well-formed beauty. Taken for a child at first, he had the stubbling on his chin that revealed him to be older. His figure was trim, but he was well muscled and smooth skinned, with no callusing. He was no normal Nubian servant. He was someone special to someone of the Fonni. His cock and balls were those of a youth, but they were in excellent proportion to his body. He had the beauty of an ebony statue.

"You are not of low estate, are you?" The king demanded, as he walked through the circle of men and stood tall and mighty at the base of the altar. "Tell me who your master is."

The Nubian did not answer. He went silent and just lay there, trembling.

"Right. You will talk while you live," the king bellowed. "But now the Sword of Zara wants you. You will talk before the might of the Sword. Tell me what I want to hear and I will dispatch you quickly. Otherwise I will tear you to shreds from the inside."

All grew silent on the sacred mound, all except for the panting and involuntary whimpering of the Nubian youth, no longer speaking, having already betrayed himself as an educated man.

The king held out his arms, which had the span of an oak. And when he did so, men pressed forward at the crouch and unlaced his armor and took it off him and did as well with his tunic and backed away, the one holding the kingly garment of linen shot through with threads of gold folding it reverently in his arms.

The king stood there in only his short skirt and his sandals that laced up his calves in ropes of gold. When the attendants had unlaced and taken away the strips of metal that had hung down from the golden belt at his waist, his only remaining adornments were gold bands on his biceps and high on his thighs, the one on his right thigh holding the sheath for a golden dirk knife.

The king himself reached to the small of his back and unlaced the waistband of his short skirt.

"I am King Zara," he bellowed to the heavens, "and this," he declared in a ring tone, "is the Sword of Zara." At that he dropped his short skirt and all in attendance, not the least the Nubian youth lying on the altar, gasped at the revealing of the longest, thickest cock on the island nation of Adrano. Hanging down behind the huge cock was a set of matching balls the size, it seemed, compared to other men, of cannon balls.

"Prepare!" the king declared, and three attendants shot forward and took turns working the king's cock with their mouths and rubbing it with ointment.

Two other attendants surged forward and grabbed the Nubian youth by his ankles, one on each side, and pulled his body down to where his perfectly rounded buttocks were on the edge of the altar top. And then they lifted and spread his legs out, rolling his pelvis up to receive the Sword.

No one present, including the king, thought that the sheathing of the Sword was going to be possible; they all assumed that the Nubian youth would expire at the first thrust. Still, they knew that even in death the Sword would be thrust inside, and the sacrifice would be torn asunder and lose his lifeblood at the base of the altar. All took a step forward, licking lips, anxious for the rarely seen spectacle, wanting to see the expression on the Nubian's face and hear his last strangled yowl as the thrust of the Sword transmitted him to the world of the dead.

Everyone looked at the king, now in full erection, and saw that his cock was as long and thick as the Nubian youth's forearm.

But this was what the Adranoans did with any stray brown person finding themselves on the island. The customs were ancient and clear. The brown people—the Nubians— were a sign of good luck for the island. But only if they were dispatched with the sword of the ruling king. No king in history had had the sword that King Zara possessed. Thrice before Nubians had been brought to him during his reign. And each time good times had come to Adrano when he had dispatched the Nubian with his sword. Only one had survived the first thrust, and then only for a matter of moments.

This was the smallest Nubian sacrifice of all.

The king approached the Nubian between his spread legs. He unsheathed his golden dirk and placed the tip under the chin of the young lad. Looking down at the Nubian, the king was in full arousal. The Nubian was pure beauty, the height of sensuality to the king. He would not make this quick if he could help it. He did not relish dispatching the arousing youth as quickly as the others. But even in death, the king would have his sheathing and plant his seed at the center of the Nubian.

The king placed the huge bulb of his monstrous cock at the hole of the Nubian and leaned over and looked closely into the youth's face.

"Tell me who you are and who you serve and how you came to be on the beach of my kingdom," the king growled.

"I am Toma," the youth murmured. "Beyond that I cannot say. Kill me if you wish. I cannot say."

The king watched with relish as his bulb gained purchase in the youth's hole, which caused the youth to shudder and his head to veer back and his howl of pain and stretching to be cried to the heavens. The king was pleased with the expression on the youth's face; it made the king feel mighty and invincible.

"The heavens cannot help you, little one," the king muttered. "The heavens favor me, and you have been sent as yet another favorable sign. Now, tell me, who do you serve and how do you come to be on my beach. It will go quickly with you if you do."

Silence.

The king, angry now, pushed his greased member in several inches in one thrust. The pupils rolled back into the eyes of the Nubian youth, and he screamed a scream that stopped in mid voicing and he had passed out.

All in attendance thought he was dead, indeed thought that the taking he had received was enough for him to be dead, but the king saw that the youth still breathed, in shallow breaths, and he signaled attendants, who stepped up and slapped the youth on the face until he was revived.

"Who do you serve and how do you come to be on my beach?"

The Nubian just looked the king steadily in the eye and was silent.

Angry again, the king started to thrust even further into the channel of the youth, but now it was he who gasped. The surprise was his now, as the Nubian's channel expanded, and the undulating muscles of his canal seized the king's cock and pulled him deep, deep, relentlessly deep into the center of the Nubian youth. And then the youth arched his back and raised his pelvis further. He jerked his ankles out of the grasp of the attendants and crossed his legs tightly above the king's buttocks and started to fuck himself on the king's staff in a steady rhythm.

The shocked king was lost in ever greater waves of arousal. He dropped his dirk, and when the Nubian raised his lips to the king's, they went into a deep sensual kiss.

The king was lost in full fuck now, forgetting tradition and custom and the sacrifice completely. And the flowing he experienced was the best he'd had in memory.

Afterward he collapsed on top of the breast of the Nubian youth, and Toma put his lips to the ear of the king and murmured, "I serve you, if you will have me, and I came to be

57

on the beach because the gods sent me to endure the sheathing of the Sword of Zara for as long as you will have me."

Recovered, the king bluffed that the gods had sent the Nubian Toma to answer to the arrogance of the Fonni and that he would be locked away in the castle to be sacrificed on the altar of the sun there, the altar of the sea not being worthy enough for this sacrifice. The altar of the sun was so sacred that only the king could approach it.

And so, Toma was locked away in the king's chambers. The first time the king called for Toma, however, Toma straightaway gave the king the answers he had originally sought.

"I will keep no secrets from you, my lord, as long as you search my depths with the Sword of Zara. Only you have brought me satisfaction. Before coming to you, I served the Duke of Sorso, who was lost at sea that stormy night, he along with all of his forces. Only I survived, being sent to you by the gods to serve you. And I gladly tell you that it is more than the forces of the Duke of Sorso who are no longer with the prince who besieges you. The Duke of Jerzu has deserted him as well, with all of his contingent. And the puss sickness has taken away even some of the prince's forces. But it is true, he is the Prince of Madness. He insists on attacking you and taking Adrano. He knows you do not have the forces to cover all of the approaches to your island kingdom. He believes he can find your unprotected underbelly."

"He does not know what I know, little one," King Zara said. He was laying on his bed of pillows, holding the small Toma to him and running his hands over the Nubian youth's body. He was transported by the brown bodies of the Nubians. He had regretted the short play time he had had with the first three sent to him. He had no idea how the youth had managed him on the altar, although he had only been half sheathed when he had given up his seed in surprise. Toma was arousing him to the heights, but he did not want to kill the lad with his sword until he had learned more from him. In the meantime, he was toying with Toma's hole with his thumb, which was larger in itself than the cocks of most Adranoans, and Adranoan men were famous for their cocking.

Toma was sighing and began to move his hips on King Zara's thumb and, without thinking about it, the king had substituted first one and then two fingers.

"He does not know that we know precisely where he will land. The oracle at Noto has told us so. It has spoken twice. When it speaks the same name the third time, we will know for sure, and that is where we will position our defenses."

"I fear for you, my king," Toma said, as he reached down and held the wrist of the hand the king was slowly finger fucking him with. The king felt the pull of Toma's channel upon his fingers, and he inserted another one.

"You are being led astray. I cannot remain silent. I must prove myself to you. I yearn for your sword, which reached further into me than any other man's. Please I beseech you, sheath your sword in me once more, and then I will tell you secrets that will shake your very soul."

"I do not want to dispatch you," the king murmured. "I needs play with you further. I am too much for you. You cannot survive me."

"Nay, sire," Toma said. And then he laughed. "Look, sire, look for your hand."

The king looked down at the hand he was using to play with Toma's hole and gasped in shock. His whole hand up to his wrist was inside Toma now, and yet Toma's channel muscles were working to pull his arm even deeper.

The king's lust knew no bounds, and he rose and pulled his fist from out of the Nubian's ass and lifted the youth up with broad hands more than encircling his waist and settled Toma's hole over his fully erect sword.

"At least I feel I must lap you," the king said, "lest I crush your body. That at least is too delicate for my frame."

The king pulled Toma half way down on his cock and began to lift him and bring him down, beginning the rhythm of the fuck.

After the initial cry and groan, Toma began to pant and moan. "Nay, my king. Sheath your sword in its entirety. I must have it all."

To the king's amazement, Toma did take it all. The king had never fully sheathed his sword; he had killed many a wife and concubine trying to do so. And after the king had given over his seed, Toma refused to release him, clamping down his channel muscles tight and demanding a second ride and then a third—until the king, virile as he was, had no more kingly seed to give, no more power in his pelvis and thigh and buttocks muscles, and just lay back, exhausted and sighing the satisfaction of total fulfillment.

Toma slithered up to where his lips were at the ear of the king now.

But the king spoke first. "You are no innocent young lad, you are a king's catamite, are you not?"

"Yes, lord, Toma answered in a whisper. I was the Duke of Sorso's catamite, but he did not satisfy me, and then the Duke of Jerzu's, and he did not satisfy me. And then both dukes at once, and still they did not satisfy me. Three men have I taken at once, and still I was not touched to the quick. I went to the prince, and he did not satisfy me. But I satisfied him, and he confided in me. And I had heard about you and that you had the most magnificent member in all the world. And so I came to you. And you satisfy me, my lord. You, today, have reached me to the very center—not once but three times. You are an elephant of men."

They kissed, the king's vanity stroked to the limit, lost in love, blind to love and his Nubian lover from this point forward.

"And in your satisfying of me, I must tell you all. I must whisper it in your ear as even the walls of your palace have ears and tongues that speak to the Prince of Madness. You must not believe in your oracle. The Prince of Madness has suborned your oracle. It is not the beach at Cefalu where the attack will occur. It is the beach of Gela, on the other side of the island. You must gather your forces there."

"But the oracle—"

"Bought and paid for by the Prince of Madness, who is not really that. He is really the Prince of Darkness. I know as no other man does. His cock is as long as yours, but it is not as thick. It is not an honest sword. It is a serpent's tongue, hissing and slithering inside me. I cannot let this prince prevail over you. That is why I have come to you."

"But I go to the oracle tomorrow."

"No matter what it says, you must announce the truth and prepare for war in the right place. But now you must sheath your sword inside me once again. The very quick of me wants to feel the prick of your blade tip."

The cries and sighs and moans emitted by Toma during this fourth cocking assured the king that he satisfied his Nubian lover in each sheathing more than the previous one.

The next day King Zara made the last of three ceremonial visits to the oracle. And, sure enough, the word that was whispered and echoed all around the smoky cave walls was "Cefalu."

"What can I do?" the king asked his new catamite when he returned. "I certainly cannot tell my people that my Nubian lover has told me the oracle of Noto lies. They would pull me apart limb from limb and feed me to the Galotes. I am not mighty enough to withstand all of the men who would align against me. And they think you are dead, anyway, sacrificed on the altar of the sun."

"There is no problem, King," Toma whispered in the king's ear as he pushed the king on his back and straddled his hips and began his own soothing ritual once more. "You go alone to the cave. Merely say that you went in and the name whispered was 'Gela.' And that as you were leaving, the cave in confusion, the oracle called you back—twice—and the name 'Gela' echoed each time, providing the three declarations that told you the truth."

"I don't know. I . . . Oh . . . my ancestors!" Toma had descended full way on the Sword of Zara and was sheathing and unsheathing it and melting away all of the king's concerns and reason.

On the day of his departure, as the king was putting on his armament before leaving the palace at Enna, Toma came to him. "Let me go with you, King Zara. Let me show my loyalty and pledge of truth by riding with you."

"No, little one," the king replied. "You ride with me as far as the village of Favara, in heavy disguise, but no further than that. You are unknown in my world, having already been thought to have been sacrificed to the Sword of Zara on the altar of the sun. I cannot give you up, but neither can I display you. And I cannot trust those I am leaving here to protect you. It's a simple village, but they are my kinsmen, and they will give you sanctuary. There will be no guards, no sign that the king's most precious treasure resides there."

On the day of the invasion of the island of Adrano, in the month that Adrano came under the sway of the country of Fonni, Toma was standing tall on the cliff overlooking the beach at Cefalu to welcome the arrival of his sovereign and lover, the Prince of Madness, and a mighty force that included the contingents of the Dukes of Sorso and Jerzu. The allied forces were already inside the walls of the capital of Enna before the army of King Zara, standing patiently and looking out to sea at Gela, even realized that they had been duped by a small Nubian spy with a talent fit for a king.

The Ambassador's Son

My head was still swimming a bit, but it was done now and couldn't be taken back. I pulled my knees in together with a groan and slipped the plump pillow from under the small of my back. I lowered my feet to the marble floor below the edge of the large lounge bed in the pool house facing the open wall to the terrace-surrounded swimming pool, light reflecting brightly off the slightly waving water under the blazing sun. He hadn't told me I could adjust my position, but he'd been so long at it in this position that I was cramping.

I turned my face toward one side and watched the slim-waisted, berry-brown body of Amir saunter off to the bathroom. His buttocks were plump orbs, but the hollows at the sides below the hips—which I had just had the heels of my hands buried in as my fingers were flared over his butt cheeks, helping to guide his thrustings—were deep. Turning my head in the other side, I looked at the used condom, plump from his prodigious cum, laying there like a bloated slug, proof that I'd let him fuck me. Beside that were the bottle of lube and another couple of condom packets. He had said nothing about how I'd done with him, but he apparently was prepared for a marathon.

When he'd left me he'd just said he needed to piss—and that I wasn't to go anywhere. He acted like I was there just to serve him. He obviously was spoiled that way, which was a given considering who he was and where we were. But then nothing I was doing could be taken to contradict that he could have anything he fancied from me.

This was all just a bit surreal. I hadn't let a man fuck me since college. I doubt if Amir would have cared even if I had told him that I hadn't, though. And, on his turf and given the bodyguards, it was rather a moot point. As he was fucking me, my eyes had gone to the ceiling over the lounge bed and I saw the frame that could be lowered on the bed and the four corner posts with the restraint attachments. If I hadn't given into to him willingly, chances were good that he would have taken me anyway.

I'd wanted the job with intelligence, using my natural skills at the technical aspects of audio surveillance. I'd restrained myself, behaving myself, so that I could pass the stringent background checks and scrutiny of my life—and I'd managed to get through all that and to my first posting, here, in this small Gulf peninsula enclave emirate, strategically important for its size not only because of the oil field it sat on but also because of where it was positioned in relationship to its neighbors and to the Strait of Hormuz passageway into the Persian Gulf.

Amir el-Basir, the pampered and spoiled son of Prince Sayeed el-Bakir, wasn't thick, but he was long, his cock curved up so that the bulb could punish the prostate as he pumped. And he had stamina. He was thin and wiry, but he was well-muscled and strong. I had resisted a bit, but I'd been tired from our tennis match on the palace courts and confused and sluggish from whatever was in the drinks he was plying me with as we sat in the pool room after the match to cool down. I had stopped putting up any kind of a struggle at all after he'd gotten his dick inside me and just went with the fuck. He was cruel, taking long, deep, rapid strokes. Fisting my knees and working my legs back and forth, thrusting as he pushed the legs out and withdrawing as he pulled them into my body.

He never asked me if I liked or wanted what he was doing to me—but I didn't use my hands to try to push him away, I grabbed his buttocks and helped guide the stroking—and when I felt him ready to blow, I held him to me, wrapped my legs around his waist and took over the stroking with my channel. So, I guess he knew I wanted it.

I had let him have his way. There wasn't much else I could do. The embassy had told me to cultivate the royals and had virtually thrust the two of us together when they learned I'd played intercollegiate tennis. Amir was a tennis nut. He'd seen me play and had expressed interest in playing me. I'll bet the embassy didn't know what he really wanted, how he wanted to play me, though—what it meant to cultivate his goodwill, to let him have his way.

Between sets he had told me that his fetish was young blonds. He said it as if he already knew I—a young blond— would take cock. Not taking him all that seriously at that point and playing like I misunderstood him—that he was speaking of blonde women—I asked him how hard such women were to come by in this Arab emirate, and he just laughed and said there was a market for young blond men, like me, here. I didn't necessarily believe him, but his eyes weren't laughing when he said it, so I didn't call him on the statement. Neither did I press the point on which gender we were talking about.

Once here, I couldn't very well refuse him with those armed guards standing at the corners of the pool house, ever vigilant, but seeing nothing. Just standing there, as we sat by the pool after—at his suggestion—skinny dipping and him plying me with liquor, speaking flatteringly of my physical attributes, and pulling similar voicing of admiration from me on his own naked body. It was his idea that we move into the shade, on the lounge bed in the pool house. He had already kissed me and held and squeezed my cock by the pool, so I knew what was coming in the pool house. I suppose I could have at least tried to withdraw then, signaling that I wasn't available. But I didn't, and he didn't act as if I had a choice or might choose other than what he wanted.

He pushed me onto my back there on the lounge bed in the pool house, where I could see the frame above me and contemplate it with some trepidation, as he knelt between my spread thighs and gave me nominal suck. We were both hard already, though, so there was little preliminary preparation, before, telling me he couldn't wait longer, he rose over me

65

between my thighs, forced a pillow under the small of my back, and thrust inside me.

I had murmured that I wasn't sure, knowing from my slurred words that the liquor had impaired my reactions, and, after it became evident that he was going to carry through, that I had been some time and could he go slowly. But, no he couldn't—and didn't—go slowly. The initial thrust caused me to scream and try to jerk away from him, but he just laughed and held on tight, reared back, and thrust again, deeper. And then again, and again, and again, faster and harder.

After his dick was inside me, I was lost. I gave in completely.

"I knew you were just teasing," he muttered.

But I hadn't been teasing. It had been long enough for me to forget how much I wanted it.

It was like old times in college, if ever so brief. But so arousing. I encircled his slim waist with my legs and held onto his sides under his armpits, the heel of my hands rubbing his nipples, as the head of his dick found my prostate and worked me there. I ejaculated and collapsed as he worked my channel, and he grabbed my legs, bent them, with my heels dug into the edge of the lounge bed, and pumped my legs back and forth to the rhythm of the pumping with fists on my knees, while I arched my back, reached for holds on the brass rungs of the headboard behind me, and moaned my acceptance of the cocking.

I came again, and he noted, with pride, how easily he could coax the cum out of me.

Once again I told him, "It's been years," to which he retorted that I was a liar—that he thought I was a pro. He had fucked harder, mercilessly, to his own ejaculation then.

I watched him return from the bathroom, dark-skinned, thin, wiry, his cock in upcurved erection again, his hands busy rolling a condom onto the long, thin staff.

I wasn't drunk anymore. There were no excuses anymore. But there was nothing to fight anymore either. It's not like I hadn't done this before.

Neither of us said anything. He was so cocky, so sure of himself. As if this was his kingdom and he could have anything—anyone—he fancied. And, in fact, it was and, as far as I was concerned now, he could. The time for diplomatically pulling away and leaving had been as we were leaving the tennis court when he put his arm around my shoulder and gave me that hungry look. I had known that look in college, but I had thought myself beyond those youthful follies. I wonder if I knew at that moment on the tennis court that he was going to fuck me. I suppose it's a waste of time to think about it, though, as he did fuck me. And having done it once . . .

I watched him roll another condom on and lather it with lube. Then I raised and separated my legs. He moved between them, pushing the pillow back underneath the small of my back, grasping my ankles and hanging them on his shoulders. He leaned over me, bringing his face down to mine.

"Be good to me this time," I begged in a whisper. "Last time you—"

"I know what you want," he growled as his lips possessed mine and his hands grasped my wrists.

I lurched and tried to open my mouth in a scream as he thrust up deep inside me, but his tongue was occupying my mouth cavity. He immediately began pumping hard and deep, and I groaned and grunted. Taking him. Taking all of him deep and hard.

Within moments knowing it was what I wanted. That didn't matter anyway. He was the son of the prince of the kingdom. This was what he wanted.

The worry kept pounding in my brain. How did he know? How did he know I'd take the cock? What gave away the desires I had that I thought I'd successfully hidden? Or maybe he didn't know. Maybe, here, in this primeval enclave of power and selfishness, it wouldn't have mattered at all what I wanted or didn't want.

I rose up against him, struggling with him, he wrestling with me—but laughing when he realized what I was trying to do. I pushed him to the side and rolled with him until I was on top and he was on his back on the lounge. It was me now lowering my face to his, taking his lips in mine, putting my pelvis in motion rising and falling on his cock. My sexual surrender to him total, although he would demand more than sex from me—and I was so lost to him now that I would give him anything he wanted, do anything for him that he demanded of me.

* * * *

When I drove back into the embassy compound and turned the keys of the embassy car over to the garage supervisor, he told me, "The ambassador has requested that you go see him when you've returned."

I was afraid of this. In fact this was much of the reason that I had let my defenses down to Amir el-Basir and then, after he'd first gotten his dick inside him, had just given way, letting all of my defenses shatter on the marble floor of his pool house. I been walking gingerly around like on broken glass since I'd arrived in the emirate, knowing that at some point I'd meet up with the ambassador.

"In his office?" I asked, hoping.

"No, in the residence."

Shit.

Hunter Sean Caldwell II. He hadn't been the ambassador when I'd first received my assignment to this country. The assignment had come as a surprise, while I was still training in tech craft, mostly audio surveillance, at Warrenton, after finishing my masters in Muslim studies. I wasn't exactly at the head of my class at Warrenton, and some of my fellow students weren't that pleased that I'd gotten an assignment so early. But then most of them were still struggling with languages. My Arabic was fluent already.

I had already sublet my apartment in Rosslyn, near the Pentagon, and sold my Mustang convertible when I'd read that Caldwell would be the new ambassador. Hunter Sean Caldwell II, the last man, before today, who had fucked me. The first man who had fucked me. Before Amir just now, the only man who had fucked me. The man who I thought was a master at cocking until I encountered Amir.

Caldwell had been both the direct ancestor of the founder of Caldwell College, a university prep junior college for jocks—my sport being tennis—and its president at the time

I came to his attention. I was on a work-study scholarship to augment my sports scholarship and I served drinks and hors d'oeuvre at his cocktail parties.

He was having a rough time in his marriage. I didn't know it then, but his penchant for young blond men was the crux of the problem. One night after a cocktail party, when his wife wasn't in evidence because she had flounced off to Europe, I was still cleaning up when all of the rest of the servers had left. Caldwell came into his living room, his tux tie undone and his shirt open to show a well-muscled chest covered in salt-and-pepper, curly hair, and sat in a wing chair, watching me under drooping eyelids and drinking scotch from a bottle. I could tell that he was keyed up.

He told me I could stop and that he wanted me to sit with him and talk with him. We passed the bottle back and forth while he told me of all his problems with his wife and the school and life in general. He also told me what a fine-looking young man I was and how well I could do in the university on the bases of a good recommendation from his school. He told me, in guarded references, of his weakness for young blond men, not spelling out the manifestation of the weakness but saying enough that I could hardly claim I didn't know what he was saying.

As earlier today, after tennis with Amir, I could have left at that point and we both could have maintained at least surface denial of what was being offered, requested. But the offer had been couched in references to my future and my good standing in the college. And I can't say that I hadn't been curious or tempted before. I can't say that Caldwell hadn't been able to read my vulnerability and natural inclination.

He could hold his liquor better than I could. I have no idea at what point he was kneeling between my thighs and giving me the first blow job I ever had from a man.

He fucked me in the backseat of his Mercedes in the garage, saying he didn't feel right about doing it in the house. But that was a one-time taboo. He had no trouble fucking me in the house for the months afterward. The backseat of a Mercedes in a closed garage is a hell of a place to lose your male-male virginity, but I was drunk, he was the college president, and I was barely making it through on combined scholarships—scholarships that he controlled.

He was gentle with me under the circumstances, my first ejaculation occurring while he was still sucking me and working my body with his hands as I was on my knees between his thighs, facing him in, the center of the backseat of his Mercedes. My ineffectual murmur of objection as he pulled me down into his lap and I felt the hard insistence of him. I can still hear the unzipping of his trousers in my then liquor-clouded mind as he had my torso bent back toward the front seat and was sucking on my nipples.

I remember murmuring that I'd never done it before and then the feel of the bulb of his cock at my entrance. The long, slow, painful journey of my channel down that pole, which wasn't unusually long but, I didn't know it at the time, was unusually thick, seemed like a telephone pole to me. And then, once I felt the curly hair of his pubes on my ass cheeks, the rocking back and forth on his cock, one of his arms around my waist and the hand of the other between our bellies, stroking my cock hard again. The pleasure rising up to overlay, and then overpower, the pain. My second ejaculation, and his bathing of my channel. He hadn't worn a condom. The kisses and his, voiced, but surely not seriously meant, apologies afterward as I continued to rock on the cock and it withered inside me were almost anticlimactic.

I remember having been slightly irritated at his insistence that I had just been teasing him about not having done it before and, worse, having maneuvered him into the tryst—all voiced to justify his own actions and weakness, I'm sure. But what was done had been done and I needed his goodwill, so I didn't argue. I have no idea what he would have done, how he would have reacted, if I had cried or railed against him. Since I didn't, obviously, in his mind, I had wanted it.

The apologies didn't prevent him from fucking me again that night and over the next few months again and again and again. And until Amir el-Basir fucked me, I thought that Caldwell was an expert at it and that I was lucky to have him servicing me once I had been accustomed and drawn to it.

After I'd moved on to Stanford to major in Muslim studies, with a full tennis scholarship, I left that behind and managed to forget what I'd had to do to get through junior college.

But that wasn't really fair. Much like having given in to Amir el-Basir once he'd gotten his dick inside me that first time, once the awkwardness of the backseat of the car and the first breaching of my ass ring by a cock was over, I had nothing left to protect, and I had enjoyed Caldwell's cocking. He must have enjoyed cocking me, because, though we parted amicably enough when I went off to Stanford and he presumably moved on to other young blonds, he'd obviously kept track of me and had requested my assignment to his embassy when he was tapped to be an ambassador.

A Filipino manservant opened the door of the residence, which was a wing of the recently constructed American embassy complex, built like a fortress in a compound that could withstand a siege or a rocket attack. No one looking at the building from the courtyard would even know what was office space and what was the ambassador's residence as well as the residences of other senior embassy officials.

I obviously was expected, as I only had to give my name to be ushered to a central, two-story foyer with a huge skylight overhead and a staircase sweeping up to a second-floor landing. The manservant gestured toward the stairs and looked at me expectantly.

"I'm to go upstairs?" I asked. "And then where?" I had never been in the residence. I'd only been in the country for two weeks and most of that was on leave in a hotel, busy trying to set up new living circumstances. The embassy admin officer was the one who actually arranged for housing. Mine hadn't been set up yet, and he seemed to be dragging his feet on getting me settled. I was still in the hotel.

"Excuse me, sir," the manservant said. "Yes, up the stairs, down the corridor, and the last door on the right." He gave me a look that seemed peculiar, but what did I know about the looks that Filipinos gave? And what did it matter anyway? Filipinos, like the Thai, were favorites as house servants for the wealthy for their ability to fade into the wallpaper and to take anything going on in the house in their stride—not judging, at least overtly, just serving, and serving well. After giving me directions, the Filipino houseboy withdrew—into the wallpaper for all I knew.

I knocked on the door and heard Caldwell's voice, bidding me to enter. The room I entered obviously was his bedroom—large, elegantly decorated, and with a commanding four-poster bed. I can't say I was surprised.

I also couldn't say I was surprised that he was standing at a full-length French door out onto a narrow balcony that looked down on an interior garden courtyard. Even though the courtyard was enclosed, mostly by the blank walls of other areas of the embassy, the view was distorted enough for me to know that the glass was thick and bulletproof. Nor was I surprised that he was in a robe of a gauzy material thin enough for me to tell, with the backdrop of the sunlight streaming into the window, that he was naked underneath. He was still in superb condition, these six years later, for a man in his late fifties—solidly built and somewhat stocky, but not fat. And he was half hard, with a thickness that I well remembered.

I stood inside the door, which swung shut on its own behind me. We said nothing for half a minute, during which he gave me a sardonic look and took a couple of swigs of whatever he was drinking out of a brandy snifter. Liquor. My softening-up vulnerability. He had made me drunk before fucking me at college. Amir had made me drunk before fucking me in his pool house earlier in the day.

Caldwell didn't offer me a drink. We were way beyond that.

"So, here you are. I understand you were playing tennis with Prince el-Basir's son."

"Yes."

"Went on a bit long."

"Yes."

"I put the word out two hours ago that I wanted to see you."

"I'm sorry. I didn't know you'd call for me today. I've been here a couple of weeks. As you surmised, the tennis went on a little long." If I had meant how long he'd left me cooling

72

my heels before summoning me as a criticism, he didn't show it. If he hadn't mellowed, he didn't really care all that much what I felt about anything. What my statement did establish, though, was that I believed I was here to answer whatever summons he made.

"And what happened afterward? Did he fuck you after tennis?"

I didn't answer. There probably was no need, in Hunter's mind, for me to answer. But that was a bit unfair. After Hunter, there had been nobody—until earlier today. Hunter obviously thought otherwise. Instead of answering that question, I introduced another topic. "I didn't know you were to be ambassador here."

"I didn't want you to know until after it was impossible for you to back out of your assignment. Does that bother you?"

"A bit, yes. I wasn't up for a foreign assignment yet. May I assume that you arranged that?"

"Muriel has left me. I'm on assignment alone. It's a tense assignment, and I have needs."

"I see," I said.

"I like the familiar. I knew of your schooling and training and that you'd fit this assignment. I didn't want to take risks, to establish new arrangements here. I knew that, with you—"

"I said that I understood."

He had put the snifter down on a table next to the window and was unbuttoning his robe. He parted the robe, which showed that he was in full erection now. He was beefy, but hard bodied. I knew that he was an avid squash player and worked out with weights. He probably still could break me in two. "It's been a long time, but I haven't forgotten. Have you?"

I knelt in front of him at the window, opened my mouth wide, by necessity, and gave him head until he growled that he wanted me naked and on the bed.

He fucked me swiftly, missionary style, to an ejaculation, and then we lay on the bed, our bodies stretched out against each other and our hands exploring, reacquainting ourselves with the hardness and suppleness of each other's

73

bodies. Caldwell was thick but not particularly long, and he never could last long at a time. Since he'd been my only one before Amir, I had thought that sex with him was quite hot. After Amir, I wasn't sure. But that didn't really matter. He was the man in control. I knuckled under easily to a man in control.

When he had engorged again, I rolled over on top of him, saddled myself on his cock, and rode the cock cowboy style, rocking back and forth on the cock, as I knew he liked. Still, there was a businesslike, perfunctory air about it. There would be no emotional entanglements. He had tensions with his job. My major job was to be to help relieve those—without fuss or demands.

I'd never really heard of a man having a male mistress, and now it seemed that I was to be one.

"You have kept in good form," he whispered when we were laying, entwined again.

"There was no one after you," I murmured. "I want you to know that. I couldn't have gotten this job, if there was. And I probably won't be able to keep the job if—"

"I can smell another man on you," he said. "An expensive cologne. Amir el-Basir? You didn't answer me before."

"I haven't lied about there being no other man—up to today," I answered. "But knowing you were here . . . I just was riddled with worry and confusion. And vulnerable. And he's the son of a prince. I didn't get the impression I had much choice."

"I understand," he said. "But you are with me now."

"Yes," I said. "I am with you now." I didn't want to tell him that I had already arranged the next time I would be with Amir. And, indeed, I was to meet and lie under Amir at least twice a week thereafter. And Amir would take much more from me than just sex and a tennis workout. He controlled me with sex in a way that the ambassador never had and never would, and I could deny nothing that he asked of me.

"I will have your things moved from the hotel. You will be staying with me here. The Marine guards think it would be safer if there was someone else staying inside the residence— one of the younger male staffers. The Marines are already

74

overstretched on duties. For propriety sake, your assigned bedroom will be just across the hall, but . . ."

At least now I knew why the admin officer had been dragging his feet on finding me an apartment.

But that too didn't last very long. Two months later I received a note in my mail slot at the embassy that an apartment had been assigned. It was only later that night, after Hunter had fucked me like a dog at the foot of the four-poster bed, swiftly and with little emotion, that he told me that his son would be arriving by the end of the week, to live with him in the ambassador's quarters, and that I would be housed separately, although I was still expected to attend him when he felt he needed it and could arrange it.

The introduction of the ambassador's son into the equation changed much and nearly spoiled everything.

* * * *

Hugh and I arrived at the chief of station's house in the embassy compound together for the reception of Tony Jacobs, the deputy chief of Mideast Ops from back in Langley. We were both a little blurry eyed that we were being included, as we were just about the lowest men on the totem pole at the station. We were essentially "it" as audio surveillance techs at the embassy went, but neither of us had done much in the way of that work since I had arrived at station nearly three months prior. Hugh had been so busy before that they'd opened up another slot, and then when I arrived, the business went dead. I had all but been reassigned to be the ambassador's gofer, which the station wasn't opposing because the Agency had little for me to do and was happy to garner the goodwill of Caldwell.

But Penny Haskell, the hard-as-nails chief of station—COS—had insisted we be there for this reception, so there we were.

Our presence was somewhat explained when she stopped us in the foyer of her residence in the embassy compound as we arrived and said, in low tones, that we were to stay around after Jacobs had been taken back to his hotel. This meant she had some actual surveillance work for us to do, evidently something she didn't want to discuss at the station in the chancery. I was a little nervous about that. As well as putting bugs in and monitoring them, our job was to find and take bugs out at the embassy. If Haskell didn't want to give us an assignment in the office, perhaps, I thought, she believed we hadn't swept the station well enough. On the other hand, she seemed willing to talk to us in her residence, which was also on the embassy compound.

I stewed about what we might have done wrong or if Penny had discovered that the ambassador wanted me around because he was fucking me—at least until I saw Sean, the newly arrived ambassador's son, Hunter Sean Caldwell III, at the reception. He was being called Sean at the embassy to distinguish him from his father.

"Who's he?" I had asked Hugh, a canapé half way to my mouth and tugging at Hugh's sleeve with the other hand.

He turned his eyes toward where I was pointing, where Penny's husband, Tyler, who ostensibly was the reason the Haskells were in this country—he was an oil company representative—was talking with a young man.

Hugh laughed. "You thought it was a mirror at first, didn't you?"

Indeed I did. The young blond man was the spitting image of me.

"That's the ambassador's son, Sean—at least that's the name he's going by here. The two of you could be twins."

Yes, we could. And that sent me to wondering about what it might be that Hunter saw in me that was desirable and what deep, darker secret it surfaced about the man. As I grazed at the food table, I worked on dredging up in my mind the young men I'd known Caldwell to show interest in in college, and they all came up as blonds with good bodies and model-handsome faces. None looked more like the ambassador's son than I did, though, and it had been me that Caldwell had been fucking back then—and had been sleeping with here until Sean Caldwell arrived.

Hugh went over to meet the ambassador's son, but I held back, wandering around the various entertainment rooms in the COS's house, nodding here and there, but not really getting into any conversations. I was nervous here among my embassy and Station colleagues, wondering whether any knew or suspected that I was fucking the ambassador—even though that had tapered off since his son had arrived in country. I wasn't much less nervous that some of them might know that Prince El-Basir's son was fucking me too.

And now I had a whole new line of thought on the presence of the ambassador's son to cogitate. I hoped he wouldn't complicate my life, but there was every reason to believe he might.

Just when it seemed the reception was going to go on forever, it was breaking up, with Tyler Haskell accompanying Tony Jacobs back to his hotel in an embassy car and those from the embassy leaving en masse to return to their offices as if everything had been staged and they all had something else to go on to—which was pretty much the case with these embassy parties.

And then it was Hugh and me sitting on the other side of a mahogany desk in the COS's study. I looked out the window and realized that the first-story study looked out onto the same embassy enclosed courtyard that the ambassador's second-story bedroom did. As the top-ranked spook in the country, Penny Haskell's house was yet another appendage on the chancery.

"I wanted to speak with you because I have a delicate surveillance operation for you two perform. It will require hours sitting in a safe house apartment."

"That's what we're here for," Hugh said.

I could hear both Penny and Hugh, but I felt like it was at a distance. I was sitting there, staring out of the window, up at the ambassador's bedroom window. The glass of that was tinted and was so thick that it would have to be night with the lights on in the bedroom and the curtains drawn for anyone to see anything from down here. That just made me think of nighttime instances that might have been like that with me up there in that bedroom—with the ambassador.

"The matter is delicate because it concerns his son," Haskell said.

I was tuned into that, but still at a distance.

"The national security adviser fought him being permitted to come here at all because he was running on the edge back in the States—pro Muslim and associating with some pretty dicey characters. This just wasn't the place for him in view of his background. And he's already hooked up with someone on our watch list here. I want to set you up to listen in for a few days to see if Sean Caldwell's visits to the palace have any terrorism implications."

"The palace?" I asked, suddenly tuned back into the conversation. "Whose palace?"

"Prince Sayeed el-Basir's palace," Haskell answered.

Hugh whistled. "We suspect that Prince El-Basir has connections to terrorist elements?"

"No. His son. Amir el-Basir."

My blood froze at the sound of his name, and I suddenly was all attention. My meetings with the ambassador may have tapered off recently but my meetings with Amir el-Basir had not.

"We want to know what, exactly, the ambassador's son is doing with Amir el-Basir," Haskell continued. "And the matter is much too delicate to coordinate with the ambassador. That's what Tony Jacob is here for—to give us the go-ahead in person, coordinated with the secretary of state, who had little chance but to cooperate after the national security adviser was on board. The operation is so delicate that we couldn't put any hint of it in the diplomatic traffic."

I suspected that I knew exactly what the ambassador's son and Amir el-Basir were doing in the palace. And then it hit me, and I had difficulty swallowing much less asking what I had to ask.

"The bugs," I asked Penny. "Do we need to put them in place? How and where?"

"That's already taken care of," Haskell answered. "And we're concentrating them around the sports area of the palace compound. Amir appears to spend most of this time there—the locker room by the tennis and squash courts and the pool house."

"The bugs are already in place?" I asked, trying not to let my voice sound like I was strangling. "When?"

"Yesterday. A grounds cleaning crew goes in once a month. This time it was local assets of ours. I couldn't see any way of getting you two in there to set the devices."

I could think of a way of getting in the palace, of course. I got in there twice a week to be fucked by Amir. But I wasn't going to volunteer that information here. Penny Haskell was being lax about not knowing it already. But maybe she did, and maybe this would be some double sting. I'd been incredibly stupid. The bugs were put in the previous day, she'd said. I hadn't been to the palace in the last three days. I let out a deep breath. Still, as delicate as this operation was for Penny Haskell and the Station, it would be like walking on eggs for me.

* * * *

I hung around after Hugh had gone and tried my damndest to convince Penny Haskell that I could handle the surveillance myself—that we didn't need two men to do it. Everything was taped, and I could go through those quickly myself, I said. I tried so insistently that she gave me a hard look and asked, "Are you saying that you don't trust Hugh?"

"Let's just say that I think I can handle it better alone than with him," I answered, which was completely unfair for me to say, but I was panicked about what he might learn from eavesdropping on Amir el-Basir's conversations before I could get to the Arab to warn him he was being bugged.

Having the ambassador's son in the picture now was bollixing everything up. There were several reasons why I would be better off not having him here—and so would Amir.

Haskell overruled me, though, and ordered us to go straight to the surveillance apartment. "If it could be a one-man operation, I'd assign it just to Hugh. You're scheduled to go on TDY to the embassy in Cairo the week after next. I'm just hoping we can wrap this up here first."

That stopped me dead in the tracks. Worse than Hugh and me doing it together would be Hugh doing it by himself without me knowing what he was picking up.

I had no time to do anything or say anything to anybody before we were riding up the elevator with our duffle bags and a box of foodstuffs and bottles of cold beer on our way to the safe house surveillance apartment.

We had been in the apartment in the high rise across from the palace and were moving through checking on the bugs in various parts of where Amir el-Basir liked to hang out for several hours without honing in on anything of interest. I was off in the apartment's kitchen getting us each a beer, when Hugh called out, "Come on back, Chris. I think I've got something."

My heart leapt into my throat and the two glass beer bottles I was holding by the necks in one hand started clinking together as my hands started to tremble. I quickly and quietly pulled drawers out until I found what I wanted—what I didn't really want, but what I needed to have—and I slowly walked back into the room.

"You think you've got something?" I asked, trying to keep my voice calm. "This soon? It's about time for your break. Maybe you should turn the surveillance over to me before you get too tied up in what you're listening to. It's recording, isn't it? I can tell you if there's anything of interest on it—my Arabic is a lot better than yours. If you feel you need to, you can play it back later."

Hugh gave me a strange look. "It's what we've come for, I think. Right off the bat. It's Amir el-Basir and the ambassador's son. I hear them through the bug in the pool house. It sounds like they're about to have sex. El-Basir is saying he wants to spread-eagle bind the other guy on a bed, and the guy isn't objecting. Gonna get pretty kinky, it sounds like. And it's the ambassador's son. Come on and listen in."

"How can you tell it's the ambassador's son and El-Basir?" I asked, trying to make myself sound skeptical. I didn't doubt for a moment, though, that it was them.

"I talked to Sean Caldwell at Penny Haskell's reception," Hugh answered. "I can tell it's him from his voice.

They're speaking English. And the ambassador's son is calling the other man Amir."

Shit.

"OK, OK, let me listen too," I said, as I crossed the room, handed him a beer, and put the other pair of headphones on my ears. It definitely was Amir doing the controlling. The other guy was grunting and groaning now, presumably the restraints having already been applied. My mind went to that frame I'd seen hanging above the lounge bed in the pool house. It didn't require any imagination for me to know what was happening there.

Amir was making the sounds he made after he managed to get his dick inside me. and the ambassador's son was panting and begging Amir to go slow with him. Yeah, right. I knew how little Amir paid attention to such requests. I went hard—which I hoped Hugh wasn't noticing—just from thinking about what stage of the fuck they were in and the feel of Amir's cock working inside the ambassador son's channel. I even envied the guy the restraints and use of the frame. I'd have to ask Amir to do me that way the next time I was there just so I'd know what it was like. I didn't know if it was the ambassador's son or not. But Hugh wasn't a dummy— unfortunately. He seemed sure it was Sean Caldwell.

What was Amir doing, I wondered. And how did the ambassador's son fit into this? And then my mind went back to the whole reason we were doing this surveillance—that the Agency thought that Sean Caldwell was collaborating with Mideast terrorists and, further, that Amir el-Basir was on the government's terrorist watch list.

Shit. This was all moving too fast for me. It was all happening too fast to me.

"Wait. There's a third voice," Hugh said, his own voice full of excitement. "And he's being invited to enter right in. A gay sex threesome. We've really stumbled onto something here. He's mumbling. Can't quite . . . no, now he's talking more distinctly. Telling Sean how to position himself—how to accommodate two men fucking him. God, I know that voice. Oh shit . . . it's . . ."

81

Tyler Haskell, the COS's husband and oil company representative, I thought. I knew the voice as well as Hugh would. And I wasn't surprised at hearing it, as Hugh had every reason to be. I was too panicked to say anything, though.

"It sounds like . . . yes, it's Ty Haskell," Hugh said. I could hear the disbelief in his voice. More disbelief than I was able to muster.

"They'll be at the sex for a while, Hugh," I said with a weak voice that didn't really even convince myself. "It will be some time before they can say anything that we want to hear. We'll have to decide what on the tapes to give to Penny. This is all so . . . going to shit so fast. It involves both the COS and the ambassador. We both could get so screwed if we don't handle this right. Go ahead and take your break now. I'll signal if and when they get into talking about anything that should be of government interest."

"The COS's husband double fucking the ambassador's son with a suspected Mideast terrorist?" Hugh asked in consternation. "Why wouldn't that be of government interest?"

"But the people involved, Hugh. This is a powder keg. There isn't anyone who is going to reward the messengers of stuff like this. Why don't you . . . ?"

"Wild horses couldn't pull me away now," Hugh answered, stubbornly.

We sat there, Hugh licking his lips, a sloppy grin on his face, and me listening in dismay as I heard Amir going through his usual long, totally dominating, routine of taking the ambassador's son, accentuated in arousal and licentiousness now by the adding of Tyler Haskell. Sean Caldwell was being quite vocal on how totally he was being taken in a double penetration. It was all I could do to keep my hand off my cock in trying to share the experience with him. I was afraid I was letting out a moan or two of my own and worrying that Hugh would zero in on how this was affecting me. But Hugh seemed lost in listening to it—and he didn't seem as reluctant as I was to touch his cock through the material of his shorts.

I started to sweat—almost to hyperventilate—when they'd finished with the sex and began talking among themselves of other matters. That damned ambassador's son.

His appearance had changed everything, might ruin everything. He was bringing everything to a head.

"Fuck," Hugh said. "Do you hear that, Chris? They're talking of an operation now. An al-Qaida operation. Two weeks. The embassy in Cairo. Fuck, Chris, did you hear that? They're planning an attack on the American embassy in Cairo. We've got to . . . Chris! What's that? What are you . . . ?"

"As Allah is my witness, I'm sorry you heard that, Hugh. I tried to push you out of it, but . . ."

"Chris! Why? Don't!"

The strong beams of sunlight coming through the window of the apartment glinted off the surface of the sharp blade of the knife I'd taken from the kitchen drawer as it rose and fell.

I hated to do it. But it had to be done. And it was just the beginning anyway.

The Art of It

"Hello, you must be Shayne. I'm Mr. Caldwell's houseboy, Jerome. Come on in. I'll take your bag to your room. He's out beyond the great room, in the pool. Go on back."

With that welcome, I entered the world of Ted Caldwell, retired supposed master spy, the man I'd been sent to the New Jersey shore to interview over the weekend for *Spy* magazine. I hadn't been looking forward to this assignment. I didn't half believe in what Caldwell said he was and what he'd said he'd done. His book had sold well, but I put that to the sensationalism in it. But Alex Jameson, the magazine's publisher, had been all keen on an interview—anything on Caldwell at this point in his book sales would help the magazine's bottom line, I could see, so I couldn't argue with that. And I was engaged to Jameson's granddaughter, Denise, so I couldn't very well wiggle out of the interview.

Ted Caldwell's "houseboy," whatever that meant—was a surprise. He certainly didn't look the least bit boyish, although he looked maybe four or five years younger than me—barely twenty. He was a chocolate brown and obviously worked out a lot. He'd answered the door in just wide-legged white muslin pants that rode low on his hips, and he was barefoot. There was a gold medallion on a string around his neck. Other than that, he was all muscle and male model looks. I could see that the New Jersey shore was a whole lot more laid back in midsummer than Manhattan was. I wasn't complaining, though. I was happy to be off the steaming asphalt of the streets of New York.

The wall toward the ocean in the great room was one whole expanse of window, and I could see the gray head of a man swimming laps in the terrace pool beyond, breaking water at a good, fast pace as I walked through the room toward the sliding glass doors to the pool area. He apparently saw me coming and was rising out of the pool as I came through the door.

Yes, indeed, the Jersey shore is far more laid back than the city, I thought, as I watched him emerge from the water. He was nude. This, I assumed was Ted Caldwell, author of the best-selling novel, *The Candy Store*, which supposedly was only a fictionalized—and toned down—memoir of his years trading gay male sex for secrets in service to his country's intelligence interests.

I recognized his face from the cover of his book and had one of my doubts blown away. The cover photo hadn't been doctored. He looked as good in the flesh in his mid fifties as he did on the cover of the book—no helpful airbrushing or lighting distracting from flaws. He was tall and trim and somehow had maintained the muscle tone of a man at least twenty years younger. His silver-gray head hair was stylishly cut to a short style and required no combing over. His chest hair, which extended down his belly and into his bush in a light matting that showed off his musculature to good effect, had speckles of reddish auburn in it, the whole downward trip ending with rather more dominance of the auburn in the bush. His leg muscles were firm, his butt well rounded, and his balls hung low. The cock was probably much longer and thicker than the norm, although who was I to judge a norm? I just knew what I saw at the Athletic Club and in the mirror.

I wouldn't normally scrutinize a man like this, but, like I noted, he unexpectedly rose out of the pool in the nude and my whole interview revolved around what I assumed would be a mild debunking of his sensationalist claims in his book. I must say, at first—quite full—view, I couldn't say he didn't fit the part of male stud—even in retirement.

I stood there, in the doorway, as he padded over to a chaise lounge, one of a pair, dripping on the hot patio stones the whole way, retrieved a pair of white, button-fly short shorts, and pulled them over his hips. They immediately turned damp and plastered themselves to his body, doing no good at all in making that cock disappear. I found my attention riveted to his midsection. I couldn't think of any other man I'd seen that fully equipped.

"Is that you, Mr. Tanner from *Spy* magazine, come to suck this old man dry?" He called out to me. "Come. Come out to my playground." He smiled, a very nice, disabling smile as I gulped through his colorful double entendre reference without being able to discern that it wasn't a well-turned and apt phrase. I had enjoyed his book—at least the writing style— and I felt yet another of my spiteful prenotions dropping and shattering on the patio tiles. It was quite possible that he was facile enough with the language to have actually written his book himself. The critical undercurrent of the structure I'd already preprogrammed for this magazine interview was quickly being shredded into tatters. I was left with trying to tie him up in lies and contradictions.

"Umm, sorry for surprising you this way, Mr. Caldwell. And please call me Shayne. And as for coming out into the hot sun . . ." I spread my arms, bringing attention to the three-piece suit I was wearing. I had driven straight from the Manhattan office building our magazine hid in. And I had learned that, with interviews, it was better to arrive overdressed than under. The latter often was seen as disrespectful and the interview was a disaster from the get go.

"Surprising me? Oh, no, dear boy, you arrived within a couple of minutes of when I expected you. So, you seem to be the obsessively punctual type. We'll have to see what we can do about . . . how we can help you prolong your pleasures. Do call me Ted—or daddy, considering the differences in our ages. Oh, no, that wouldn't do. Jerome calls me daddy, and it would be so confusing when the three of us were together. Oh, sorry, I'm prattling again, and you've dropped your jaw."

I indeed had dropped my jaw. The innuendo he was throwing in there, the breezy "but of course we all are on one page with this" talk. It was straight out of his book. It should have put me off in reading the book, but, strangely enough, it hadn't. It had made me feel warm and wanting to think of the possibility of being in his world, which seemed so open and easy. It was like chocolate; I had felt evil in indulging in the book, but I read it to its completion and wondered what deeper level he could talk to that he hadn't put in his book.

This feeling that I only now was intellectualizing, coupled with the man just standing there toweling off his head and chest, with the water dripping down the white, now nearly transparent front panel of his shorts, was making me feel a little woozy and dangerously aroused. But Caldwell had prattled on while I was spaced out.

"No suits allowed on the Jersey shore in the summer, my boy. What you are wearing will not do for another second. Take that off on the spot. Here, here is a swim suit. Put this on right this instant. Here. Then you can take a cooling swim, and Jerome will bring us some drinks. I have a special cocktail for you to try. It's got passion fruit juice in it."

He was moving toward me, holding out a skimpy Speedo and capturing me with laughing eyes that were a pale blue.

"Uh, OK. I'll just take this and find where your Jerome has put my bag and be back out in a moment."

"No, no, I said instantly. You can strip all of that hot stuff off—and I'll admit that you do look very hot in it—right here, and Jerome will pick it up and take it to your room. Chop, chop. Or should I undress you myself?"

What was I to do? I slowly stripped down on the spot, with Caldwell standing there and smiling at me, taking in an eyeful. I did turn from him when I exchanged my briefs for the Speedo, and Caldwell just laughed.

"Now, into the pool. Then we'll lay and laze and bake and you can start your interview."

Caldwell stripped off his shorts again, walked over to the side of the pool, and neatly dove in. I followed him at a slower pace. We swam laps for a while and then we moved to the shallow end and hunched down and lay against the side of the pool, next to each other.

"You look like you work out, but that you could be getting a little bit better definition in the torso," he said while we were talking about gym work and what we did.

"Uh, well, I can't shake loose a lot of gym time in Manhattan. Work, you know."

"Yes, no doubt," he smiled, "And all of that extra exercise time with Denise Jameson, right?—I did hear right, didn't I, that you were shacking up with the publisher's daughter?"

"Well, um?"

"Big breasts, hasn't she? And those hips. Perfect for sport. Do you well in bed, does—?"

"Uh, well, everything good there. I do have to get material for an interview. Maybe we should be—"

"How'd you like the torso of that Jerome?" Ted asked, switching gear. "Your chest and six pack aren't bad, but how'd you like to be cut like Jerome is?"

"Well, um."

"You know, he looked no better than you did when he came to me, and now look at him. Here, move around and stand out and let me take a look at you. Yeah, hmm. Raise your arms."

I stood, feeling embarrassed and then feeling tingly and knowing I was trembling as we both stood up in the shallow water, up to our knees, and Caldwell ran his hand over my biceps and shoulders and chest muscles and then let the hand glide down to my lower belly and just rest there as he prattled on about exercises and equipment that would tighten me right out and bring out the definition.

I looked down and saw that he was half hard. And I'm ashamed to admit that I was too. I didn't look down, but I knew it from the sensations I felt.

I fell back into the water with a splash and sat on the floor of the pool, with water up to my neck and my eyes on his half-hard cock.

"The interview. I think we'd better get on with the interview," I croaked. "I've got a lot of questions, and it's just tonight that I plan on staying."

"Yes, that would be splendid," Caldwell chirped happily. And he gave me a happy smile—I'd like to say a pleased, satisfied smile, as that seemed more fitting—and turned and streamed off in a perfect breaststroke toward the pool steps.

The next two hours were quite productive for me, although I was being warmed by more than the cancerous rays of the sun. Caldwell stretched out on his back on one chaise, fully reclined and fully nude, and responded to all my questions in a witty, slightly risqué stream of fully coherent, well-organized, rich baritone expostulation. He was filling in background on things he had only hinted at in his book, and I wasn't able to catch him in a single inconsistency. My preconceived line of attack that I had wanted to use as a tongue-in-cheek approach to covering his whole life with a question mark and a whisper of scam in my *Spy* article was sliding off in little chunks and smashing to the ground. I found myself searching for a whole new line of foundation for the article, and the clearest concept I was being able to come up with was something ricocheting back and forth between "Wow" and "Hot."

The heat was getting to me. The heat of the sun beating down on our bodies, the heat of the stories behind the stories in his book, the warmth and relaxation and tingly feeling coming from those cocktails Jerome kept bringing out to us, the increasing warmth of the reactions of my body while watching Jerome deliver the cocktails in his billowy muslin pants and seeing his long feet and plump toes, the heated looks Caldwell was casting my way as I lay on the chaise lounge with the laptop propped on a basket that betrayed that I was having very disturbing feelings and reactions, and, above all else, Caldwell lying there, lazily running his nails along his slim, well-muscled torso and then down to fondle his half-hard cock.

I felt myself breathing heavily and my voice becoming thick as I asked the questions and then tried, with not the greatest success, to enter the gist of his fascinating, but definitely not family-rated stories into my files—when he suddenly hopped up off the chaise lounge, reached for his now-dry shorts, stepped into them, and announced, "Nap time.

I can tell you are getting drowsy, and it's time to take a nap. Shower and rest in your room, and the house will go completely quiet as I do the same. Dinner is at 7:00. Jerome grills a mean steak, and we have some lovely wine—unless, of course, you would like to continue with these cocktails. Like them, do you? Give your cock a little twinge do they?"

There was little I could say in response to the torrent I was growing accustomed to from Caldwell. And he left me speechless with that last comment, because, now that I thought about it, that's exactly what the cocktails did for me—they gave my cock a twinge. And it was far from an unpleasant experience, although it was with great embarrassment that I now thought about it.

I showered and pulled clean boxer shorts out of my bag and stretched out on my bed, drowsy, and my eyes watching the slow-moving paddles of a ceiling fan above the bed. The room was in shadows when I awoke. I don't know what woke me, but it seemed to be a bell somewhere. When reflecting on it later, I quite suspected that I had been awakened on purpose.

I lay there, trying to decide whether to get up and review my notes or drift off to blissful sleep again. I was leaning toward the latter, because I woke in a mellow mood and my cock was hard. I must have been having a pleasant wet dream, but, as with most dreams, I couldn't remember a bit of what that was except for waking with a pleasant feeling and slightly panting. In my world that reflected a sex dream.

It took a while laying there before I heard the sounds, and it must have been the residual randiness that pulled me out of my bed to investigate what were pretty clearly identifiable sounds. I padded down the hall.

They had left the door open to the master bedroom and they were both on the bed, naked. Jerome was on all fours and Ted was hunched over his hips, fucking him in long strokes. I watched Ted's cock pull all of the way out, which was a long journey, and then slowly, inch by inch, work its way in to the root, followed by three quicker strokes and then the long one. Ted's hands were wrapped around to Jerome's chest and were latched on to the chocolate god's nipples. By the

91

expressions in their faces and the moans being emitted by both, I knew they were at the height of passion.

I turned and fled back to my room—and laid on my back and masturbated, trying, without success to replicate the moanings I was hearing from down the hall. I was in a whole new world here. I'd never reacted this way to men before in my life. And I'd certainly never caught the reality show version of men having sex with each other.

I was scared. And what scared me the most is that I didn't get up and put on my three-pieced suit and just walk out of there.

Dinner was delicious, taken at a long table in the dining room, overlooking the shimmering lights in the pool and the relentlessly pounding surf of the ocean beyond. It also was an eerily quiet dinner; not a word was spoken on anything that had happened earlier in the day. Ted sat at one end of the table, still only in his shorts, and Jerome, still only in the muslin pants, pattered about delivering food and pouring wine. There was soft pseudo-Brazilian samba music in the background, Brazil 66, if I wasn't mistaken—or something similar, at least. I sat at the other end of the table, with the laptop open and humming on a chair beside me, trying to pick up on and file away the nuggets of gold being rattattattated at me from Ted's end of the table in a rich, rambling unloading of his spying exploits—most of which left me gagging on my food and blushing.

Afterward, we adjourned to the adjacent living area and sat at opposite ends of a huge, curled sectional sofa facing the ocean while Jerome padded about in the kitchen area, cleaning up the dishes.

Ted had told me that I could have this time to backtrack and ask questions about what he had already told me in his long, fascinating, extremely hard-to-believe save for the believable detail monologue. And while we talked, and Ted continued to weave a web of contentment and slight sexual stimulation around me, Jerome appeared with another of the cocktails we'd had earlier in the afternoon. I didn't intend to drink the one he set in front of me, but as Ted and I talked and I became engrossed in our discussions, I noticed Jerome taking away an empty glass and putting down another full one, and then another one after that.

I was feeling woozy and fully contented and more than just a little tingly when Ted suggested we needed to take an evening swim, with the pool just lit by the under-the-subsurface lights.

I don't remember at all being convinced I didn't need a swimsuit for that swim. I do remember being embraced and kissed by Ted in the middle of the pool. I vaguely remember being asked if I'd ever had a blow job as I lay on my back on the deck at the shallow end of the pool, my butt on the rim and Ted standing between my spread legs. I remember that, because I said no, but I lied—just barely, though. I'd let a guy do it at my prep school for college in the bathroom of our dorm, because in that year I was trying anything new and forbidden. But I didn't feel all that guilty about saying no, because that prep school blow job wasn't anything at all like Ted's sucking—or his bringing me to the brink and laughing and holding me still until the moment passed and then starting to suck my bulb and flick my piss slit with the tip of his tongue again and deep throating me until at last he let me come—and swallowed it. And then came over me and laid his chest on mine and kissed me.

I was with it enough to moan and object when he asked me if I'd ever been fucked. And, ashamedly, I was also lucid enough when, after moving his head down and tonguing my hole and working my cock again with his hand, his face loomed above mine again as well as his hand with the disk of a condom between two fingers, and he asked me if he could, and I moaned not just my acceptance but also my need.

He was gentle and took it slow and praised me when I took it all and stopped long enough after I cried out at the beginning of the stroking that he was too big for me for my walls to stretch to accommodate him. And I remember rising to new, never-before-experienced heights of pleasure as he fucked me for what seemed like forever.

And I was mostly "with it" when I let Jerome kiss me while he was toweling me dry, and I must have had at least some of my faculties when, after he had led me to my bed, and stretched out beside me, I begged for Jerome to fuck me on all fours, like a dog—just like I'd seen Ted fuck him. And he did.

I woke in the middle of the night, sandwiched between Ted and Jerome, and I remember murmuring my pleasure when Ted moved my body to where I was stretched out on his body, my back on his chest, and his arms wrapped around my torso, and he raised his knees between my legs and spread my thighs with them and slowly entered my channel and rose deeper and deeper inside me and worked my nipples with his fingers, as I moaned and moved my hips, fucking myself, and beginning to drift off again as Jerome took my lips in his and encased my cock in his hand and started to stroke me. If this all sounds confusing and disjointed—and overwhelming—that's pretty accurately how I experienced it at the time.

I was alone when I woke. My muscles felt tired, my channel was sore, and I was remembering only bits and pieces of what had happened. But I remembered enough to know that it had happened—and that I hadn't walked out the previous afternoon before it did happen.

Ted was at the table for breakfast, with the same cheeriness of the night before, not indicating that anything momentous had happened—and it struck me that, for him, it undoubtedly hadn't been anything new or special. What he had done—what he and Jerome had done—fit in perfectly with their world—the world Ted wrote about in his book and described to me in the interview. This was my own disconnect with reality. I was the one out of touch with the world—at least of the world I had intruded into for this interview.

Jerome padded over from the kitchen counter, in his muslin pants, and poured coffee for me—once more just Ted's "boy" doing all of the domestic chores. He smiled, but it wasn't the knowing "I fucked you good last night" smile that I expected—and that I deserved.

By my second cup of coffee, though, Ted's world became much more complicated and evil—and much closer to his book theme—and invaded and possessed my world just as surely as his cock had taken my channel the previous night.

Carrying his cup of coffee and a stack of paper, Ted came down the side of the table and sat down next to me.

What he was carrying were glossy photographs, which he fanned out in front of me as he sat down.

They were photos of Ted and Jerome fucking me in the guest room bed. They were taken from several edge-of-the ceiling angles, and they clearly showed me enjoying the cocking I was receiving.

"What is this, Ted?" I asked when I could manage to say anything. I spilled my coffee when I first saw the photos, and Jerome dutifully came over and sponged up the spill and topped my cup up.

"This is fairly obvious, Shayne. This is you fucking two men on a bed. I'd show you some photos from the pool, but they didn't turn out nearly so good—or graphic."

"Why?"

"This is how we do it, Shayne. Now, I don't think we want your Denise or her grandfather to see these, do we? It's not just a marriage—and to a fine set of tits and a big butt—but the money as well, don't you think? It's also your job on the line. A whole future career."

"What do you want, Caldwell?" I asked. I tried to make my voice cold, uncaring. But it came out in a weak squeak. I needed the coffee badly, but I didn't think there was any way I could hold the cup without spilling it just now.

"Not much," Ted answered chillingly. "There's a safe in Jameson's office. I think you could get the combination to the safe and manage to be in the room alone for a few minutes. Don't you agree?"

"I . . . I don't know. This is all just too. . . . It's just happening too fast. Too much of shock. Yeah, I guess I could manage that."

We sat there and stared at each other for a long moment, and I blinked first and lowered my eyes.

"What's in the safe that you want?" I asked weakly.

There was a long pause, and Caldwell said, "Nothing. There's nothing in the safe I want, Shayne."

I looked up, and he was smiling. How could he smile at a time like this, I wondered.

"I don't understand," I mumbled.

"This was all to make a point, Shayne, although you do have a beautiful body, and a fine ass, and a nice, tight hole. And I always enjoy being the first. But we did it to make a point. I don't want a damn thing out of Jameson's safe. And we can burn these photos together—unless you want them for your trophy case."

"I still don't understand," I stammered.

"Jameson warned me that you didn't believe my book. That you didn't believe that normal men could just be seduced and suborned to do illegal, unpatriotic things for sex. I—with some help from Jerome and lots of cooperation from you— have just proved you wrong. I want you to write a better article for *Spy* than one of disbelief and dismissiveness. I think now that you can't possibly write your piece from disbelief that it could happen. There is an art to it. You've just been had by the art, and it took less than twenty-four hours."

Again a stare down, and this time I just couldn't help myself. I started laughing. First a nervous giggle and then a full, uncontrollable session of belly laughing that was only stanched when Ted put his arms around me and his lips to mine and rocked me back and forth in my chair.

"Do you need more notes, Shayne, or are we done here?" Ted whispered in my ear.

"I think I could use a few more notes," I said. I couldn't take my eyes off the photographs. More and more of what happened the previous night was coming back to me. And I couldn't deny the pleasure I saw in these photos and remembered from the actual coupling.

"Do you think you'll be staying the night again, then?"

"Yes, I think maybe I'd like that."

"And maybe a bit of a swim in the pool now—and maybe Jerome can join us?"

"Yes, that would be nice. I'm not sure I know where the swimsuit you gave me is."

"I don't think we'll be needing that, Shayne. Do you?"

"No, no, I guess not," I murmured.

The Brigade

They had first met in an insurgent camp outside Yogyakarta in the Indonesian jungle, far from their own country of the Philippines. In the Philippines there was little chance that they would have met, especially while the Americans were still there in force, but even in more recent years when the government had been weak and taken up with internal squabbling. Rahib, long-time leader of the Moro National Liberation Brigade, was seasoned and deliberative and Islamic, and he came from the Moro people in the southernmost island of Mindanao. Hilario, in contrast, was young and vibrant—a regular fire brand—and was nominally Catholic and the result of an excellent mix of native Filipino and Spanish blood and came from the northern island of Luzon.

And beyond this, Rahib and Hilario's father, Humberto, had been political rivals and enemies from the earliest days of efforts by such Third World leaders as Sukarno, Nehru, and Castro to bring all of the undeveloped world together to stand against the Western nations. And in those efforts, these leaders had worked—seemingly unsuccessfully in Rahib's and Humberto's cases—to bring all of the charismatic revolutionary leaders together, and to combine their forces to stop fighting each other for control over a nation that was in the hands of yet other forces.

Humberto was long dead and his original organization defunct, but out of the ashes of that had arisen another insurgent organization that had become the bane of the Americans and the Manila governments they supported in an urban warfare environment. And the leader of this Philippine Nation Brigade was Humberto's young son, Hilario.

In a never-say-die effort of the old Panchsila doctrine leaders, Rahib and the son of his nemesis were enticed to meet with insurgent leaders from other countries for the first time in a congress of remnant revolutionary groups across Southeast Asia. Hilario was still open to high thinking and had a fire in his belly for change, and he was susceptible to the principles of Panchsila. Rahib who had been around long enough to know that Panchsila stemmed from an effort to keep Islam spreading in Southeast Asia was not.

However, Rahib was sexually attracted to Hilario and could not help but notice that Hilario was attracted to him even more, like a puppy sniffing after a bone. And Hilario was highly sexed and was a pushover for more mature, well-muscled men. The two came together, interestingly enough, for exactly the same selfish reason—disrespect for Hilario's father, Humberto.

As the conference wore on under the heaviness of high-flown speeches that were dusty from decades of useless delivery, Rahib's amusement at the thought of fucking Humberto through the puppy following him around turned into a possibility and then an intention. With Hilario, it started with the attraction to Rahib, the man, solid and mature, well-muscled and silent until discussions were at their deepest quandary and then cutting in with the wisdom of many years on the trail and in the insurgent hunt. And those many hard years were etched in the man's body. The primitiveness of the jungle camp did not accord much privacy, and Hilario saw Rahib in the showers. His body was powerful, his Moro tattooing was intricate and fascinating, his cock was thick, his balls were heavy, and, most intriguing of all, his body was pocked with the medals of combat that can't be properly symbolized by colorful and shiny baubles.

Only after Hilario decided he wanted to be fucked by Rahib did he start thinking of what a delicious revenge that would be on the unloving and abusive father who had never had a favorable thing to say about the Muslim insurgent leader.

Hilario was the aggressor. Rahib had planned the taking, but he was always deliberate and slow in unfolding his campaigns. Hilario was impulsive and direct. He started by wearing nothing but low-slung jeans and always being in Rahib's line of vision. His was a lithe, berry-brown, and perfectly proportioned body that came with the delightful mixing of the genes of dramatically separate races. He moved gracefully, like a dancer, and his beautiful body was always in motion. Rahib was not the only man to watch the youth in motion and want to grab that, and hold it, and penetrate it deeply as it slowly melted down at his feet.

On the day Hilario entered the shower room when only Rahib was there and directly asked Rahib if he'd like to fuck him, Rahib turned the smaller, younger man belly to the concrete wall, crouched below him, and willingly thrust his thick cock up into the soft core of his enemy's son. With each thrust, Rahib declared a death to each person and force that stood between the disparate Philippine revolutionary groups and seizure of the mutually hated, American-influenced government in Manila. Hilario answered, between groans and moans of pleasure, with a pledge of assistance and cooperation. If the Moro leader ever needed him, Hilario said, his insurgent band would be there to help.

And in that strange way of zealots always putting their zealotry at the center of their lives and natural functioning, an exorcism of a mutually hated, long-departed man was consummated, and the seed of future cooperation was sown just as surely as Rahib's seed was implanted deep in Hilario's channel. In addition, the conference attained probably its only success toward meeting its goals—and never even knew it.

For the remainder of the conference, the two very different leaders bedded together, while Hilario endeavored to introduce Rahib to sophisticated and refined sexual positions and Rahib trumped that with lost-to-the-fuck power ravishment. The one technique that Rahib readily absorbed

99

from Hilario's preferences was bondage. Hilario liked to be lightly controlled with strappings and entrapment when he was fucked.

At the end of the conference, ironically enough, while Hilario returned to the Philippines to insert his band of young, energetic insurgents ever deeper into the major Philippine cities and his forces grew, Rahib took his Moro insurgent band to the north island, Luzon. Although in time he was successful in displacing American influence there—especially around the former U.S. service recreation center at Baguio—as the U.S. forces were being pulled out of the region, the toll of combat on his own forces was significant.

As the Americans left, the government in Manila began to take on more of its internal defense responsibilities, and within months of declaring Baguio insurgent held, Rahib's Moro National Liberation Brigade was trapped in the dense forests on the nearby Mount Pulog and the Philippine army was poised to announce that yet another insurgent band had been wiped out.

At that point, Rahib's long-ago rivalry saved his life. A small army of young, inspired hot brands streamed out of the cities and into the highland jungle of central Luzon. The forces of the Philippine Nation Brigade under the leadership of Hilario was reconstituted in the foothills of Mount Pulog and merged with the battered and combat weary remnants of Rahib's Moro band.

The two leaders met, all smiles. They agreed on the spot to merge their forces, without regard to the real differences in doctrine, religion, ethnic origin, and political goals that had made them separate forces. And, not being able to readily agree on a name, they settled on the only shared word in their individual titles, and the combined force now became known only by the bland name "The Brigade."

"We must celebrate tonight," Rahib said with a big grin, knowing full well that the equal nature of the merger was a farce—that to the extent he controlled the impetuous young Hilario's ass canal, he controlled all of the insurgents gathered. He had just rejuvenated his own forces at the mere cost of a title. "We will dine alone, you and I, in my tent."

The look Rahib gave Hilario left little doubt who would be dining on what.

"I should like to bring my lieutenant along with me," Hilario said, reaching back behind him and pulling a tall, solidly built man of greater years than Hilario and most of those in his youthful band forward into the circle of senior combatants. "This is Fernando," Hilario said.

Rahib took one look at the seasoned combatant Hilario had brought forward and at the way Hilario held the man's arm, and Rahib instantly knew that this was competition. He marked himself for a fool for not realizing that the impulsive and randy Hilario naturally would have a lover, and he decided he needed to establishing the poking order from this new beginning.

"I would love to talk with your lieutenant further and to give him full position in our counsels, Hilario, but I would like this first evening together to be a meeting of the minds of just we two principal leaders. I would be happy to see you at my tent at 7:00 p.m., please." And then he turned and left, not bothering to check the glances exchanged between Hilario and Fernando.

That evening, the wily and experienced Rahib did manage to establish the poking order. He fucked Hilario, with Hilario's wrists tied above his head on the tent's center pole, and Rahib lifting his legs off the ground with hands grabbing Hilario's hips and pounding up inside his channel. Rahib had figured that Fernando had not guessed that, although Hilario said he enjoyed exotic positions and refined fucking, what he melted to was just a controlled deep pounding by a thick cock.

And when Rahib was finished with Hilario, he sent him back to Fernando immediately as a "try to top this" challenge. Fernando's stretched out, sensual, slow-fuck side splitting of Hilario inside their combined sleeping bags did, indeed pale in Hilario's unconsciousness in comparison with the exciting domination Rahib provided him.

During the following months, Rahib managed to walk a precarious but ever-more-steady line in sublimating the many differences in temperament and beliefs and goals within his expanding insurgent force and keeping Fernando in a distant third place, all through his cocking mastering of Hilario. And as time went on, his position and hold strengthened, and the insurgents slowly regained control of the Baguio region and the government troops began to cordon off the region rather than continuing to try to wipe the insurgents out—and to complain of outside support of the insurgents to their American allies.

At that point a new element entered in the mix.

Rahib, Hilario, and Fernando were standing in the center clearing of the main camp one late afternoon—dancing around an argument over Rahib's minimizing of a one-time goal of the Philippine Nation Brigade and Hilario just standing and slightly frowning as Fernando lost point after point with Rahib—when a commanding, Western-visage, shockingly out of place figure strode into the circle.

All around the periphery rifles were raised and safeties were clicked off, but the figure continued his measured strides right up to where the three insurgent leaders had been conversing. He was a large, hulking figure, cut to demanding military standards, dressed in jungle combat garb with brown camouflage fatigue trousers over combat boots and a brown athletic T stretched over an expansive muscled chest descending into a narrow waist. His biceps were like trunks of trees, and he was easily shouldering a duffel bag over his shoulder, carrying a submachine gun in one hand, and dangling one of the insurgents' perimeter scouts under his other arm. The scout was minus his trousers and briefs and just collapsed and moaned in the dust when the stranger dropped him.

"Not the best of welcomes," the stranger barked, "You'll find another scout out on the trail. Not the worse for use, I hope."

Rahib stayed the progress of the insurgents from the periphery of the circle, who, rifles still raised, were closing in around the stranger.

"Who are you, and who sent you?" Rahib asked, challenge and no fear in his voice.

"They call me Sling," the intruder answered. "And Osama sent me."

"What is this?" Hilario said, turning to Rahib, who obviously had heard the answer to his challenge that he wanted to hear and was motioning the insurgents to lower their rifles.

"He is an expert in commando operations, Hilario," Rahib answered. "We have agreed, you and I—and Fernando—that, as exuberant and motivated as your men are, they lack the training for rural warfare. You have been fighting in the cities. And when we put my men with yours for training, there has been too much friction. Sling here is an expert trainer. He comes to us from comrades in Colombia. He will help make us strong."

"But, he said Osama. That isn't—" Fernando muttered, the concern clear on his face. And there was more than one reason he felt an uncomfortable concern. He had his eyes on Hilario, who was staring intently at the stranger. Fernando knew that look. Hilario was so hard to control. He was a randy brat; he'd open his legs for any mature, muscled man, if Fernando didn't keep him under control. Fernando was already losing ground to Rahib with Hilario. And now here was a brand-new threat. Fernando was listening out of one ear to the conversation between the insurgent who had knelt to help the disarmed scout, and the scout was saying that the hulking Westerner had fucked him after disarming him and he was babbling something about a strap.

"Come, Sling and Hilario," Rahib interjected forcefully into the discussion. "We will go to my tent and discuss plans for the training. It could not have come too soon. We've heard that the government forces are building. They may be planning a dry season offensive."

Rahib did not want to dwell on who actually had sent Sling. He wanted to minimize the Islamic connections. But these connections were key to Rahib's plans for the future. In his mind the insurgency group was fundamentally promoting the interests of the Islamic nation, even if the youths Hilario brought into the mix considered themselves nationalistic Catholics.

Hilario had trouble paying attention to the formulation of plans during the meeting—which Fernando tried to attend but was turned away from at the entrance to the tent by two of

Rahib's right-hand men. Hilario's eyes were glued to Sling's pecs and the quarter-sized nipples pushing through the material of his athletic T. Hilario had also heard the scout say that the stranger had fucked him, and Hilario was lost to arousing speculation from that moment.

Sling started his training immediately. It did not go smoothly, although Sling obviously did know his craft well and he was a good enough instructor. What Fernando noticed in watching him at work, though, was that Sling was slyly fomenting unrest between the members of the two disparate bands that had been flung together with little preparation. When he was working with Hilario's men, he slipped in disparaging remarks about Rahib's seasoned combatants. And when he shared rations with Rahib's veterans as they all squatted around the fire, he criticized the abilities and talents for rural combat of the brash and snotty young men from the cities.

When Fernando tried to speak with Hilario about this at night when he was making gentle and slow love to his young leader after Rahib had sent him back to his own tent, Hilario just turned on his side and drifted off to sleep, exhausted at the bound cocking Rahib had already given him.

At the first chance Hilario could get in the next few days, he spied out Sling in the showers, simple woven bamboo-paneled sections set on stone floors with hoses set in frames above them. And the small, young revolutionary gasped at the sight of the man naked. His body was more magnificent than Rahib's even. He was younger than Rahib, his muscles were rock solid, and the cock and balls hanging down from his bush were, if anything, meatier than Rahib's. And, like Rahib, his body displayed the honor of combat scars. On him, they just made him seem more dangerous and desirable.

Hilario let out another gasp when he became aware that Sling saw him watching and Sling turned to him and, with soapy hands, began to work his cock, giving it almost impossible length and thickness.

Two evenings later, rather than going to Rahib's tent, Hilario decided that he needed a shower as he watched Sling, only in his combat fatigue trousers striding toward the showers with soap, a towel, and some sort of black leather thick strapping over his arm.

Hilario entered the shower enclosure naked. Sling turned to him and gave him a half, "I knew it" smile. He was working his cock up with soapy water again.

They stood there, staring each other down, for a long minute. Hilario was unsteady on his feet, and his rising cock was betraying his interest.

"Have you come for this?" Sling asked, moving his hand on his cock.

"Yes," Hilario said in a small voice.

"Come here, kneel, and blow me." Sling growled.

As Hilario knelt and took Sling's cock in his mouth, Sling added, "And work yourself."

After a few minutes, Sling pulled Hilario up, standing, close to his chest.

"Work them both," he directed, and Hilario took the two jutting cocks together in his hands, while Sling palmed the young man's buttocks and then, using soap under the cascading water from the overhead hose, spread the orbs with his palms and began working his fingers into Hilario's channel and opening him up.

Sling reached over to where he'd dropped his towel and came up with the thick black-leather strap Hilario had seen slung over his arm when he was walking to the shower.

"Ever used one of these?" Sling asked. "It's called a plow belt—and that describes what it's used for quite well."

"No," Hilario answered, but the way he said it indicated that he clearly was interested in what it did. It was about four feet long and ten inches deep and padded. It had hand holds at either end.

Sling took one handle in one hand, flipped the sling around Hilario's back and grabbed the other handle in the other hand.

"Climb my cock," Sling directed. And he crouched down, jutting his midsection forward, as Hilario positioned his hole over the head of Sling's cock and, with the help of his hand, moved the cock inside him to the rim of its bulb head.

Sling pulled the plow belt tight under Hilario's buttocks and pulled up in a strong motion as he quickly rose from his crouch, sending Hilario's channel on a deep dive down the length of Sling's long, thick, hard cock.

Hilario cried out at the taking, flung his arms around Sling's neck, climbed Sling's hips with his legs, and held on for dear life as Sling used tightening and releasing of pressure on the strap slung under Hilario's buttocks to stroke Hilario deep with his cock.

Hilario came before Sling did, and then, when Sling came, he just dropped one end of the belt and let Hilario collapse down his legs onto the stone floor of the shower enclosure.

Sling picked up his towel, the sling, and the bar of soap and walked out of the enclosure.

Two nights later Hilario told Fernando it was time for him to go sleep among the insurgents for a while and work on their morale. This had been Hilario's answer when Fernando tried to tell him again that Sling appeared to be sowing dissension between the two insurgent factions. When Fernando was gone, Hilario asked Sling to move into his tent.

At the same time Hilario stopped visiting the tent of Rahib in the evening.

In short order tension had mounted and tempers had gotten as short among the leaders of The Brigade as they were among the insurgent underlings.

Two days later, in the midafternoon, with the temperature so hot and the sunlight so intense that the men retired to their tents and to the shade for their midday siesta, Sling was fucking Hilario in Hilario's tent. Sling was standing in the middle of the cleared area inside the tent, in a half crouch. Hilario was bent over the plow belt held at each end by one of Sling's fists and suspending Hilario's belly above the ground, his asshole connected to Sling's midsection by Sling's impaled cock. And Hilario was moaning and groaning in deep passion as Sling raised and lowered the young insurgent leader on his throbbing cock with the black sling under his belly. This was the third such fucking using the sling in this position, and Hilario had begged for it rather than taking a nap.

Sling was standing to where he could see out into the center of the camp from the sheltering shadow of the tent interior. He saw Rahib standing out there, shouting something, and then Fernando lurched into view, facing off with Rahib and waving a pistol. Sling could see the figures of other insurgents, moving about, forming up two opposing lines.

While Hilario was still crying out at his own ejaculation and begging for Sling to finish him, Sling lowered Hilario to the ground, dropped the ends of the plow belt, and reached for Hilario's throat, his thumbs seeking out the vein that would black the young insurgent leader out.

Hilario wasn't quite out, but definitely was stunned, when the first shot rang out in the camp center. Sling crouched low, grabbed up his fatigue trousers, and pulled the knife out of the sheath attached to the trousers' legs. He was at the back of the tent in a flash, picking up the duffel he's stashed there in one hand and slitting up the wall of the tent with the knife held in his other hand. He turned and, at the sound of automatic weapons fire, Sling saw, past the figure of Hilario, who was groggily fighting to sit up, both the body of Rahib sprawled on the ground and the body of Fernando slowly falling to the ground. Stray bullets were zinging into the tent and pinging against this and that, and although Sling didn't stay around to see anything else clearly, he thought he saw Hilario jerk and grunt and start to topple over in the periphery of his vision.

Silas "the Sling" Collins, a senior member of the Agency's special ops unit that was informally known as the Candy Store, could still hear the gunfire coming from up the slope of Mount Pulog when he was half way down the mountain. But he also was beginning to tune his ears into the sound of the chopper coming to pick him up, the chopper he'd summoned with the GPS device hidden in his duffel that he'd set off as soon as he felt he was safely away from the fire fight that was imploding the recently created Philippine insurgent Brigade.

It had been a fairly easy and quite effective operation, really. The hardest part was for whoever managed to make Collins believable as a connection between mainstream Islamic terrorism and Rashid's Moro insurgent group.

As he drew close to the whirlwind caused by the blades of the hovering chopper, Silas laughed when he looked down and saw that he was still clutching and dragging his favorite sex toy, the plow belt. He was happy he wouldn't even have to replace that.

The Glass Cube

(This is the opening chapter of habu's novella *Last Call*)

"So, will you go with me?"

I looked across the table in the open-air area of Effendi's Restaurant on the Kyrenia Harbor quay, and I could see the need in Tahir. I had known he would ask me that question. That was why I was here, in the Turkish zone, on my last night in Cyprus.

Make him happy, the chief of station had said. He hadn't said how to make Tahir happy, and it was something that had to remain unspoken, but both he and I knew why I had been here in Cyprus and why I had been assigned to run Tahir—and how I was to make him happy. Tahir was well placed in the Turkish Cypriot prime minister's office, and the station knew exactly what Tahir's weakness was—what could be used to win him over, to suborn him to keep providing the information we needed to know about what the Turkish Cypriots were up to.

Thus far I had kept Tahir interested and productive by the big tease. A bit of lip work and furtive hand jobs and, when his interest seemed to be lagging, a surreptitious blow job, with the excuse that we had to be extremely careful in our contacts and a promise of paradise "someday soon." And even though my tour was now up, Tahir was still producing ever-more-interesting material, and thus this was a delicate time in the asset's life. Tahir also didn't know that my time was up, that I would be turning him over to someone new.

"Make him happy," was the last thing the COS had said to me before I had crossed the border from the Greek side of the divided island for the last time. "Make him look forward to your replacement," the COS had said.

I didn't answer Tahir's question immediately. I was thinking about the other man at the table, his warm, hard-muscled thigh pressed maddeningly against mine.

Tahir had left word by the usual means that I was to meet him at 11:00 p.m. at Effendi's Restaurant. I'd never met him here before—never before in such a public place. But it was my last night, so it didn't matter to me if it didn't matter to him. And I couldn't have hoped for a better place to spend my final evening on the island.

We were dining on the quay of the small, picturesque Kyrenia harbor, the ancient horseshoe-shaped fishing village with the Byzantine castle at its eastern end, wrapping around the small inner harbor to the Dome Hotel and the breakwater holding back the waves of the Mediterranean to the west. Lining the stone quay in the curve between the castle and the hotel were multistoried stone buildings from the same era as the castle. At one time, when Kyrenia was one of the main trade ports of the ancient island, these were all merchant storage houses, set into the sharp incline up from the seaside. The lower stories of these buildings, facing the sea, were the storerooms and trade houses of the merchants; the upper stories, facing out onto the street ringing the harbor, were the residences of the merchant princes. The buildings abutted each other and functioned in ancient times as a city wall protecting the harbor. And to the south, looming over the coastal town and splitting the island from east to west, was the ragged-peaked Kyrenia mountain range.

Now Kyrenia was a major tourist center of the island—or as major as a blockaded island territory no country but Turkey recognized and that was in perpetual belligerence with Greek Cyprus occupying the southern half of the island could be. The harbor had been made into largely a pleasure yacht basin, and the lower stories of the ancient buildings were restaurants with tables stretching from the entrances into their dimly lit interiors, used only during the colder winter months, down to the edge of the quay and the start of the masted sailboats. At night, with the fairy lights strung in the rigging of the boats in the basin, on the ramparts of the castle, and around the periphery of the restaurants, and the people strolling among the revelers of the restaurants, Kyrenia was a treasured last memory of a very pleasant foreign assignment.

The magic of the night started at 10:00 in Kyrenia, the dinner hour of the Mediterranean culture, and I had arrived at the restaurant an hour later, at the height of the evening.

Tahir had been waiting for me, the look of longing on his face, hopeful in the opportunity to bed me at last—the possibility that I had held over his head for months while he was feeding his government's secrets to me.

Tahir was very nice to look at—slim but well muscled, hirsute in a way that I liked. Black curly hair. A handsome, swarthy face, with a very nice smile.

Everything should have been just fine. But I liked my men appreciably older than me, experienced, controlling, and slightly cruel. A touch of danger went with why I was in this business at all. Tahir was younger than I was, and he gave me the impression that I would have to be the aggressor. As badly as he obviously wanted me, I felt like he would want me to dominate—but not much. Tahir wanted romance. And that wasn't what aroused me. Still, it was probably what made Tahir so easy to run as an in-place asset. And he had earned his reward.

I knew I had to try to please him—not only so he could be passed on, but also because he had done well by me. I owed him. If I left him unsatisfied, I wasn't being fair to the agent who replaced me. Tahir would know we were leading him on, soaking him for as much useful information as we could before cutting him off—or if he had been valuable enough to us, before we extracted him and gave him a new life somewhere far less exotic and friendly than Turkish Cyprus.

As I walked up to the table, I was smiling suggestively at Tahir, signaling that tonight was the night. And all of that time I was telling myself that somehow I had to become aroused enough to satisfy him.

But then my smile froze and I became genuinely aroused as a figure passed between Tahir and me. It was the restaurant host, asking me if I wanted a table, hearing Tahir call out that I was with him, and then giving me a broad, knowing smile.

A smile that melted me.

He was Tahir twenty years from now. Dark, much more substantial than Tahir. The same handsome face and melting smile. But older, more in control. The same dark hair, but streaked with gray and longer than Tahir's, banded into a ponytail. Not fat but solid, heavily muscled. Substantial. This stood out in stark contrast with Tahir's youth, puppy-dog diffidence, and hesitancy. He was the older, more world-wise, form of Tahir, giving me a knowing look as he escorted me to the table. He was guiding me with a beefy palm to the small of my back. And with that he was branding me as his—if he wanted me. Somehow he knew the decision was his; that I would have no choice.

"This is my Uncle Fazil, Jack," Tahir said—almost unnecessarily, as we reached the table. "Can you sit with us, uncle?" Tahir asked.

Yes, yes, I was screaming in my brain.

"Perhaps a bit later, when the customers are settled," Fazil answered. A beautiful, smooth baritone voice, with a charming Turkish-British accent. That was an interesting aspect of the island system; once a dinner party was seated, they were there for the duration.

I sat across from Tahir, and we talked about not much of anything, he fidgeting and nervously waiting for me to become mellow on the wine and atmosphere and delicious food, and me waiting for his uncle to return.

Tahir was giving me that puppy-dog look, afraid to ask what he wanted to ask. I relieved his anxiety by reaching over and playing my fingers down his forearm, through his dark matting of hair. He shuddered in recognition of what that meant. He took the fingers of the hand I wasn't lifting the wine glass with in his hand and gently stroked my fingers. I leaned across the table and let him kiss me lightly on the lips.

As we were coming out of the kiss, Uncle Fazil was there, beside our table, and he sat down next to me and turned toward me and smiled. And I melted to him.

I had to think of something to say to him. I wanted to make whatever connection I could. It was lame, but it was a start.

"So, you work at this restaurant, do you, Fazil?"

Fazil just smiled an indulgent, knowing smile at me.

"Uncle Fazil owns the restaurant," Tahir said, his voice full of pride. "Uncle Fazil lives in Istanbul and just comes home occasionally. Uncle Fazil is an importer. See that big yacht right out there? That's Uncle Fazil's too."

Bells were going off in my brain, flipping through the cables I had to review daily in the vaulted Station area of the embassy. Fazil. Fazil Fikret, the arms smuggler. I tried not to change expression. The illusive Fazil Fikret. He'd been a major intelligence target of ours for years, but so far no one had been able to come close to him. And regardless of this, at the moment I only could think how much more I wanted to go with him tonight than with Tahir.

I tried my best to remain unfazed and even to turn most of my attention to Tahir. This is what I had been trained to do. But every fiber of my being went to the outside of my thigh, which was touching Fazil's warm, hard-muscled thigh under the table in the closely packed restaurant.

More than once I felt that Fazil was about to reach out to touch my arm, even while Tahir was holding my hand and stroking my fingers. But he didn't do it. I had no idea what I would do if he did. I owed Tahir this night.

The ship's bell was ringing at the bar inside the restaurant and the barman was announcing "last call."

That's when Tahir haltingly asked me the question. "So, will you go with me?"

I turned to him and smiled. "Yes."

"Now?"

"Yes."

I heard Tahir take in his breath, almost as if he didn't believe how easily I had agreed, and, unless I was mistaken, I felt increased pressure on my thigh from Fazil's leg.

"Where will we go?" I asked.

"How long? When do you need—?"

"All night," I answered, looking at Tahir levelly, hoping at least that he would take some control, lose some vestige of his off-putting timidity now that his goal was being achieved. "The embassy doesn't expect me back in the office tomorrow." This was true; the embassy expected me on a flight home tomorrow, not back in the embassy. And then I repeated my question. "Where can we go?"

"My uncle has a flat here in this building," Tahir said. But he said it so tentatively that I suspected there was more to it than that. "He owns the whole building."

"But?" I said, because the way Tahir said it, there obviously was a "but" involved.

"We can use Uncle Fazil's flat, but only if—"

"Only if I can be there. If I can watch," Fazil finished for him.

I started to shake, and Tahir, feeling it in my hand and wrist, was quick to say, "But I'm sure there is a room at the Dome, if—"

"No, that's quite all right with me . . . if you don't mind, Tahir," I answered in a low voice. Tahir had mistaken my shudder for squeamishness when it was more a response to an answered prayer. Still, it didn't warm me to Tahir. He never seemed more of a wimp than now.

We rose from the table, and Tahir led me through the interior of the restaurant to a flight of wooden stairs rising to the floors above. Fazil was behind me, guiding me with a broad, cupped hand on my butt. My dick was hardening, and I was grateful for that. Tahir would think it was for him.

We went up four flights of stairs and came out on what was once the roof of the old stone structure. I gasped as we entered Fazil's pied-à-terre at the top of the building. I had been in the Kyrenia harbor many times in the last two years, and yet I never had noticed this flat. It was nearly all window glass, with a narrow terrace running around all four sides. Only in the southeast corner of what was a cube, about thirty feet on each side, was there a short span of rock wall, enclosing a bathroom and a section of a kitchen wall, where all the utilities must have been run. The staircase came up in the southern section of the room, separating the kitchen and a small dining area from the larger room, but not visually cutting off the view.

And the view was magnificent. To the north were the fairy lights of the yacht basin and the hulking Kyrenia castle bastions—and out beyond that the silent sea. To the east and west was the undulating Mediterranean coast reaching out into the distance, and to the south loomed the purple majesty of the Kyrenia mountain range, dotted with the twinkling lights of isolated villas.

The great room itself was nearly empty, except for a large platform bed, covered with red silk, in the middle of the room and a few tub chairs circled round it.

When we reached the top of the stairs and while I was taking in the view, Fazil went into the kitchen and poured himself a large snifter of brandy and selected a cigar from a wooden humidor. He was moving slowly, deliberately, but I felt his eyes burning into me. And he had not lost his knowing smile.

Tahir walked up behind me and encircled my chest with his arms. I turned my face to him, and we kissed. He started unbuttoning my shirt, and I flinched.

"Can you turn off the lights? We are rather exposed," I said. And, indeed, we were. Our glass cube, nearly in the center of the buildings ringing the harbor and hovering over the yacht basin and taller than the rest, was well in sight of many of the windows of the surrounding buildings, and even from the breakwater that served as an inviting promenade to help settle a heavy meal.

"If you would prefer," Fazil said from the kitchen. And he gave a low laugh.

"Yes, please, I would," I answered.

The lights went out, but it didn't go dark. The lights from the harbor side below and from other surrounding buildings cast an eerily glow into the glass cube. Tahir resumed unbuttoning my shirt and pulling its hem out of my trousers.

115

We were kissing lightly again. Everything he was doing was slow and tentative, as if I might put a stop to it at any moment.

This wasn't the way I liked to fuck. I liked a man to take me quick and hard, to dominate me and take my breath away—to let me know we were fucking and that I would never come away from it the same man I went into it.

I was standing at the foot of the platform bed. Shirtless now, I felt Tahir's hands cover my chest and play with my nipples, as he stood close behind me and kissed the hollow of my neck. He was shirtless too, and I felt a chill of pleasure at the tickling of his chest hair against my shoulder blades.

I gave a low moan, because I knew that was what he would like.

Fazil had come over to one of the tub chairs beside the bed. He had stripped naked but was still holding the brandy snifter in one hand and the lit cigar in the other.

The room was dimly lit by the dancing lights of the still busy town below us, and I shuddered at the sight of Fazil. He was magnificent to me. Solid and muscled, thick stomached, but not fat. A Zeus against Tahir's Apollo. His dick wasn't particularly long, but it was one of the thickest I'd ever seen, and his balls were heavy and hung low. Many men would be scared of him and would back off. I was scared of him, and if Tahir hadn't been embracing me, I would have run to him.

I kept thinking that this man was dangerous. An international criminal. Someone to fear. And I did fear him. I feared what he could do with that cock of his. And at the same time, I ached for him to use it on me.

Tahir had unzipped me and pulled my cock out, finding it hard. No doubt pleased that his lovemaking was arousing me. But if he only knew.

Time to go to work—to pay my dues—to complete my assignment.

I pushed my trousers to the floor and stepped out of my loafers, and then I turned and pivoted Tahir around and laid him gently on his back on the bed. Kneeling between his knees, I unzipped his trousers and pulled them off his legs and crouched over him. Holding both of his wrists out at the side on the bed, I started to tongue down his heavy matting of chest

116

hair, wetting his curly hair down and moving my lips down his belly and into his pubic hair and sucking on his hairy balls before taking possession of his long, thin cock with my mouth. Tahir was trembling with pleasure, breathing in short gasps. Lost to me.

All of the time, when I was able, I was looking over at Fazil, who was sitting in the chair, his brandy snifter and cigar on the table beside him, and languidly working his cock with one hand and running his other hand through the heavy matting of his chest, living vicariously what I was doing to his nephew on the bed. And I was also looking out at the magnificent view from the glass cube, the setting sensual and arousing in its own right. It made me feel like I was floating on the clouds between purple mountains and dark blue sea.

Tahir was groaning and sighing under my attentions, and he tightened up and ejaculated in my throat the first time I took him entirely in and held there, my teeth lightly pressuring the root of his cock.

He mumbled an apology, but I pretended not to hear it or to notice that he had come so quickly and kept on giving him deep-throated cock play.

But when I looked up at his uncle, there was a derisive twinkle in his eye as if he was signaling that we were in the presence of a rank amateur. The languid look he gave me conveyed that he thought I needed something else. Something more vigorous and passionate—something more dangerous. And he was right.

Tahir was young and in good shape, and thus he was filling out quickly enough again. He pulled out from underneath me and helped me up to my feet. For a moment I thought he had no idea what to do next, but then he was behind me and I spread my legs and leaned over the bed, with my fists in the red silk coverlet. But my eyes were locked on Fazil's as Tahir knelt behind me. He pulled my dick through my legs and began kissing and tonguing and sucking my balls, dick, and entrance in alternating patterns of slow, sensual lovemaking.

It was a pleasant sensation, and I managed to stay hard as I watched Fazil play his own body off to the side of the bed, his eyes boring into me.

I felt Tahir's cock at my hole, and then he was inside me and taking me slowly in long strokes. I panted and groaned for him, and he murmured his pleasure and appreciation as he covered me close from behind and kissed my neck. Again, the feel of his chest hair on my bare skin helped me. But Fazil's hair fascinated me. He was a real bear of a man, thickly matted nearly everywhere, black, but with gray highlights, which shone in the reflected light of the outside world. My eyes fixated on his hands, his fingers, his hairy knuckles, and I moaned and moved my hips in imagining him finger fucking me with those hands, the fingers thicker than some men's cocks.

Misjudging the source of my arousal, Tahir shuddered and gave a little cry and fucked me faster—but only briefly, as he came again and collapsed on me, sending us both down onto the surface of the bed.

I heard Fazil give a low laugh. I don't know if Tahir heard it too. Probably not. Tahir was lost in ecstasy at what he no doubt thought was a world-shaking fuck.

We lay there for a few minutes, and then Tahir murmured that he would shower and then I could do the same. And after that, he said, we could retire for the night—if that was what I wanted, if I was willing to stay the night. I brought his face to mine and kissed him and thanked him for the fuck and whispered my regret that the night was so short but that it was, by no means, over. Then trembling with pleasure, he rose from me and trotted off to the bathroom, to all appearances glowing with accomplishment.

I sensed more than heard Fazil rise from his chair even as the bathroom door was shutting, and I barely had time to turn onto my back and spread my legs and lift my pelvis before Fazil was upon me, roughly grabbing my waist in both of his powerful hands, leaning his face down, whipping my cheeks with the long strands of gray-streaked hair he let down before he came to me, forcing his searching, possessing tongue between my lips, and thrusting his thick, throbbing cock hard inside me.

I gasped and gurgled and grunted loudly at the onslaught, the sound muffled, I hoped, by the stream of water in the shower, and arched my back and dug my hands into Fazil's chest matting and tried to push him away. I struggled against him, trying to pull out from underneath him, as I knew he wanted me to do. And he bit me on the lip and reared up and backhanded me across the face. He also pulled his pelvis back and thrust hard forward again, driving his cock deeper inside me—as he knew I wanted him to do.

We fucked like animals who didn't believe in tomorrow, him attacking my nipples with his teeth and me clawing my nails into his hairy back and drumming my heels on his calves. He smelled of brandy and cigar and male lust, and I loved him for it. He reared his hairy chest off me and grabbed me by the throat, causing me to choke and gurgle, and beat my head up and down on the mattress mercilessly, as he pistoned his pelvis between my thighs in rhythm. I counterthrust with my hips to take every inch of him inside me that I could. I came quickly and prodigiously, and he ejaculated shortly thereafter, slathering my depths with his hot cum.

He was back in his chair, calmly smoking his cigar and sipping at his snifter, a secret, satisfied little enigmatic smile on his face, when Tahir emerged from his thankfully long shower, rubbing his hair dry with his towel.

I moved slowly, painfully to the bathroom, as Tahir pulled the coverlet off the bed and started pulling the sheets down. He yawned and said I'd find him in bed. And I assumed he would be out like a light. Sometime in the dawn hours, I decided I would wake him and beg to be fucked again. And he would feel the virile man as he turned me on my belly and rode my ass languidly like swelling waves on the sea as I watched the sun rising out of the Mediterranean through the transparent glass walls and dreamed of Fazil's cocking. And maybe that would keep him content to continue to feed state secrets to my successor.

Fazil mumbled something about going downstairs for a few minutes, and he picked his trousers up and headed for the stairs.

But he bypassed the stairs while Tahir wasn't looking and pushed me into the bathroom and fucked me hard again from the rear against the tiles of the shower under the running water, his hairy-knuckled fingers digging into my waist, and his strong hands sliding me up and down, my nipples and belly sliding up and down the slick, soapy tiles of the shower wall, as he played my channel on his cock and reached for my tonsils with his thick, possessing tongue.

"I leave for Istanbul on my yacht in the morning," he whispered in my ear as he released my bruised lips and continued pile-driving his cock up inside me.

"Yes," I murmured.

"You will come with me," he said.

"Yes," I murmured again.

"And from now on, the lights will remain on when we fuck," he said.

"Yes," I answered between groans as he rotated his thick cock inside me, punishing all of my channel walls in a movement that was driving me crazy with passion.

The COS would be pleased that I had wormed my way into the inner circle of the notorious arms smuggler. But that wasn't the only reason, by any means, that I'd be sailing to Istanbul with Fazil Fikret on the morrow.

The Golden Question

Sometimes the simplest of questions require the greatest amount of preparation.

"The golden question for this week the same as for last week?"

"Yep," my boss answered.

We were sitting in the office of the chief of station, the highest-ranking CIA agent in country, in the Nicosia, Cyprus, embassy and, as usual, I was trying to see if I could see anything at all through that small, rectangular bulletproof window beside his desk. It was a shame as gorgeous as the vistas of mountains in two directions were from the American embassy in Cyprus' capital that we were stuck with these security windows, which only gave the illusion that we weren't in a secure fortress. No one laughed about it, though. An ambassador had been shot dead a couple of decades ago through a window in the old embassy building.

"What is it exactly?" I asked. Each week the station got a new shopping list of intelligence questions for that embassy's region from CIA headquarters in Langley. The question at the top of the list was known as "the golden question." You got points from the chief of station, Ted Jamison being the one here in Nicosia, for providing the answer to any of the questions. But Ted was so hardnosed that only answering the golden one would earn a pat on the back. The said getting the answers to the other questions was our job—just what we were being paid for.

"The elite Maroon Beret commando unit of Turkey's 9th Corps, currently stationed on the Iran border, is moving to either the Iraq border or here—to the northern, Turkish zone of the island. The question is, which is it?"

"The importance being?"

"They have been undergoing special training in cross-border infiltration. Presumably the training is leading up to crossing someone else's border. Any way you cut it, that's not good for U.S. policy."

"And we know that how?" I asked. ". . . that they are getting such training."

"We know it because it's our own Green Berets who have trained them for such an operation. And that training includes covert redeployment."

"And we couldn't just ask the Turks where the unit is going?"

"Oh, certainly not. The Turks are among our most valuable—and sensitive—allies. They are probably aching for us to ask so that we can get embroiled on the consenting side. Either we'd have to agree with the action, or they'd claim we did and it would somehow leak that we knew about it in advance. If the unit is going to the Iraq border, it will be messing around with the Kurds, and we couldn't approve of that in the slightest, so we don't want to officially know anything about it. In the same vein we have to prepare for it if that's what is happening. The same thing here in Cyprus in spades. We don't want to officially know about anything, but we damn well better be prepared for what we're going to do about it. Nothing is harder in diplomacy than balancing off two allies of ours who are enemies of each other—and that's what we have with Turks and the Greeks. What we'd much prefer is for them to stay right there on the Iranian border and harass Tehran. But indications are that they will be on the move from there."

"And why do we think they may be coming here?"

"Satellite photography shows new construction at the Turkish army base on the mountainside below St. Hilarion castle and above Kyrenia. Why are you asking, Ron? You got an answer to this one?"

"Not that I can give right now. But one I think I can get. I think I can get to some of the soldiers at the base here. If there's construction, the soldiers will have some idea what's happening."

"Using your special services?"

"Yeah."

"You know how hard it is to get to mainland Turks assigned to the military based on the other side, don't you? They're kept on a short leash. Rarely let off base. Never in fewer than groups of three—to keep each other in line."

"Yeah, I know. But I may have a way. They may be on a short leash, but Turks are well known to be randy—and to like variety. And to consider any hole as worthy to be filled." Ted was right, though. The troops on the Turkish-held northern coast of Cyprus, with the lower two-thirds a Greek republic, had proved impossible to pick off one by one for intell purposes.

"More power to you then. What do you need?"

"A few days loose from anything else. And can Logs fix up two bottles of Johnny Walker Red for me?"

"Knockout or lethal?"

"Slow-working knockout would be best—both of them. I'll be on the other side for a few days. Can I use the safe house on the beach at Karavas?"

"Sure, as long as you don't bring any men back there. Don't want it being noticed."

"Right, Ted, we wouldn't want the Agency connected with any gay activity, would we? Even to get a golden question answered."

We both laughed. The irony of homosexuality being a cause for instant dismissal laid against the Agency having a "Candy Store" unit to use that basic preference to its advantage wasn't lost on either of us. Still it was a thin wire for anyone in that unit to walk. At any point that the Agency decided it wanted to separate you, it could be quickly accomplished.

* * * *

I had formed the idea of how to get around the short leashes on the Turkish soldiers problem while I was fucking Musa on a lounge bed beside the pool at Angie on the Rocks the previous day. The Angie of the club's name was a zaftig British expatriate prostitute who had come into some money and opened a Mediterranean-side pool bar at Lapithos on the northern Cyprus coast to the west of Karavas, which itself was to the west of the picturesque medieval harbor town of Kyrenia.

I enjoyed fucking Musa. He was young, not long legal, and berry-brown, the result of a Turkish mother and Moroccan father. Nicely formed, lithe, and fully compliant. But what I enjoyed most about Musa was that others who frequented the well-fenced off pool bar enjoyed fucking Musa too and found him to be as good a listener as a lay. Angie had a great layout here. There was a nice-sized pool with a lot of terracing around it, poised on the rocks above the Mediterranean surf. Off to one side was a restaurant area under a long, covered verandah. And on the land side of that were a kitchen area and a set of small rooms, where Angie and her waiters and waitresses made extra money on their backs. The flat for Angie and her Turkish Cypriot policeman husband—the perfect spouse for a business like Angie had—was above these rooms. That the husband made extra money himself by filming the activity in the pool area below from his bedroom window and selling the videos on the streets of Istanbul was something that few knew. I knew, however, and always managed to do my fucking on lounge beds out of range of that window.

The glory for me of Musa being such a draw for others was that the pool bar was considered the exclusive domain of expatriates living in northern Cyprus and UN soldiers and the diplomatic community from Nicosia on the other side of the guarded Green Line between the Greek and Turkish zones. Diplomats could traverse this border and came here to escape the glare of the attention in Nicosia. And here they murmured of the problems of their workday as they lay on their backs and Musa rode their cocks.

Musa, one of Angie's waiters, one who specialized in taking care of the male clientele, was an asset I ran, one of my sources for information on what happened behind the scenes in Cypriot affairs and in embassies located in Cyprus. But Musa also liked the cock. And he really liked my cock, so a combination of money and attention kept Musa happy and me fed with a couple of useful reports home whenever I had a chance to go north for a swim.

On this night, Musa was comparing my cocking to that of Turkish soldiers, complementing me on taking my time and giving him as much attention as he was giving me—but, as an afterthought, saying that rough sex with a grin and no frills was nice to have occasionally too. I was agreeing with him on Turkish men in general. No one fucked with gusto and a smile like a Turkish Cypriot man did. And young Turkish Cypriot men had the bodies of gods, often pleasantly hirsute, until their late twenties, when, almost universally, but not always, they quickly began to deteriorate into either a leather balloon or an emaciated bag of bones. At any age, though, they cocked with gusto and few, if any, inhibitions, all white-teeth smiles in grinning brown faces and vigorous thrusting. If you liked to be manhandled and taken hard, but not in anger, a young Turkish Cypriot man was what you wanted.

But then it hit me. He was talking about Turkish soldiers.

"You mean mainland Turkish soldiers?" I asked. Raising myself on the hands planted on either side of his chest on the lounge bed and pulling my cock up to where the bulb was lodged just inside the entrance. He was panting hard and had the heels of his feet dug into the small of my back above where my buttocks flared out.

"Oh, god, don't stop. Finish me. I almost was there," he whined, digging his fingernails into my shoulder blades.

"You mean mainland Turkish soldiers?" I asked again, more insistently. "Tell me and I'll finish you."

"Yes. Soldiers from the base on the side of the mountain below St. Hilarion."

Mainland Turkish men could be even more arousing and fulfilling than a Turkish Cypriot man if you wanted to be overpowered and taken brutally. "When were you fucked by Turkish soldiers from there? They hold their soldiers close."

"Every Tuesday afternoon. They let them out in threes occasionally. Turkish soldiers are as randy as any and they sometimes get tired of fucking each other. God, let me have the cock. I'm almost there."

"But you. How do they get to you?"

"The same three, every Tuesday. Angie has a deal with them. She supplies booze for the commander, a Colonel Erlugu, up there. He sends soldiers to pick it up. On foot. I meet them just off the road up to St. Hilarion, in a pasture. The soldiers pay me for a fuck and an extra bottle. They like Johnny Walker Red. They are tight with each other, like to talk about bodybuilding and flashy American cars while they fuck me and . . . and . . ."

"And what, Musa?"

"Oh shit, don't leave me this way. Fuck me. Oh, god, yes!"

Once, twice, three times I dove my cock deep inside him, twisted it with the revolving of my hips and pulled back up.

"And what, Musa?"

"And they fuck rough. They like to take turns doubling. It sometimes takes me to the next Tuesday to recover. But when you've been fucked by a Turkish soldier—by two Turkish soldiers—you've been fucked. Oh yes, please, yes, like that. Yessss!"

I fucked him hard as he writhed and panted under me—and then fired off up my belly—forgetting, I hoped, anything but the fucking he had gotten. Forgetting what he had told me, which meant more to me than he could realize.

"God, almost like a Turkish soldier," he murmured when we were done. I took it as a compliment.

* * * *

The afternoon after getting the "go" from Ted, I pulled up in my BMW convertible to a rambling beach house on a nearly deserted stretch of beach between Salamis and

126

Famagusta on the east coast of Cyprus, still in the Turkish Cypriot zone. I parked next to a bright red 1959 Cadillac convertible—the one with the outrageous tail fins—that was in pristine condition. Looking out toward the Mediterranean, I saw Onur sitting at his easel, facing out to sea and painting. The multicolored caftan he was wearing, which was billowing in the wind, was more arresting in color than the paints being applied to the canvas. He wore a white turban on his head, the end of which was loose and was beating on his cheek when it wasn't floating out across the sand in the air currents. He didn't seem to notice.

I took my shirt, shoes, and socks off, stowed them on the trunk of my car, and then walked down the beach and stood behind him. I looked out to sea, where a large sailing yacht was bobbing up and down, and then at the canvas where the naked figure of a young man was appearing. No sign of water or a boat on the canvas. The young man was very nicely equipped, though. Onur was especially fond of nice equipment on a young man and I was always flattered when he told me I was one of his nicest young men.

"What is it you want, Ron?" he asked me in a low, bass voice. He hadn't turned around to see me either arrive in the car or walk down the beach to him, as far as I could see. "Mustafa is off in Istanbul, accompanying the prime minister. He's been gone since the last time you visited."

Ah, so he hadn't forgiven me yet for having caught me with Mustafa in high rut on the beach that night.

"I know. I just came to visit. I'm lonely for the company of crazy old men. I see that Sami is gone too." I recognized the model in Onur's painting. It was his sometimes houseboy, who easily got into a snit and went back to his boyfriend in Famagusta, only to return to Onur when he got hungry—and into a snit over something his boyfriend had or had not done. Onur couldn't go a day without seeing Sami, even if he had to paint an image of him in his absence. Onur's paintings of the young man showed that he knew every inch of Sami's body.

"He's been gone a week this time."

"And you've had no one to . . . model for you since then? You know I could—"

"You'd have to take off more than the shirt and those shoes and socks."

"If it will make you forget about that night on the beach, I would be happy to. It was your fault anyway—that cheap wine—and leaving us alone. You know Mustafa better than that."

He sketched me, naked, reclining on the low wall of the long loggia that ran across the sea side of the sand dune-hugging villa. I was leaning on a Moorish column, one leg on the wall, knee bent and my seaward side arm propped on the knee. My other leg stretching down to the tiles on the floor of the loggia, my toes reaching for the floor. My landside arm stretched loosely onto the thigh of my stretched leg, the fingers of my hand, at Onur's direction, pointing to the goods dangling between my legs. I was half hard, also at Onur's request, although I had to dredge up some pretty exotic thoughts to become that way.

"Very nice," he said after about twenty minutes. I knew he was referring to my half hard-on and I also knew he had the sketch finished then. He always was in a trance while he was painting or sketching.

I came around to his side of the easel and gave a little laugh. Everything was done in subdued, almost sketchy strokes except for my package, which was drawn in great detail. Still, it was a masterful work, something to respect as well as chuckle at. "Not too subtle," I said.

And it wasn't subtle. He wanted me to fuck him. I probably wouldn't be forgiven for Mustafa until I had done so.

"When a young man is as hung as you are," he said, "I like to focus on what is important. This will sell quickly in that gallery behind the gallery in Nicosia. I can use the cash. Now, what is it you want from me, Ron? And what else are you willing to do for me to get it?"

Onur was another one of my regular assets. The wrist he had a pulse on that was of interest to me was that man named Mustafa, of the seductive ways, who now was personal secretary to the Turkish Cypriot prime minister. Mustafa had been initiated by Onur decades before, and the man had remained close to Onur ever since. That had been a specialty of Onur's. Initiating young men. Garish and flamboyant, from a wealthy merchant family but with a genuine talent for art—especially for nudes of young men, Onur was an institution of decadence in Cyprus. He left Cyprus at the first hint of a Turkish invasion and the resulting division of the island and had come back to retire quietly in one of his family's villas after an arrest and imprisonment on the Turkish mainland for debauchery and sodomy—apparently of young men in families that were too powerful with sons who were a bit too young.

He was a large man, thickish of waist now, but still solidly built. He once had been beautiful and had had no trouble being a pied piper to young and curious and beautiful themselves barely men. Not yet completely gray, he had a beard and mustache to be proud of and a hairy chest, arms, and calves. There was no hair on the top of his head, though. He was bald, which was the reason that he had worn a turban for decades. He was still a man who was vain about his appearance and used deflections to take the eye away from what no longer was perfection in his body—an earring, multiple rings on his finger, and, when the caftan came off, nipple rings and a gold serpentine band encircling his cock, the tail wrapped around the base of the balls and a cobra head flaring over the bulb.

He had taken the caftan—but not the turban—off when he'd started to sketch me. He obviously hadn't been fucked—receiving now being his favored position—since Sami had wafted off in a snit. And Onur, even at sixty, was a highly sexed man. Despite his nonchalance, he was happy I had come to see him. In his own way, he was trying to seduce me. He wanted me to fuck him. This sketching of me in the nude and his disrobing with the excuse that it was hot in the loggia were foreplay.

After many an encounter such as this, we understood each other perfectly.

I wanted a favor from him, so I would fuck him. I would have fucked him just out of friendship, of course. I was fond of him in terms that went beyond his usefulness as an intell source. Knowing what the Turkish Cypriot prime minister was thinking and doing was fine and helped pay for my usefulness in the station, but in all the time I'd been in Cyprus, we hadn't received a golden question about the Turkish Cypriot prime minister. Washington didn't seem to give two fucks about the Turkish Cypriot prime minister. The mainland Turks controlled Turkish Cyprus. It was what the Turks did in relationship to the island that was of interest to us.

"Stop asking me what I want, Onur. Can't a man drive all the way across Cyprus just because he fancies a blow job from an old friend? Don't you realize how irresistible you are?"

Onur put his sketching pencil down and looked up at me, glowering at me from under his bushy salt-and-pepper eyebrows. He had a slight smile on his face. "Fuck you, Ron," he said. But he had that slight smile on his lips.

"No, fuck you Onur. But you really must be quick about it. This cock can go either way in a hurry. Hard or soft. Which do you want?"

I had unconsciously returned to my pose on the loggia wall after taking a look at the sketch. He came to me and knelt next to my extended leg, cupping and slightly distending my balls with one hand while letting the other glide up to my chest and find a nipple. His mouth took all of my cock. It would have been a chore for most men. But Onur wasn't most men. Swallowing cock whole and then letting his tongue and inner mouth and throat walls make love to it was a specialty of his. Old age doesn't diminish some talents. I leaned back into the Moorish column, moved the leg that had been posed, bent on the low wall, to rest on his broad shoulder, closed my eyes, and let him take me to arousal heaven.

I fucked him on his throw pillow-strewn studio couch, taking him from behind as we lay on our sides. His belly didn't challenge the depth the cock could get in that position. I held his upper leg up to give me deep penetration inside him. He particularly enjoyed deep penetration and always complimented me on being able to reach farther into him than most men. He sighed and panted lightly and purred as I stroked him slowly at first and then, giving him the assurance I knew he loved losing control in the fuck, pushed him over on his belly, straddled his hips, and rode him hard. He ejaculated before I did and was reduced to deep moans and expressions of pleasure as I focused on finishing myself. After I shot off, I lay close on top of him, my cock still buried inside his ass, kissed the hollow of his neck, and let my hands play in the thick hair of his forearms.

I knew he loved this attention afterward. Something, along with the inability to fuck hard and to attain positions that permitted deep penetration of a heavy-set man, Sami had yet to master. I didn't care if Sami never learned to master it. I wanted Onur always to be happy to see me when I came to milk him for intell.

He turned his face to me, we kissed, he murmured his appreciation for the attention to an old man, and then he gave me that glower of his. "Now can you tell me what you want of me?"

"I want to borrow the Cadillac for a few days. I'll leave the BMW here. You can drive it into Famagusta and bring Sami back. He loves the BMW."

"I allow no one to drive the Cadillac. You know that."

"Which is why it needs the exercise." I knew he was just posing. For a fuck from me, he'd give or do just about anything. He always had before.

"Perhaps. Perhaps with a bit more persuading."

"You know I always give you a second one—when you give me what I want," I murmured. And, indeed, we both could tell that I was managing to go hard inside him again.

This time I fucked him just as we were, in close embrace, me plastered to his back. Just my hips moving, giving him a slow and deep fuck—until he begged me for more, and then I vigorously finished him again.

"The keys are on that dresser over there," he said when I finally rose off him and padded toward the bathroom to clean up. He couldn't resist saying in my wake, "I would appreciate if, just once, you came just to make love to me."

I gave a chuckle. He was still so old school that no matter how debauching the fuck was he referred to it as "making love."

After slipping the loafers on my feet and stuffing the socks in my pocket, I opened the trunk of the BMW and took three bottles of scotch out, looking carefully at the subtle markings on the labels to keep them straight. All of them were Johnny Walker Red; only one of them was unadulterated. We had tried to impress our assets one Christmas by moving up to black label for their presents and had received a resounding— and not particularly polite, considering they were supposed to be gifts, not straight-out bribery—confirmation that they all wanted the cheaper red label. I don't know how they would have reacted to the blue label.

I put two of the bottles, after carefully examining them, in the trunk of the Cadillac and the other one on the floor of the backseat. I waved at Onur as I left and watched him, after he had come over to the Cadillac and, having lovingly stroked the finish on the trunk and giving me the "there had better not be a single scratch when it returns" look, strolled down to the beach. He was quite a sight, with his caftan and the tail of the turban floating in the breeze. He settled down on the stick chair, dug off kilter in the sand, and returned to the canvas he was painting of the absent Sami in naked repose while he was facing the surf of the Mediterranean.

That night I visited Angie on the Rocks, which was just west along the beach from the safe house in Lapithos. As I was leaving, I told Musa, "Not this Tuesday. Fail to show up to deliver the liquor in the pasture this Tuesday. I've arranged it with Angie. The story is that Angie sent you to Kyrenia for a new shipment of liquor, but it didn't arrive. So you missed the connection and didn't have liquor to give anyway."

* * * *

Early Tuesday afternoon I parked off the road in a field far below St. Hilarion Castle and the Turkish base below it. I trained my binoculars on the entrance of the military camp until I saw three figures emerge and tramp down the hill, in my direction. When they left the road, moving into the pasture where Musa said he met them, I drove up above that point and, before reaching the entrance to the military base, turned the Cadillac around, parked off on the side of the mountain road, and lifted the binoculars again.

The three soldiers, all beefy and thuggish and looking like I'd get some enjoyment out of this caper, were gathered around a man in a blue uniform. Angie's Turkish Cypriot policeman husband. The soldiers clearly were not pleased with what he was telling them. I thought it fortuitous, though, that Angie's husband was a policeman. I couldn't think of anyone else who could safely deliver the news to three Turkish soldiers—the Turkish army was known for its brutality—in a remote pasture and walk away without a scratch. Wearing his uniform was a nice touch, but it had been necessary. I'm glad he thought of that. I hadn't. Having seen the three now, chances are he would have been roughed up for giving them the bad news otherwise.

I waited for the three to get back on the road and to start marching, clearly angry and afraid of what their colonel would say and do, up toward the base. I revved up the Caddie and bore down on them at full speed, making them jump off the road and into the brush as I swept past them. I stopped the car with a screech and waited from them to pick themselves up and run for the car.

The one that got there first grabbed me by the throat—I was only wearing gym shorts and sandals, so there was no grabbing me by my shirt—and hauled a fist back, preparing to pop me one.

This was one of the trickiest parts of the operation, but it went smoothly enough. I think the vintage red Caddie helped.

I lashed my hand out and grabbed his battering arm at the wrist, calling out, "No, please, I'm sorry. I didn't see you." Happily the other two soldiers were content with letting the first arrival deal with me. They were busy walking around, admiring, and touching the gleaming red car.

"Please. I'll make it up to you. There's liquor in the backseat. And maybe you see something else—someone else—you might like. I've got to say that you three are the hunkiest men I've seen today—and I've had an itch for hours." I spoke Turkish. That both set him back a bit and sped up the

133

negotiations. I gave him "that" look. And I could see the wheels spinning in his little mind.

Then the clincher. I blurted out as I let my hand go to his bicep, "God, are you that big all over?"

The only "little" thing about any of these men would be their minds. They all were bruisers, young, handsome, every bit the Turkish hunk. Two of them had taken off their tunics for the trudge under the sun and were magnificently built. One was extremely hirsute. They had made me hard just from seeing them run for the car, and I shifted my gaze down to my lap so that the Turk at my side would follow my shifted gaze and could see that I was hard.

They'd been expecting a lay in the pasture and hadn't gotten it. I figured they'd be up for a substitute. They obviously were.

"Look at me," I said, guiding his eyes with mine to my crotch. "See what you do to me? Can you soldiers help me with that?"

The Turk at the window told the others, obviously the fact that I spoke Turkish not fully registering with him, that the "nice piece" behind the wheel wanted to be fucked.

"Yes, that would be nice," I added, which brought his head snapping back to me. "You guys want to take a ride in my car? Any of you want to ride me? Any two of you want to ride me?"

They were being a little thickheaded, I thought, but the mention of a ride in the Caddie brought the other two around to the driver's side, and the car door opened.

"Any of you drive American cars, or should I take you for a drive?"

Another tricky part, and this one didn't start out very well.

"I drive American car," one of the men, the hairy one, said with a proud ring to his voice. "My family in Turkey has Chevy older than this and I fix cars before army."

I had hoped none drove and that I could stay behind the wheel. I spent no more time behind the wheel while the soldiers were with me, though. The two other men, identified as Ahmet and Emin, manhandled me out of the driver's seat and into the back, as Kerem slipped in behind the wheel and started driving back down the mountain. The saving grace was the Kerem hadn't lied. He knew American cars and he was a good, if recklessly fast, driver.

Ahmet found the bottle of Johnny Walker Red in the backseat and opened that, took a swig, and started passing it around, while Emin got his pants off, and then my gym shorts, and grabbed and squeezed my balls and pulled me over into his lap, facing away from him, and onto his hard cock. I raised and spread my legs wide, the balls of my feet pressed into the backs of the front bench seat, to open for him. I leaned my torso forward and grabbed the tops of the seat in front of me too to give him a straight angle for the slide of his cock. I burbled quite a bit as, his rough hands grabbing my waist, he forced himself into me—rearing back and thrusting again when the going got tough. I'm glad I lubed myself up beforehand, because none of these guys seemed to care if they split me apart or not.

I laughed a guttural laugh and egged him on, knowing that it was important for me to let them know I was game for the fuck.

After Ahmet passed the bottle to the front seat, he turned, slipped under my thrust-forward arm and leg, came up facing my chest, and hunched down between my thighs, which Emin had pulled wide and up, and wasted little time in getting his cock inside me on top of Emin's. In short order I was being double fucked in the backseat of the Caddie as it sped west on the northern coastal road.

I was careful to continue to let them know this was consensual to encourage them not to get ugly with it at the hint that I would—or wanted to—resist. We all knew that this already was way beyond resistance.

So, they hadn't just been paying attention to the offer to ride in the car. They'd also caught on to my offer to take two of them at once. At least I hoped that they considered that I had offered. Musa had told me that they weren't shy about double fucking him without consulting with him first.

It was a good thing that I'd been warned by Musa that these boys played this way and that I'd had experience being doubled before. Both of the Turks were young, hard-bodied hunks, with normal-sized cocks, so I didn't mind. And I gave them a good time, so they didn't seem to mind a bit either.

Arriving back in the pasture and driving far enough off the road not to be seen, Kerem, the hairy one, got his turn at the DP. Ahmet sat at the wheel, turning it and making vroom, vroom noises, while Emin, again under me, reclined on the trunk of the Cadillac, embracing me, and inside me from underneath, while Kerem pumped me from in front. I indulged in the luxury of running my hands through his pelting and sharing kisses with him as he fucked me. He had the biggest dick of the three, and I let him know I preferred him.

I also gauged that he was the most talkative, opening up increasingly as he drank more of the scotch.

The bottle was nearly empty, and the men were noticing and mourning that as they finished fucking me on the trunk. Free from them for a moment, I opened the trunk, and making sure they couldn't see inside, hauled out one of the other bottles of Johnny Walker Red I'd stashed there—one of the bottles that I'd gotten station Logs to spike for me. The one they'd already been drinking hadn't been doctored.

Making nice, nice to Kerem and telling him I wanted him to fuck me again—in the backseat—just him, whispering to him that he was the best cocker of the three, which pumped him up and wasn't a lie, I handed off the bottle to the other two, who were happy enough to go squat nearby in the pasture and trade it back and forth. The nearly empty bottle I gave to Kerem while I was cajoling him into the backseat and praising the size of his cock, which was, indeed, praiseworthy.

While he sat in the middle of the backseat, one hand on my waist and the other one wrapped around the scotch bottle, I rode his cock, facing him, with my forearms around his neck, nuzzling his face with mine at first, and then lowering his mouth to my nipples so that he could take turns sucking on the scotch bottle and the nipples.

"God, you have one big cock. I want to see you again and have you inside me," I murmured in Turkish. "Will you be here much longer?"

"We rotate out next month, but we come down here on Tuesdays. We can do this again," he answered between grunts as I moved my channel on his cock.

"Another month? I've heard that special troops are coming in after you."

"Special troops? Where you hear that? What special troops? Just another unit of the Cyprus Special Forces Regiment. Just more like us. New recruits mostly. But a bigger unit than ours."

"A bigger unit?"

"Yes. More men. They are building more barracks now because more men come. And replacing a few that are falling down."

"Bigger men than you? Bigger cocks than yours?"

"My cock plenty big for you."

"Yes, I know. I can't imagine one any bigger," I whispered, taking his head, which also was getting bigger from my praise, in my hands, moving his lips to mine, and kissing him deeply while I revolved my channel on his cock.

He came out of the kiss sputtering. "Turkish soldiers don't kiss; we just fuck," he growled.

"But it felt good, didn't it? I felt it in your cock."

He didn't contradict me, so I honed in on the information I was trying to milk from him while I milked his cock.

"But I heard they were very special troops. Are you sure—?"

"Look. I big man in camp. I know everything. Ahmet, Emin, and me, we handle commo from the green line. We see all messages Colonel Erlugu get. We know what unit is come and why new barracks is built."

"God, yes, you're a big man. A very big man. The green line. You mean the Green Line running across the island and dividing Turks from Greeks."

"No, green line is special commo circuit back to mother Turkey."

"Ah, confusing," I said—trying to use a tone indicating I didn't really understand and had lost interest in the point.

"But look. Your bottle is empty. I have another one in the trunk of the car. You want it?"

He did want it. He took several big slugs of scotch from the bottle while I resettled on his cock. He didn't bother to look over to see that Ahmet and Emin were collapsed in the pasture, dead to the world.

Not too dead, I hoped. I wanted the soldiers to keep this tryst secret. That would be hard if two of them were dead and that Colonel Erlugu of theirs started to investigate.

"Fuck me. Fuck me hard. Biggest cock I've ever had," I cried out, grabbing for his nipples nestled in his thatch of chest hair, rising and falling faster on the cock. He lost interest in the bottle of drugged scotch—although he'd already swigged enough to satisfy me—grabbed my waist, groaned deeply, and slammed my channel up and down on his cock. It was a race with time. I wanted him to come. He was a beautiful, young, hard-bodied man. I wanted him to come. I wanted him to make me come.

When I did, I let out a howl, and leaned into the back of the front seat. He was looking at me, eyes wide open, a big grin on his face. I moved my butt in a circle and squeezed my channel, and then he came. Almost immediately thereafter his head rolled back onto the top of the backseat, and he began to snore.

I took a moment to run my hands around on his hairy chest, feeling the hardness of the muscles, regretting a bit that the fucking was finished. Then, with a sigh, I pulled off him and dragged him out of the car and over to where his friends lay. Taking both of the spiked bottles of scotch, I walked deeper into the pasture and emptied the bottles. I tossed all three of them into the trunk of the Caddie and went looking for my gym shorts.

It took me a while to maneuver the convertible out of the pasture. Kerem had driven it in far enough that the ground wasn't conditioned for the weight of an old American car. But I managed.

I only stopped at Onur's long enough to do an inspection of the car for damage and only letting myself breathe when I couldn't find any. The keys were still in the ignition of the BMW. That meant Onur hadn't gone to Famagusta to find Sami. It also meant I needed to leave quietly, or I'd be stuck here with another sketch and fuck with Onur. I wouldn't have minded that—not that I hadn't gotten enough sexual exercise today already—but there was the golden question to answer. So I left as swiftly as I had arrived.

* * * *

"So, that's the answer to the golden question?"

"Yep. The Maroon Beret commando group isn't for here. It's just a normal rotation of the Cyprus Special Forces Regiment, but a larger force coming in, so they are adding barracks and replacing a few of the old ones. That's what the satellites see. The satellites can see. It takes humans to figure out the why, though."

"You know this from some officer in a bar or bedroom?"

"Better source than that. Got it from the code clerks who actually handle the communications."

"Ah, yes, that is better. All of the colonels are careful. The enlisted men boast. You found an enlisted man who boasted?"

"Three." I didn't add that they backed up their boasting with well-wielded cocks.

"It would be nice to have some sort of corroboration."

"Throw it to Ankara station to confirm," I said. "The colonel here is named Erlugu. The communications circuit is called the green line. It's a commo circuit, not the line separating the Greeks from the Turks on Cyprus. They probably are using that name to make anyone who hears the reference assume it's referring to the physical board. Our commo guys might see that as an explanation for some confusion in the Turkish traffic they're reading. Get Ankara station to hit the commo files of the Cyprus Special Forces Regiment headquarters in Ankara."

"That's a thought. Being first, the answer to the golden question would be our get. And it's a very nice get by you, Ron."

139

We were standing. He was patting me on the back. This was as good as praise got from the chief of station.

"I trust I don't want to know how you got this intell," Ted said to me.

"I trust you're right about that, Ted."

"Hope it wasn't real hard. It was really a pretty simple question."

Yeah, it involved a few things that were real hard, I thought. But what I said was, "Sometimes, Ted, the simplest of questions require the greatest amount of preparation—and require something hard."

"Ain't that the truth."

Somehow, from his lopsided smile, I think Ted got the double entendre.

The Invisible Man

"He is known as the Invisible Man, and your job is to make him visible to us."

We were dining in the Bel-Etage restaurant of the Sofitel Hotel in Zurich on tender roasted veal with potato pancakes, not a great distance, but several centuries in amenities, away from the north African country of Bulla Regia bordering the Mediterranean.

"But why the need for this sort of operation?" I asked. I waved away the stiff-carriage waiter who had stepped forward from the shadows and refilled Sam Winterberry's wine glass the instant it had been drained and who had then offered to top off my half-filled glass. I was taking my liquor very lightly these days. I was still having headaches. I hadn't been told why the procedure I'd undergone was necessary until just now.

"Are you all right, Guy?" Winterberry asked, his face full of concern. Winterberry always knew the proper expression to show in public. No doubt that had been part of his Agency training back in the day.

"Yes, why do you ask?"

"You winced and touched the spot. Don't worry, the occasional pain and reminder will pass in time. But you do need to be aware of it and not draw attention to it in the meantime."

"Oh, sorry," I said. "I haven't had the formal classes, you know. But, again, why the need for this sort of operation, and why me? This could take years. And he's the president of the country. Surely—"

"Yes, it could take years, but we are hoping it won't," Winterberry answered the last question first. He paused to take a long swig on his wine, which drew a smile; Sam loved good wine. In fact he was reveling in the whole Sofitel experience and the looks he gave me reminded me of life with Sam Winterberry when he was on a high.

"But even if it takes years," he continued, "this is an operation that is worth it. As for why it's not a direct sanction, first, the Lieutenant is a wary one—and a thus far very successfully wary one. He moves constantly, never spends more than one night in a single location, and there is no pattern to his movements. Second, we are planning something much more subtle than a simple sanction. We want to control what follows. His nationalization of the oil companies has made quite clear that some more complex response is needed here."

There were a few moments of silence as Winterberry savored his tender veal in its own gravy and while I contemplated the target. He was known as the Lieutenant because that was what he was when he miraculously mobilized the Bulla Regia armed forces to overthrow the decadent and decaying monarchy and set the country on the path of his own personal brand of mixed socialism and dictatorship. The Western world had called him mad and had ostracized him. He, in turn, had nationalized all of the Western holdings in a country that was floating on oil and had proven himself not too mad to have survived, standing alone against the pressure of the Western world, for more than a decade now.

"And why me?" I repeated an unanswered question.

"Why you? Because you can be inserted easily. We have a position available as professor of Arabic literature for you at the national university in Altiburos, and your true credentials take you back to your Ph.D. in literature at Canada's Calgary University. It was a mere hop, skip, and jump to documenting you as a Canadian citizen. Of all the Western nations, only

Canada, which had no companies operating in Bulla Regia to nationalize, is still on good terms with the government there."

Winterberry looked down at his plate and started to cut up another bite of veal. He was looking entirely too pleased with himself, though.

"Is that it? Is that the only reason?"

"Of course it's not the only reason, dear boy. I'm here; this is one of my Candy Store operations. You were chosen because the Lieutenant likes his men blond and young and submissive. And I can see his point."

The look Winterberry gave me was quite enough to tell me that my engagement calendar was booked for the night.

Sam Winterberry wasn't one of my favorite people. By far. I could have had an entirely different life if it had not been for Sam Winterberry. I had been young and idealistic and had steeped myself in Arabic literature and culture—and, unfortunately politics—in my graduate years in Calgary. I had been judged brilliant, the youngest man ever to have reached the doctorate level at the university. And, although I was an American, I had gone to school in Canada rather than the United States because I wanted my education to be as free of prejudice as possible. That too was probably a mistake. I found myself taken up with a group of Arab students who pushed the envelope beyond the philosophical and who actually included the nucleus of a cell of terrorists biding their time and laying in wait for a plan and direction to strike a blow for Islam in the United States.

I never was drawn into this cell—although in time there might have been an offer. In my idealism, I was attracted to what they said in public. I, of course, had no idea what they were planning in private. So I floated around the periphery of this group and became close to a few of the cell members.

One of the cell members was fiery and handsome, dark, hirsute, and built like the seasoned soldier that he really was. He was older than most of the others, and clearly a leader and an initiator and risk taker. Ahmed paid considerable attention to me, at first because of our professed shared love of Arabic literature. He was a persuasive conversationalist and spoke in honey-toned poetry. And one night when I was half drunk, he

143

pulled me down on his bed and stretched all along the length of my body, touching me closely everywhere and showing me that he wanted me by the hardness between his legs. He kissed me and fondled my body with his soft hands and whispered sweet poetry to me. And when he put his hand between my thighs and coaxed me to open for him, I did, with a sigh, despite my fears. And when he slowly pushed inside me, he covered my mouth with his and kissed away my cry of pain and shame as he unburdened me of my virginity. As the pain subsided and he began to move inside me, I moved with him, willingly, with him chanting his poetry in rhythm to the stroking of his cock inside me and to the pattern of my panting and moaning. Ahmed opened the gates of heaven to me with a flood of love that left me with no regrets and no doubts about what I was and what I wanted.

I never knew what happened to the cell, but I learned soon enough what Ahmed was. Not only was he a U.S. government plant in the cell, but he also was a recruiter for a special unit of the Agency informally called the Candy Store, headed by none other than Sam Winterberry. On the same night I had all of my doubts about my sexuality and my preferences wiped away, I was compromised and recruited into the world of intelligence. And not just the surface world, but into one of its most closely guarded secrets—the existence of a unit that gained intelligence through sex.

And here I was, a world and three years away from my innocent exuberance in Calgary, the excellent meal now finished, nibbling on the last of the chocolate torte and superior-blend coffee.

Winterberry delicately patted his lips with a fine white linen napkin and turned a smile on me.

"Now, there are a few more details we should talk about with a bit more privacy."

I looked around the dimly lit restaurant with the widely spaced tables. I couldn't think of any place with more privacy than this. But, looking at Winterberry's smile, I guess I could.

"Shall we adjourn to my hotel room?" Winterberry asked. But I knew it wasn't a question.

When we were in his room, three flights up in the hotel, he turned and, in a matter-of-fact voice said, "Now, sweet Guy, would you please disrobe and sit on the edge of the bed over there."

I sucked his cock as he stood before me at the bed and gave him what he wanted. But I kept it on an edge, where he knew it was all mechanical, that I didn't really want him. And I tried to maintain the same tone when he spread my legs and held them out under his arms and thrust inside me. But as he began to pump and thicken and mined ever more deeply in my channel, my instincts gave way and I began to move my hips with him and to pant and moan, and his heavy breathing and groans had a synergistic effect on me. And soon we were fucking in earnest, me wanting it as much as he did. Maybe more. I couldn't help myself. I loved a man's cock churning inside me.

But Sam Winterberry is a cruel lover, and he had noted how hard I'd tried to stay mechanical with him. And he knew what I was, what I was unable to stay away from. As I was about to ejaculate, he pulled out of me and held me tight, not letting me go over the edge.

"Please, Sam," I panted.

"Please what, Guy?"

"Please, oh please."

"Say it, Guy."

I gritted my teeth. "Please, Sam, please finish me. Fuck me. Ahhhhhh." He slid deep inside me again and began to pump, once again showing me who was boss.

I came and he moved as to pull out of me, roll off his condom, and ejaculate on my belly, but I cried out, "No, please. Inside me, please."

And, with a shudder of pleasure, he continued pumping until he had filled the bulb of his condom deep inside me. I knew that I had pleased him—once again.

There being no better time than that moment, as we were both calming our breath, I said. "My parents are both dead, Sam. Did you know that?"

"No, I did not," he warily answered.

"And it's been a long time since that business with the terrorist cell in Calgary. And anything coming out of that now would be pretty fuzzy, you know—especially with what I might have to say about what transpired afterward if push came to shove."

"What are you saying, Guy?" Winterberry asked in a low, nervous voice.

"I'm saying that I'll do this operation for you, but when it's over—if it's successfully concluded, I want to ask a favor of you that you will pledge now to honor."

There was a slight pause, but then Winterberry answered wearily, "If you must."

At that moment, I think we both knew what my request would be. I had done quite enough for the nation.

* * * *

"Have you seen the Roman ruins on the cliffs of Albia yet, professor?"

It had been asked innocently enough, but I hoped it meant some progress was being made. I'd been teaching Arabic literature at the national university in Bulla Regia's capital city of Altiburos for some four months now, and as hard as I was trying, progress had seemed to be slow.

When Winterberry had briefed me, he had given me a list of names of young men students at the university who both would be interested in what I had to offer—beyond the instruction in Arabic literature—and who could give me a natural entrée to the ultraprivate Foxes Den club near the government officials' residential enclave, the very secret place where the well-heeled and powerful men of Bulla Regia went to meet other men. The ultimate target here was the army marshal General Iken ibn Tariq, who was considered to be as closely associated with the Lieutenant, Mezian al-Masmud, as anyone in Bella Regia could be.

Yunes ibn Afalku, one of the pampered sons of the ruling class, which still managed to rule society despite the Lieutenant's so-called socialist revolution, was one of the students in my Arabic literature class. He also was on my list of intermediary targets. He was maybe four years younger than I was, one of the older students. He had already served his army duty and was in extremely fit shape. He was a national-level bodybuilder, narcissistic to an extreme degree, and thus, of course, a name on my list. And he dabbled in Arabic literature. He wasn't a full-time university student; he had just signed up for my class because he had accompanied his younger brother to orientation and had talked with me over a punchbowl.

I knew from the outset he was interested, and he was the main mark I was working on. But it took me four months to prime him to ask me this question.

"No, Yunes. I haven't seen the ruins. I would love to, though. I just haven't had the chance to go outside the city. Visitors like me are fairly closely watched here."

"No one I'm with is watched," Yunes said. "And I have a van. I'd be pleased to show you the Roman site."

The mention of the van was not lost on me, although I assumed Yunes thought he was being clever. I'd seen Yunes drive onto campus. He drove a Mercedes sports coup.

I was not surprised to find that the van had no windows in the back. Yunes drove it up to the edge of a cliff, within the outer reaches of the perimeter of a small, ancient Roman city colony that hadn't really had time to blossom before the local, highly warlike tribal bands had wiped it out. More of the old city ruins lay at the base of the cliff, where there had once been a small harbor reaching out into the Mediterranean. From up here, looking out of the front windshield of the van, I could see the tops of the crumbled stone of the protecting wings of the manmade harbor quay under the surface of the water. A light rain squall was going through, and Yunes suggested we wait in the van until it passed.

I toyed with the idea briefly that Yunes represented such ingrained power in Bulla Regia society that he could conjure up a convenient rain squall on demand.

"Are you enjoying the Arabic literature class, Yunes?" I asked.

"Yes, very much so, professor. But tell me, do you not read the books of Ali Ghanem, Albert Cossery, and Rachid

147

Boudjedra? Why have you not included their books in the course?"

There it was, the opening, checking me out. All three of these Arabic-theme authors wrote homoerotica.

"Yes, I have read Ghanem's *Seven-Headed Serpent* and Cossery's *Proud Beggars* and Boudjedra's *The Great Repudiation*."

"And enjoyed them?"

"Yes, yes, of course, I found such literature very . . . compelling." Yunes turned his torso toward me and, seemingly inadvertently, put a hand on my knee.

"But then why not include these in your course?"

I put my hand on top of his and slid them both up my thigh and onto my basket. Yunes took in a deep breath.

"Do you really think the authorities would permit me to teach those authors, Yunes? But haven't you noticed that I do include Naguib Mahfouz's *Midaq Alley* and *Sugar Street* in the curriculum. He is just too famous for the authorities to censure. Haven't you read those? There are passages in those that remind me of you when I read them."

"You find me attractive, professor?"

"Yes, very much so," I answered. "Can't you feel that through your hand?" And, indeed, I had managed to harden up for him nicely. "I have watched you in class. I think you must be a very powerful, forceful man. But you have seemed a bit shy. I would have thought you a man who saw what he wanted and took it."

I sucked Yunes's cock with him turned to me in the driver's seat and kneeling in the seat and me leaning over him and raising and lowering my mouth on his erect tool while he moaned and controlled my head with hands buried in my hair. For a brief moment I worried that a hand would stray to the nape of my neck, but it did not do so—and even if it had, I'm sure he was too preoccupied with my expert blow job to find anything amiss.

After he had come, we moved to the back of the van, which he had prepared with thick oriental carpeting, and we stripped and he laid me on my back and covered my body with caresses and kisses and paid considerable attention to my cock, balls, and hole while he regained his youthful virility. I thrilled at the feel of the firmness of his cut muscles, and I ran my trembling hands over his chest and torso and arched my back and gave a welcoming roar of genuine delight as he spread my legs, wedged his knees under my butt cheeks, thrust himself deep inside me, and began to pump hard.

We met frequently in my apartment thereafter for about a month until I was sure he was besotted and would do whatever I wanted him to.

"Have you heard of the Fox Den club?" I asked one afternoon as I lay inside his embrace, my back to his front, and his cock churning slowly and deeply inside me.

"Yes," he answered with a grunt.

"I think I would like to go there. Do you happen to know anyone who can get us in?"

"Yes," he answered. "I can; I'm a member."

On the third visit to the club, my next target, General Iken ibn Tariq, made his move. He had been there during our previous two visits too, but during the first visit he and I had only exchanged meaningful looks across a dimly lit room. During the second visit, he invited us to his table, where he sat, with two bulky bodyguards standing at attention behind him.

Yunes had not been pleased at the invitation to the general's table, and this was probably the touchiest part of my assignment, where I had to continue to please Yunes while beguiling the general. Somehow I managed.

While we were chatting and the general was, rather professionally, interrogating me with a friendly smile on exactly who I was and ever had been and was doing in his country, I asked him if he was a reader of Arabic literature.

"No, my reading is other worldly, Professor Breeden," he answered. "Have you perhaps heard of Henry Spenser Ashbee or Ulrike Heider or Trevor Jacques?"

I could tell that Yunes was out of the "know" here and, thankfully, saw that his attention was drawn to the sex scene going on on the stage, a quite tall and bulky Bulgarian stuffing himself into a small Nubian in a particularly flexible position.

"Yes, yes, I've heard of those authors." I said, willing myself to blush and lowering my eyes. All wrote on S&M homoerotica, mostly from the nonfiction stance. I wasn't either surprised or shocked. I'd been briefed on the good general's proclivities.

"And?" the general said, looking at me intently and squeezing my knee under the table.

"And . . . I have never, but . . ."

"But?" he pressed on.

"But I do find it . . . interesting."

"And inviting?" he asked.

"Yes, a bit. But, of course, this in Bulla Regia. It's not something to really even consider here, is it?" At this statement, I raised my face with as much drama as I could and looked directly into his eyes. His hand had gone up my thigh, and I had willed myself hard for him.

"And how do you find me, professor?"

"Fascinating," I responded, and I looked him directly in the eyes when I said it.

"And it does not shock you that I read Ashbee and Heider and Jacques?"

"No."

"You do not fear the light lash, the binding?"

"I don't know, to be honest. It rather excites me."

At that point Yunes had turned his attention back to us and General Tariq had withdrawn his hand. Not long afterward Yunes said he was bored, we said our good-byes, and he took me back to my apartment and fucked me in the inventive position he had watched the Bulgarian use to take the Nubian in the club. Yunes cocked well. I was somewhat sad to move on from him.

On the third visit, the general once more invited us to his table, an invitation Yunes could not decline, as the general trumped his family for the moment in the national power positioning.

And Yunes made the mistake of needing to go take a piss.

I made my move. "About those authors you mentioned last week, General."

"Yes."

"I've been reading them. Some of the milder things they talk about."

"Yes?"

"Well, those seem very interesting. Very . . . arousing."

The general was smiling broadly. "Would you like to see my new villa by the sea?"

"Yes, that would be nice. Perhaps we could set up a time."

"Now," the general said. His breathing told me that he was, indeed, very interested in a visit now.

"But Yunes," I said.

"Now," the general repeated.

The general's special room was in the basement of his villa. I was strapped into a black leather sling suspended from the ceiling, with my arms and legs running up the four corner chains and bound there, which I didn't much like, and a choke collar on a leash that the general tugged on with each of his thrusts, which I liked even less, and a riding crop flicking at my flanks, which I didn't like at all. But I didn't mind the cocking. And the general was pleased enough to schedule a return visit—and then another.

On my third visit, I only got as far as his foyer.

"We are not going downstairs tonight, Guy," the general said. His two goons were standing close to me on each side.

"Then perhaps—" I started to say, wanting to make this sound good, but hoping that it was ultimate show time at last.

"Doctor, if you would," the general muttered, and from out of the shadows a figure emerged in a well-cut suit and goatee—and with a syringe in his hand.

I started to back away, but the two goons held me fast as the doctor inserted the needle into a vein in my arm and I began to black out.

* * * *

I came to in darkness. The darkness of being blindfolded in a darkened room. I was encased in billowing softness, which I took to be a mass of pillows. And I was uncomfortable from being trussed up. I was on my back. There

151

was pressure on the back of my neck, and I feared it would ride up to my hairline and that something awful would transpire. Whatever was wrapped around my neck was connected to why my legs were being held spread and my wrists were bound close to my spread calves. When I tried to move my legs, the pressure increased on the back of my neck.

Hands were gliding all over my body, flesh on flesh, and it struck me then, for the first time, that I was naked. The hands centered on my cock, and I was being stroked and greased fingers were working inside my hole. I stifled moans, not wanting whoever was working me to realize that I was conscious.

I came fully conscious, however, as the bulb of a cock was presented at my hole and started working itself inside me. I moaned then and groaned, and begged for mercy, not being able to gauge yet what would be the most arousing for the invader—when I cried out for mercy with the general, he took it as an invitation to be more cruel, which was all the more arousing for him. I hoped this was the fulfillment of the plan and this was a crucial point.

The cock, having entered only a few inches at that point was withdrawn and the hands were working my cock again and caressing my torso and there were lips on my nipples.

The mercy had been shown. The taking was tentative. I realized I'd used the wrong technique.

So, I begin to moan and groan and tell whoever was doing this of the pleasure I was being given. And then, after this had been going on for a while, I started to whine for the fuck.

"Please, please," I murmured. "Please take me. I can't take any more teasing. Please, someone fuck me. I need someone inside me."

When the slide of the cock came, I was well open for it, and it just went deeper and deeper and deeper. He wasn't thick, but he was extra long.

I cried out that what he was doing was exactly what I wanted, and when he was completely embedded and started to slowly pump me, he gasped as I started to roll my hips within the limited freedom I had, going with the fuck, and causing my channel muscles to make love to his cock.

I told him how much I loved having him inside me and begged him to do this and that, and he responded.

"Please, though, not like this," I murmured. "I want to make love to you too. Free me so that I can make love to you too."

A command was voiced, several pairs of hands worked at my bindings, and I was free. The blindfold came off, and whoever had freed me slinked into the shadows of the room. I was looking up into the face of the Lieutenant—Mezian al-Masmud, the president of Bulla Regia. Exactly as planned.

I was on my back in a mountain of pillows. We were in a large tent of some sort, and there was a soft glow beyond the tent walls. But it was still very dark inside the tent. Mezian was crouched between my spread legs, leaning over my torso, loosely embracing my chest in his arms. He had come out of me during the untrussing.

He was a handsome fellow. Early forties perhaps, with a delicate, sensual face, milk-chocolate eyes, and black, curly head hair. He had a long, lean body covered with a matting of curly black hair. The cock jutting out of his bush was also long and lean.

"Please, please kiss me," I murmured. And he leaned down and took my lips in his and gasped as I reached down and took his cock in both of my hands and guided him back inside me.

We fucked slowly, sensually, completely, for hours, in the end with him on his back on the pillows and me riding his cock in slow, deep-penetrating rolling of my hips, like a ship riding the waves.

At dawn, men in flowing, sparkling white *dishdasha* Arabic robes came into the tent, Mezian disengaged from his full-body embrace of me and left with a few of them. The remaining men washed my body with tubs of water and sponges and dried me and put a white *dishdasha* over my head. Then they bound and blindfolded me as the tent was being struck around me.

We traveled for hours in vehicles. I knew there was more than one, because I could hear more than one motor around me. Sometime during the trip I was seized and inspected closely by someone they called "doctor," and a sample of blood was taken from my arm.

When we reached wherever we were going, I once more was deposited in a pile of pillows. But this time I was inside a mud brick room. The windows were barred, but we seemed to be in a town of some size. I was taken to a primitive privy in a small room off the larger one I was in, and then I was fed a simple but nourishing meal and then bathed and massaged and rubbed with ointment by a masseur whose massive hard on told me that he wanted me too, but that he dare not take me—although when I moved his hand to my cock, he enjoyed stroking—and then sucking—me to an ejaculation. I needed to cultivate the need for any man here for me. I could not discount any help I might get from someone I'd pleased.

I was clothed in a clean, white *dishdasha*, and I sat in the pillows, demurely, until Mezian appeared. He was in a *dishdasha* as well, and looked magnificent.

He came down into the pillows and embraced and kissed me and ran his hands under the hem of my *dishdasha* and all over my body as I sighed and moaned. I was stretched out beside him, when he took a sharp knife, giving me a moment of panic, and slit the side of my *dishdasha*. He barked a command and an attendant came in and took away the knife. Then he ran his hand into the slit and took possession of my cock and, while holding me close in his embrace and kissing me whenever I turned my lips to his, slowly stroked me to completion, ignoring all of my entreaties for him to fuck me.

I thought he would take me then, but he didn't. He lowered his hand to my balls and fondled those as I sighed and moaned for him, and then he went even lower and entered me with his fingers. My hole had been well greased, and he finger fucked me as I became hard again and writhed and moaned for him to exchange the fingers for his long cock. Then he took my cock in his hand and stroked me to a second ejaculation.

I was exhausted and worn out, but that's when he told me to stand, and he pulled the slitted *dishdasha* over my head and pushed me over to a wall with my back to the cool mud bricks. He didn't take his *dishdasha* off but merely hiked it up around his waist and crouched down as he spread my thighs with his hands and moved the head of his cock up to my open hole. I settled my channel on his cock and then grunted and lifted my legs to encircle his waist as I groaned and groaned and groaned with his cock pushing my back up and down on the coarse mud-brick wall as his cock moved inside my channel. He wore no condom this time—bringing to mind the visit I'd had by a doctor while en route to here. He had been checking me out to see if I was clean and could be barebacked. I cried out in a passion that pleased him as he set forth his flow deep inside me.

The ritual was repeated the third day when we were in yet another town, this time near the sea. We didn't fuck that night. That night I made love to Mezian's body, playing his body like a violin with my caressing hands and my lips, giving his curly body hair a sensual bath and taking his cock in my mouth and draining him three times so that he drifted off to sleep before making any more use of it.

The fourth night, in a tent again, out on the desert, I lay on my belly as Mezian rode my ass in reverse, reaching down into my channel in angles that had me howling my lust and passion. And the next night, still in a tent, but miles away from the previous encampment, I was laid on my shoulders and the back of my neck, with my torso raised, while Mezian crouched over my hips and held my legs spread with his hands and fucked down into me deeper than he ever had before.

All the time I was with Mezian in those days before the end, he never fucked me the same way twice. He told me that he was besotted with me and that there were a thousand and one ways he wanted to take me. And I told him that no one had satisfied me sexually as he did or made me as happy—and I was telling the truth.

On that last night, after sex that entailed me riding his lap, we lay there and kissed and cooed to each other.

"What sort of literature do you read, sire?" I asked.

155

"Romance, nineteenth-century European Romance," he said.

I laughed, said I was happy to hear that, and gave him a kiss.

At nearly that precise moment, all hell broke out, and after a short firefight outside the tent, commandos streamed into the tent and seized Mezian. He stood and turned his face to the tent flap and spat out a "You!"

I looked in that direction, and there was a twin of Mezian standing at the entrance. And behind him was Sam Winterberry.

Mezian was bustled out of the tent, and Sam Winterberry handed me a *dishdasha*, and waited until I was covered, to speak.

"You did very well, Guy. The homing device we had implanted at the back of your head worked a charm. We've been tracking you for days. I hope we've arrived soon enough."

I said nothing.

"Oh, and let me introduce Mezwar al-Masmud, Mezian's brother. I think the people have seen Mezian so rarely now that his brother will be able to pose as him. They might be surprised, however, at the slow, but relentless improvement in Bulla Regia's relationship with Western nations and oil companies."

There was a swirl of activity, but then I was alone in the tent with Winterberry.

"The Lieutenant?" I asked.

"Oh, don't worry, he'll be treated like a prince. He'll live better than he has here. He'll just be a bit restricted in his movements—well, more than a bit. We have very nice, out-of-the way places to accommodate men like him. We won't kill him. Never know when he might come in useful. Now he can become the invisible man he always wanted to be."

"Sam," I said. "About that favor. I think I earned it now."

"Want to retire, do you?"

"Not just that, Sam. I want to go wherever you send Mezian. I want to be with him."

Winterberry raised his eyebrows, but he didn't tell me no.

The Message

I took one last look in the dingy bathroom mirror of my Strand Hotel room, opening my mouth in a wide, toothy grin to make sure everything was in good order, and then I took a deep breath, muttered a "OK, then, let's do this" to myself, and turned to the door. "Can't keep the general waiting too long."

I would have said something to the hotel management about the condition of the bathroom, but from what I gathered of the conversation in the dining room the previous night, I had one of the only functioning bathrooms left in the establishment. As I walked down the corridor to the stairs, not trusting what was offered as an elevator, I did what I could not to look at the smoke-damaged, peeling wallpaper of what had once been the celebrated Rangoon gem of the necklace of colonial grand dame hotels extending from New Delhi, down through the Southeast Asian nations, and up to Hong Kong. I hoped that someday the hotel would again regain its glory, but that was unlikely to happen as long as General Ne Win, now in his twenty-fourth year since he seized power in Burma in 1962, held his stranglehold on power here.

I would be honored to be able to be any part of whatever changed that.

I entered the dining room, where there was just a smattering of diners, just as there was only a smattering of lodgers at the hotel. Most Burmese were not permitted to

159

lodge or dine at the Strand, and most foreigners weren't even able to get into the country. It was a minor miracle that I was able to be here myself, especially considering that my request for a visa was based on an intent to interview the imprisoned emotional symbol of the freedom fighters, Kyine Nyunt, whose father had unsuccessfully led the struggle for a return to civilian rule and had died in the attempt. Kyine Nyunt, who had written elegantly and spoken eloquently in favor of the freedom movement throughout the world, had returned to Burma, only to be imprisoned and held with little contact outside of Mandalay, a long distance north of Rangoon up the Irrawaddy River. Along with the opposition's even more important intellectual leader, Aung Htun, who also had been imprisoned in some unknown place in Burma, Kyine Nyunt, was the heart of the country's freedom movement.

I was here, in the Strand dining room, because the key to my being able to land an interview with Kyine Nyunt for my International Press news agency was sitting at the best table in the room, separated by a considerable distance from any of the foreign diners. General Soe Ye, once (and still) the warlord of a major opium-producing enclave somewhere upcountry in Burma on the Thai border, was dining here this evening. I had known that. There was a whole network of informers willing to put me into contact with the whereabouts of General Soe Ye. The good general was also one of General Ne Win's backers and main supporters. If anyone could get me to where I needed to go, it was General Soe Ye.

My entrée was that I had met the general before. I had been covering an ASEAN mutual cooperation conference in Bangkok that General Soe Ye attended for the Burmese. "Mutual cooperation" was a euphemism for military alliance, but, as ASEAN was not supposed to be a defense organization, all of their talks on cooperation were couched in economic terms. I was covering the conference for the IP. General Soe Ye was royally bored by the economic framework given for the talks, and his eyes wandered. His eyes wandered to me—repeatedly—which was noted by those with interest in the freedom movement in Burma. As they also knew what General Soe Ye's weakness was, they had come to enlist my cooperation. My own inclinations didn't rail at the assignment, and the general had, in fact, propositioned me before leaving Bangkok and invited me to come to him in Burma, so, with their help from the Thailand end in me getting into Burma, here I was. Making myself available—for a worthy purpose.

Soe Ye saw me, and his face lit up in a big smile. It's not that I wasn't expected; I wouldn't have even gotten this far, to Rangoon, without his intervention. But he nonetheless was happy to see me. As, no doubt, was the waiter, who, when the general's attention was switched to me, managed to slip away from the hand that had been squeezing his buttocks and retreat to the kitchen.

"Mr. Jansen," he said in excellent, if perhaps somewhat overenunciated British English, "welcome to Rangoon. I trust you had no trouble clearing customs."

"Nothing that two bottles of Johnnie Walker Red didn't smooth over," I said. "But thanks for all of your help," I quickly added, having seen the touch of anger my first comment had caused to flit across the general's face. Corruption and bribery were widely practiced here in Burma during these years; it just wasn't anything you would talk about openly, especially not to one of the senior generals of the ruling cabal. "And do call me Gene," I added, giving him a sunny smile, which changed the expression on his face considerably. "I'll call you general, of course, but you certainly needn't be formal with me . . . given the circumstances."

"So, you have considered the little proposition I made you in Bangkok, then, have you . . . Gene? And, please do sit down and have a drink." I sat while he motioned for a waiter. "What is it you'd like to have, Gene?"

"I'll take a vodka screwdriver," I said to the waiter. I wasn't that fond of screwdrivers, but I had winked at the general—playing him—when I'd said "screwdriver," and he'd appreciated the little joke.

The waiter stammered, reluctant to admit the hotel's limitations in front of the all-powerful general. "I'm sorry, sir, we are unable to serve vodka here."

"Oh, that's OK," I said, understanding that to mean they didn't have any vodka to serve. "I'll take whatever beer you have available then."

While he was leaving, Soe Ye leaned over to me and said sotto voce, "I have vodka upstairs in my suite. And a screwdriver too. We can go up there directly to entertain each other with them." His lustful smile was unmistakable.

"That, I'm sure will be very . . . entertaining," I answered him, with a smile of my own. "But first things first. I must serve my masters—I do like to serve masters." I saw the chill of a thrill zing through his body when I said that.

"As you know, I have been sent here with a purpose. My news agency wants an interview with Kyine Nyunt. It would mean so much to my standing there if I could get one. As we discussed in our letters, certainly. The authorities can review the text of the article, of course—before I leave Burma. That's a given, naturally."

Such a game we were playing. I knew the Burmese government didn't want an interview with the emotional symbol of the opposition of any sort floated, and they would have been donkeys to not understand that a censored article run now wouldn't preclude an entirely different version being published once I'd left Burma. But it was all a game within a game, and much of it hung on the lust of General Soe Ye and on what he convinced himself was worth giving up to get what he wanted in the short term.

"Yes, quite all right," Soe Ye said. "And you have a guide to take you up to Mandalay?"

"Yes," I answered. "He's right over there—his name's Saw Win." I waved to the local Burmese guide my friends in Bangkok had hooked me up with, and he smiled back. Soe Ye wasn't smiling. He was looking at Saw Win speculatively. I wondered if Soe Ye had, by instinct, recognized the competition. Saw Win was quite talented and heavy on the muscle, good looks, and assessing eye. I had only met him yesterday afternoon, at the airport, at the arrival of my Air Burma plane from Bangkok. But he'd already spent the night in my hotel bed, fucking me masterfully like we were long-time lovers.

"Shall we go up to my suite now?" Soe Ye asked in a tight voice. I'd pulled his attention away from Saw Win by placing my hand on his thigh, just above his knee, and giving it a little squeeze.

"The letters of access and of passage up the Irrawaddy," I said gently. "I believe we had agreed that I would receive them first."

"Yes . . . I . . . I." The general was struggling for control now. I'd moved my hand to his basket, holding what gave me a lurch of fear and anticipation through the material of his trousers. This was a tricky moment, and I needed to have him in my control and panting for me.

"Here, right here. I have them," he said. And he produced a packet of precious passes worth their weight in gold—certainly worth what I was about to do.

After looking the passes over, I motioned to Saw Win, who approached the table. I gave them to him and he left the dining room. Soe Ye watched Saw Win intently as he walked away, with seeming mixed feelings. Another obvious rooster leaving the hen house; but leaving with high stakes that Soe Ye had placed on the table in the playing of his hand.

Soe Ye was a forceful, and cruel, and demanding lover. It was all about him; his pleasure. And part of his pleasure was in inflicting pain, receiving full service, having full control. The preliminaries were all about me pleasing him. Me massaging him and sucking him to the heights of desire and the hardness of steel. And the main event was focused on him taking me—by force, at his direction. My struggling against the taking was instrumental in him getting as much passion out of the fuck as possible. I massaged his ample body and gave him suck until he rose up and slapped me hard across the face, sending me to the floor. And then he was upon me, covering my back, with me on all fours, and thrusting inside me as I struggled, on the tired, almost threadbare carpeting of his room, trying—at his direction—to scrabble out from underneath him and slither to the door. Putting me in a headlock and screwing me to the floor with the force and size and insistence of his cock then, he fucked me in a lengthy campaign for his ejaculative satisfaction, while I whimpered and moaned and groaned at the onslaught.

163

Then he held me there, me panting, close to exhaustion, while he had barely broken a sweat. He was recharging, but while he did so, I remained his prisoner, pinned to the carpet by his bulk and by the ramrod drilled into me, nailing my pelvis to the floor.

When he was ready again, he pulled me up off the floor, flung me onto the bed, on my belly, the balls of my feet on the floor, my legs spread, and he beat me with a riding crop on my back and thighs and buttocks while he rode me hard to a second completion.

Afterward, he sat, calmly, in an arm chair next to the bed, chain-smoking cigarettes and drinking scotch and humming to himself, as I lay, exhausted and covered with welts, still panting hard, on his bed. He had his eyes turned to me. Clearly viewing the result of his work on my body was a large part of what aroused him.

"You please me," he said, blowing rings with the smoke of his cigarette. "You will come back to me here after your trip to Mandalay."

It wasn't a request or a question. I could not leave the country without his acquiescence. If all went well, however, I had no intention of meeting him here at the Strand again. And if I was guessing right, he didn't really have any intention of that either.

My guide, Saw Win, was waiting for me in my room when I returned from being debauched by the general. He was all cluckings and soothing words. He gently rubbed salve on my welts—both of us having known what the general would do with me—and then he stretched me out on the bed on my side and covered me close from behind and made languid and deep-delving love to me with his master cock until I drifted off to sleep.

I reveled in such attention. I couldn't get enough cock, which is what had led me to be in this situation to begin with.

* * * *

Saw Win suggested that, since I had managed to get into Burma and most likely would not find it easy ever getting

164

in again, that we should break our trip up the Irrawaddy on a series of river trader steamers at the ancient temple complex at Pagan, which rivaled Cambodia's Angkor Wat at setting the mouths of archeologists of ancient Asian civilizations drooling. It was here that the expedition turned ugly.

I was exhausted from a full day of moving from one ruined temple to another in a World War II vintage Jeep. Saw Win was an excellent guide. He knew so much about the long history of the building of several hundred temples at Pagan on the banks of the Irrawaddy. And he also was so attentive to me. And loving.

The facilities were primitive, and we showered together in the evening under the drizzle of a water pipe in a half-enclosed shed, soaping each other up and rinsing each other off, running our hands all over the tired curves of muscles and into the inviting crevices of one another. He was magnificent and masterful, and I was panting my want for him while he toweled me off and guided me into the guest lodge, parted the mosquito netting for me to lower myself on my back on the bed, and then spread and raise my thighs, so he could maneuver himself between them, slowly glide inside me, and start filling and stretching me with long, languid strokes.

During the lovemaking, we whispered to each other, discussing what lay ahead of us, knowing that if anyone was spying on us, all they would hear were two lovers in high heat, their bodies undulating against each other in primeval passion, whispering what they want to feel or do next.

I had been led to Saw Win by friends of the Burmese opposition forces in Bangkok. So I knew that he knew there was more to my coming than gathering an interview with Kyine Nyunt that would be chopped to pieces before I filed it—if they let me actually talk to her at all, which in itself was highly unlikely. It was time to tell him more. I had been told to tell him more at this point in the journey.

"I am not really here to . . . oh, god, that's good. Again, please. Oh, Shit! . . . to interview her," I whispered. His cock stopped in its probe at that point. He held us there, not moving a muscle other than the throbbing of his centering muscle inside me. I was panting, waiting for the next thrust, wanting the next thrust. But he was waiting to hear the rest of what I had to say. I could feel him beginning to tremble, in anticipation, no doubt having waited for this since that first day in Rangoon.

"Go on," he growled.

"I'm not gathering," I whispered. "I'm giving. I'm carrying a message for her. Something so important that it has to be conveyed this way."

"A message?" he asked. Holding, trying to hold us in suspense. I moved my pelvis against him, trying to get him to push me over the edge, but he placed the palm of a strong hand on the small of my back where it descends into my crevice and held me there, waiting.

"Yes," I murmured. "It's in code. In my interview notebook. A page that looks almost like the shorthand of the rest, but not quite. If . . . if . . . oh, god, YES!" he had started to pump me slowly again. ". . .If anything happens to me, could you? . . . Oh, oh, Ahhhhhh!"

We had been stretched out almost flat, Saw Win's pelvis between my thighs. But now he went up on his knees, rolled my hips up to him, pushed his cock a couple of more inches inside me, and began stroking me hard and fast, as if there was no tomorrow. He was sending me over that edge I had been seeking. I arched my back and thrust my hips into his pelvis in a counterpounding, lost in the fuck, wanting every single inch of him and the tiniest dribble of his spouting deep inside me. Pounding against each other endlessly, both crying out in lust and passion.

When we had both ejaculated and collapsed into a sweaty, spent heap, I started to doze off. I was not yet asleep. Saw Win might have thought I was, though, from my regular, shallow breathing, when he rose from me, parted the mosquito netting, and padded over to the doorway, which had been covered by matting.

The shadows of two monstrously muscle-bound men raced across the ceiling in the light of the small bedside lamp, and I was being manhandled, fucked vigorously by one bulky, cruel attacker after the other, as Saw Win stood off to the side of the room, rifling through my things, looking for my interview notebook.

* * * *

The truck journey east, away from the Irrawaddy, not north toward Mandalay, but east toward the Thai border area, was a rough one. The track we moved on could hardly be called a road; there was little if any suspension in the bed of the truck, where I was huddled between two burly Burmese hulks, both of whom prodded and pulled at my naked body to their great enjoyment. I wasn't hooded or kept from watching my surroundings in any other way, which I took as an ominous sign that they had no reason to care whether or not a knew where I was being taken.

Saw Win wasn't with us. I had seen nothing of him after he had found my interview notebook and left our room in Pagan, while the men who had invaded the room were still fucking me.

Hours later, the truck pulled up into a jungle compound, walled and consisting of several pavilion-style, leaf-roofed buildings set against the side of a steep ravine tumbling down into a rushing stream far below. The canopy of the trees met far overhead, making the compound virtually invisible from the air.

I was hauled out of the truck and set down on my bruised feet and forced to turn around. I was standing right in front of . . . General Soe Ye.

"Welcome to my kingdom, Gene," Soe Ye said. Then he laughed and ordered me to be taken into one of the pavilions and slapped down onto a rough table on my back. My wrists and ankles were bound to the legs at the four corners. And then General Soe Ye, entered, naked now, swishing his riding crop, and smiling an evil smile.

He beat and fucked me almost into unconsciousness, declaring that I couldn't fool him, that he knew I wasn't in Burma just to interview Kyine Nyunt, that he was too clever for me, and that he would hold me here and play with me until I was all used up. No one, he said, would know what happened to me after I'd left Rangoon. I was in his world now, and there was no leaving it.

I moaned for him and whimpered and told him that he was the greatest lover and that I didn't need to be bound. That all I wanted to do was please him; that I couldn't get enough of him. That he had the best cock I'd ever had.

Afterward, I was unbound and led to where I could stand under a water pipe and sluice the fucking of so many men off of my bruised and broken body. I was given a native sarong to twist around my waist and led to a small pavilion near the back of the compound. Unlike the other pavilions, its sides were set with iron bars. It was a cage of some sort.

I was pushed through a barred door, into the cage, and the door shut tightly behind me and was locked.

The area inside the small pavilion was dark, but I was able to see the rustling of material back in the corner, and, as my eyes became adjusted to light, I could make out the figure of a small, emaciated man. He turned and I checked the memory of the photographs that had been shown to me back in Bangkok.

"Aung Htun? Is that you? You are Aung Htun, aren't you?"

The figure rose up off the bench and shuffled toward me, reaching for the light.

"Who? What?" he asked through parched lips, in a ragged voice having grown unused to conversation. Aung Htun, erstwhile leader of the National League for Democracy, the coalesced umbrella organization for the Burmese opposition. The intellectual underpinning of the movement.

"Your friends in Bangkok have sent me with a message," I said. And I laughed to myself. A message for Aung Htun, not for Kyine Nyunt in Mandalay. All a game within a game, the opposition in Bangkok knowing that their intellectual leader was being held by General Soe Ye somewhere— although no one knew where. Needing someone to lead them there.

"A message?" Aung Htun asked, in confusion. "But you come almost as you were born. Where is this message? Why have they not taken it from you?"

"I am the message," I said. And then I smiled a broad, full toothed smile for him, reached two fingers into my mouth, and pulled out a molar. "In this false tooth is a transmitter," I said. "When I found you, I was to extract it and disconnect it. That was the signal that where I was, there you would be also. I would suggest that we both stand back toward the back of the cage now, if you don't mind. And perhaps go under that bench. In a few minutes, I think it's going to get very busy around here."

The Negotiator

I wondered what he could tell about me that no one at home or the office—at least I hoped and always had thought—knew. He had introduced himself as Hal when he'd appeared beside me in Business Class and I'd stood from my aisle seat so that he could get over to the window. He'd had a friendly smile, and if I hadn't been busy during the first two hours over the Atlantic from New York going over the papers for my discussion in Birmingham at Smythe and Withers the next day, I'm sure that he would have wanted to chat.

I didn't like to work on business matters while I was flying, but there were hundreds of millions of dollars at stake in this bid we were making to provide a revolutionary model of catalytic converters to the British automobile manufacturers. Smythe and Withers were the manufacturer's agents, and my company was bidding against a French firm with a design of its own. We were well versed in the automobile industry, but almost nothing had been able to be gleaned about Smythe and Withers that would give our bid an advantage. I was my company's premier negotiator, but I didn't like to go into talks knowing so little about those I was negotiating with. As soon as I could use my laptop, I got busy trying to pull something more up from the Internet on that firm than I already had.

It was a frustrating hour and a half, and I perhaps had at least one more drink from the accommodating stewardesses and stewards than I normally would have if I wasn't distracted. Finding nothing new, though, I sighed with frustration and closed my laptop with a click.

"Working on an important presentation?" I looked over to the window seat. I had lost all realization that there was someone else there.

"Yes. One that's both important and frustrating," I answered. For the first time I focused on him. He was a few years older than I was and considerably better put together. We hadn't exchanged much in the way of a conversation, but he had one of those upper-crust British accents that companies like mine liked to have their chief operating officers to have to fool their stockholders into thinking they knew what they were doing. He was debonair, perfectly groomed, and designer dressed. His face was tanned and Hollywood-star chiseled, with those distinguished, precisely trimmed gray sideburns that spelled casual wealth and near-effortless success at anything he endeavored to do. He certainly seemed to exude self-confidence.

And there was that big smile he gave me whenever I looked his way.

Almost as a flood of revelation, three awarenesses hit me at once that took me away from business, which only served to show how focused I'd been before in finding out whatever else I could about this Smythe and Withers firm. But I could afford a side diversion now; there wasn't anything else I could do up here at altitude, although the thought of that took my mind to a joke made in the office before I left on this trip about maybe getting lucky and joining the mile-high club. That was an arousing thought, although I didn't know why it had occurred to me.

I pulled my thoughts back to business. I knew everything that was needed to know about the French firm, and I felt good about their end of the negotiations. They always sent the pompous ass, Jean Claude Dupre, to such bidding wars—and he always seemed to screw up his presentations and upset the very people he was pitching. I wondered what sort of power he had in that company not to have been shunted aside already—although, since "Dupre" was in the company title, I could guess at his leverage.

The first awareness that made my mind wander from business—the thought of mile-high clubs not having registered in my awareness—was that increasingly my drinks were being delivered by a flouncy steward with dark eyes and hair flopping disingenuously over one eyebrow. The other eyebrow had a silver ring in it, and I briefly wondered when airlines had been lax enough to let their employees make such statements. But when he was serving me, all of his attention was planted on my seatmate, Hal, who rewarded him with the same warm smile I was getting.

The second revelation came as I followed the steward's gaze over to Hal's lowered seat tray, where the steward was placing a fresh martini and taking an empty martini glass away. There were two other objects on the tray that almost took my breath away—and seemed to be what was twitter-pating the steward as well. One was a paperback novel, with a familiar screaming title on the cover in gray and scarlet letters. I'm sure that most people had no idea what was inside the covers of John Rechy's *City of the Night*, but I had every reason to believe that it was a classic—and explicit—gay novel. And my seatmate, Hal, had it sitting out in plain sight.

And not only that. He also had a foil condom packet sitting there and was fondling it—that's the only appropriate verb I could use for the play of his long, sensuous, manicured fingers as they played with the packet.

It was obvious that Hal was projecting a clear message. I assumed it was for the steward, who was almost beside himself with interest, but, when Hal turned his smile on me and when I noticed that his thigh was right up against mine when there was more than enough room for us to be separated in our seats, I couldn't be sure.

And the reason I couldn't be sure was that Hal was just the sort of man I melted to. But secretly. It was something I'd never shared with either my family or my company. I led the perfect trophy blonde wife and two preciously beautiful children wealthy suburban life. And my company was perhaps one of the most conservative in the United States when it came to anything close to gender bending.

But I was instantly interested in Hal—perhaps even more than the steward who was virtually drooling over him was. What I found shocking was that Hal seemed to know that I was. I wondered, almost in panic, what had given me away.

But when Hal climbed—none too quickly—over me when the plane's interior lights had been dimmed and people had gone quiet and spoke in hushed tones to the steward in the aisle and both disappeared for nearly a half hour, I worked hard at convincing myself that it wasn't me that Hal had set his net for, but the steward. This impression was helped along when I noted that the condom packet no longer was on Hal's tray and didn't resurface for the rest of the flight.

My mind went back to the mile-high club references, and I admit to more than slight regret that the image wasn't involving me.

The swishy steward's back pressed against the wall over the toilet in the confining Business Class toilet, his bare knees pressed into Hal's chest and his head bent forward by the curve of the plane's fuselage. His tongue is hanging out and he's making little yip, yip sounds as Hal, expensive trousers and briefs around his ankles, holds the little bleach blond against the wall and thrusts a manly cock up into a tight hole. Again and again and again. A side-angle camera angle that shouldn't have been possible in the space showing the long, ribbed-condomed cock pulling nearly all the way out and then slamming home again. Repeating. The blond steward shuddering with each thrust. The camera focuses to the floor at Hal's feet, picking out the torn, now-empty, condom packet. Welcome to the mile-high club.

I shook my head, realizing that I had dozed off, if only momentarily, in a reverie. It had been long enough, however, for me to go hard. When Hall returned, his zipper was at half staff and his shirt wasn't tucked in as neatly as it had been when he'd left.

In Birmingham, as I struggled, half groggy from the effects of the trans-Atlantic flight, out to the taxi queue, I was completely disarmed and flummoxed when the rear passenger door to a black limousine opened in front of me, Hal leaned out of the door, and I heard him say, in a rich, matter-of-fact baritone, "Shall I give you a lift to your hotel room, then?"

* * * *

Hal proved to be an expert lover. He seemed to understand instinctively what I wanted—to be dominated and driven hard, but expertly. He took the initiative in everything, which was exactly how I liked to have my sex with men.

It started in the back of his limousine. As soon as my luggage was stowed in the trunk and I'd entered the back of the car, Hal pulled me close to him.

"Tell me I haven't guessed wrong about you," he said.

I had to admit, in a hoarse, near whisper, that he hadn't, although I was in somewhat of a stupor and was trembling from his directness and assuredness.

He called out for his driver to take the long route to the hotel I identified as the one I was booked in, the Radisson Blu Hotel, and only then turned toward me.

"You don't mind that we take the long way, do you?"

"No," I said, breathlessly, hoping that this meant what I was taking it to mean.

"And you understand why I offered you the ride?"

"Yes," I answered in a tight voice.

"Which means I'm going to fuck you. I've wanted to do that all across the Atlantic."

It wasn't a question. He already had an arm around me and the other hand working my belt buckle.

"Yes," I managed to croak.

He didn't bother to do more than unzip himself and I was squatting in front of him and sucking his meaty cock erect. I just flipped the split foil condom wrapper on the floor of the car—with a vision of the one I'd imagined on the floor of the airplane toilet—after I'd rolled the disc down over his cock. Then, jacket, trousers, and briefs off, shirt unbuttoned, and tie being used as reins as Hal wished, I rode his cock. I first faced him, with the two of us kissing and him working my nipples with his mouth. Then I faced the front seat with him arching my torso back to him by pulling on my reversed tie and his other hand snaking around and milking my cock.

A second opened condom packet lay next to the first on the limo's rear seat floor. A spent condom, thick as a slug with the cum inside it, lay between the packets.

In the hotel room, after we had both taken a quick shower, him first, he took me again, hard, doggy style on the carpet before we'd reached the bed. We were both naked this time. His body was magnificent for his age. His cocksmanship—stroking vigor, staying power, and reload ability—was superb. Triple A in all departments. And a hunk on top of all of that. He brought a briefcase up with him, which he placed on the desk by the bed and opened to reveal a pile of condom packets, tubes of lubricant, and various toys, including a plow belt.

"From your responses in the car, I think you know what this is for," he said.

I didn't answer. I well knew what a plow belt was for. I had started to tremble in anticipation the moment he'd taken it out of the briefcase. He whipped the strip of black leather with hand holds at each end over my head, upending me on my belly, and proved that he could support my whole weight with his hand grips on the handles of the plow belt as he thrust his cock into me and moved my channel on his cock.

He played me like a rag doll, totally dominating me, giving me exactly what I loved from a man.

I had no idea how he knew I'd let him fuck me let alone what I wanted in a fuck partner—but the experience was just too glorious for me to question. I probably should have questioned more, been more cautious in acquiescing to what he wanted to take from me, to give to me.

I slept, exhausted, after he'd pounded my ass for a third time on the bed. And when I woke, he was gone. There were no notes or any other indication of who he was or where he was. I doubted then that his name even was Hal. But that was OK. I'd been fucked well—and all of the tension of the coming negotiations for the catalytic converter bid had melted away.

Well, most of it.

I wasn't picked up for the meeting at Smythe and Withers until the next afternoon, Friday, which was meant to provide me sleep time. But its only real effect was to give me time to sharpen my nerves again over the coming meeting. I just wasn't used to knowing so little about those I was negotiating with. I had found references to the firm, and they did have a Web site, but they obviously were one of those old staid British firms that hid behind the doors of their exclusive gentlemen's clubs. At least that gave me the clue that I'd best dress and act ultraconservatively.

I wondered what they would think if they knew that I'd let a stranger I'd barely met on an airplane into my hotel room to fuck my lights out with a plow belt immediately upon arrival in Birmingham. I almost was reduced to nervous giggles by that thought.

A vintage black Rolls Royce sedan with a stern-looking uniformed chauffeur met me at the hotel door to whisk me away to what proved to be not more than a four-block ride into a garage under a modern steel and glass high-rise building. It wasn't at all what I expected the building would be like that housed the Smythe and Withers offices. I was expecting something Georgian in ivy-covered dressed stone.

The chauffeur parked in a remote, barely lit recess of the garage and waved me toward the distant elevator doors with the comment that I could find the offices I was looking for on the thirty-third floor. I wondered if it was a Britisher's way of putting an upstart American in his place by not letting me off at the elevator doors, but I was too preoccupied with the order of my presentation to take umbrage.

I almost was too preoccupied as well to notice the tableau I passed en route to the elevator doors.

If the ceiling light hadn't been on in the interior of the sleek forest-green Jaguar I was passing, I probably wouldn't have looked over at the automobile. And if I hadn't looked over there, I would have missed why the interior light was on. The passenger door was open, and with slight difficulty I discerned a pair of bare, pale legs, ending on argyle socks and tan loafers with tassels waving in the air, trying to find purchase on the door frame or to wrap themselves over the shoulders of the man who was hunched between them, fully suited in a black and gray silk pinstriped suit—obviously very expensively cut—and obviously fucking the young man lying on the small of his back across the bucket seat. The receiver's white knuckled fists were scrabbling at the upper reaches of the door frame, evidently attempting to keep his back from being bruised by the gear shift between the seats.

The bottom was being very vocal. But not in English. It sounded like French to me.

I lingered momentarily, watching, my mind connecting this taking with what I had gloriously experienced the previous evening and wishing that it was me being fucked. I liked everything that was assailing my senses with this encounter— the passionate cries of the bottom, the richness of both the automobile and the suit-clad taker, even the element of danger in the public nature of the sexual act and the incongruity of the dark garage and the lit Jaguar interior.

It was with a heavy sigh that I turned and walked toward the elevator doors. When I heard the cry of the bottom that he was coming, ejaculated in language that even I could understand, I turned and saw the man fucking the bottom tense and then fall on top of the other man, who hugged his assailants back closely with his bare legs, the tassels of his shoes swaying in air.

Again, as I waited for the elevator doors to hiss open, I wished that it had been me on the small of my back in the Jaguar. What I'd experienced when I arrived in Birmingham was still making me horny. In fact, with the difficult negotiations imminently facing me, I wished I was anywhere else, doing anything else.

I was kept cooling my heels in a mahogany-paneled reception room that could have come out of a seventeenth-century English castle for nearly an hour and then for twenty more minutes in a conference room with floor-to-ceiling glass windows overlooking downtown Birmingham after I had been introduced to a clutch of sour-looking old goats, as conservatively dressed as I had imagined, at the other end of the table from where I had been told to sit. I didn't remember all of the names, but I made sure that I latched into the two oldest goats of the lot, Robert Smythe and Halston Withers, who obviously were owners of the names on the door.

Neither one of the patriarchs seemed pleased at the delay. But it wasn't my delay. We obviously were waiting for something else to happen—or someone else to arrive.

And then it happened.

The first "happening" was the appearance, wearing a silk black and gray pinstriped suit that was expensively cut but perhaps a bit rumpled today, of the Hal of my airplane flight followed by my dance on the clouds. I went numb but not numb enough not to catch him being introduced as Halston Withers Junior, who, to my terror, was going to handle the project contract negotiations for Smythe and Withers.

The second "happening" descended as Hal was apologizing for being late because he had been late in gathering up the negotiator for the French firm, Sean Dupre, who entered the conference room in Hal's wake. This quite obviously was not the sloven Jean Claude Dupre I had faced— and easily bested—in negotiations before. It was his very young, willowy, and handsome, in a sultry, Lord Byronish way, son, Sean. My eyes went automatically to his feet and my greatest fears were realized when I saw the tan tasseled loafers with the argyle socks peeking out below his trousers hem.

Now I knew what the chauffeur didn't let me off at the elevators in the garage. The negotiations had already begun, and Hal had made sure I understood that.

The greatest consternation of all was that Hal didn't even flutter an eyelash when he was introduced to me. He had known who I was all along.

My fears were confirmed after the two presentations were taken and hard questions asked of both but no indication was given of which one they favored. Darkness had already fallen on the city of Birmingham and the night lights had flickered on when Hal declared that we would resume discussions on Monday—that he was off to his country home for the weekend and, most alarming of all, that he was taking Sean Dupre with him.

I was half-heartedly invited to weekend with one of the junior partners, but he seemed relieved when I said I really should spend the time consulting with my company on the answers to some of the questions the negotiating firm had shot at me.

"May I see you for a moment before you leave," Hal Withers Junior said to me as the others were jacking themselves out of their chairs to the tune of more than one letting gas and milling about waiting for the session to dissolve.

I didn't know what to expect when Hal took me to his office. What I wanted was for him to lay me on his desk and fuck me to ecstasy. But that's not what happened.

"I personally find your proposal the better of the two—although neither is acceptable yet," Hal told me when we were alone.

"Hal . . ." I started to say, wanting to talk about something else entirely.

"Over the weekend I'd like you to reconsider all of your figures, Doug," he continued, very businesslike.

"It's a fair offer, Hal," I said. "Better than the French one if you look at the whole package."

He wasn't looking at me. He was fanning photographs out on the top of his desk. My heart nearly stopped when I leaned over and looked at them. They were of Hal and me doing our sexual exercises in my hotel room the previous night. The briefcase. The one he'd put on the desk. It had had a camera embedded in it.

"I understand you work for a very conservative firm," Hal was saying, although I was too numb to pay too much attention to what he was saying. "And you have a lovely family—two children, I'm told."

That was like a dagger slipped between my ribs.

"You knew who I was on the plane, didn't you? And you meant for me to see what happened down in the garage, didn't you?" I asked in a strangled voice.

"But of course. That's what good negotiators do—scope out and use their counterpart's vulnerabilities. Luckily

180

for you, Doug, the negotiations are still open. I am still working on Sean Dupre's vulnerabilities."

I wanted him to say more—to say something that validated our time together. But when he did speak again, he was still focused on the negotiations.

"Monday morning, Doug. I think you can come up with a lot better deal by then."

And then he was gone.

* * * *

What stung the most was not Hal's failure to tell me that I was the best he'd ever had in the sack—or even that he had targeted me for sex. It was a fetish of mine to be dominated by a tinge of cruelty. No, what hurt the most was his suggestion that I was an inferior negotiator. I was the pride of my company in negotiations.

I would not take this laying down, I thought. But then I laughed a bitter laugh. I certainly so far had taken it laying down—with my legs open and begging for it.

When I got back to the hotel, I ordered dinner in and got right to work on the computer. I even called the research unit in the company back in New York, which was five hours behind the time in Birmingham, early for their day. Where a barrier against information had been erected around the firm of Smythe and Withers, Robert Smythe and Withers, father and son, were people and may not be as well cordoned off as their firm. Hal had been right about vulnerabilities. I needed to know theirs.

In the end, Hal's base vulnerability was the same as mine. He had a wife who was quite active in charity events and children—ones both by the current wife and by a former one. And there was no hint in the public record of Hal Junior fucking men.

The public record also told me where Hal Junior's country home was—in the Cotswolds, a two-hour drive south of Birmingham.

Because I wasn't used to driving on the left and had trouble figuring out the road signs, most of which were covered with tree branches and couldn't be read until you were driving beyond them, it took me nearly three hours the next morning to reach his country house. The first people I encountered when I pulled into the forecourt of a rambling English Tudor residence were a young couple looking to be in their early twenties, who were decked out in tennis togs and who were swinging tennis rackets. They introduced themselves as Halston Wither's older children, Victoria and Edwin—Vicki and Eddie—and I introduced myself, daringly, as an American business acquaintance of their father's who their father had invited down for the weekend.

I hoped not only that I was bearding Hal in his lair sufficiently to keep him from declaring I hadn't been invited and sending me off in embarrassment but also that the house had sufficient bedrooms to make it believable that I had been invited. From the size of the edifice that I could see, though, that wasn't likely to be a problem. It could as well be a country hotel as a country house.

At the bottom of the briefcase I was carrying up to the front door of the small castle were the photographs Hal hadn't taken with him when he left me in his office the previous evening—but that I had had the presence of mind to snarf up. Those photographs could be used both ways, especially now that I knew that Hal had a wife and children just as I had.

"Jolly good," Eddie said. "Daddy is off on a shoot with that Frenchie he dragged home for the weekend. Won't he be surprised when he finds you already settled in when he gets back?"

"I haven't the slightest doubt about that," I answered.

"You're just in time for tea," Vicki said. "Eddie can show you to a bedroom and then you two can join Mam and me in the conservatory."

It was a piece of cake—or biscuit, I guess, in the British lingo. There I was, sitting all smiles between the newer Mrs. Withers and daughter Vicki, with son Eddie across the tea table from me and with a third cup of tea in my hand, when Hal entered the conservatory all abluster with what he termed to be a splendid shooting day. He was so well tailored that he looked like he'd just walked off a movie set rather than a slog through forest and marsh. He said that Sean Dupre was all in from the day's sport and had already gone to his room.

As I was sitting where I could see the grand staircase in the foyer and had seen Hal and Sean enter the house and mount the stairs a good thirty minutes earlier, I had a fair idea what Sean Dupre was tired from and what else other than stairs Hal had been mounting.

I had to hand it to him. Hal acted exactly like he really had invited me. Only a wry smile on his lips revealed to me—and I trust to me alone—that he was both amused and bemused by my bringing the negotiations to his country house doorstep.

I stood to greet him, and as I did, the two senior partners of the firm, Robert Smythe and Halston Senior, came in from a side door, in their hunting togs and carrying their rifles at the ready rest. I had really stepped into it here. This quite obviously was a gathering I was crashing. Still, the French negotiator had been invited. So, I would press on. The worst thing that could happen would be that my company would lose the bid—and it seemed to be doing that anyway if Sean Dupre was invited for the weekend and I wasn't.

I was desperate, and although I'd been skittish to try this ploy, desperate situations called for desperate means.

Neither of the senior partners seemed the least bit upset I was there and Hal Junior was still giving me his amused look.

"Must you bring your guns into the conservatory, Father Withers?" Hal's wife asked as her hand holding the tea pot was poised over my cup. "You know I abhor firearms in the house." Her delivery was calm and offhand, as if this was an old sore that she knew wasn't going to be salved.

"Well, it's no longer my house, Muriel, and you seem to have moved the gun cabinet. I couldn't find it. Perhaps you can come show me where I can put my gun."

Mrs. Withers blushed, but, having finished pouring my tea, she rose and said, "Shall we go up then?"

Robert Smythe broke in just as Muriel Withers and her father-in-law were leaving the room with a blustered voice query for Hal Junior. "Where's the Frenchie got off to? We were to go for a ride after the hunt. I sure as hell hope he's better at that than hunting."

"He's not bad, Bob. He's tied up upstairs; you can find him in the Green Room, if you wish, though."

As Smythe headed for the main staircase hall, Eddie leaned over to his sister, Vicki, and said, "I'm in the mood for another game. Shall we?" And, with Vicki's consent, Hal Junior and I were suddenly alone.

"Couldn't live without me, could you?" Hal said in a quiet voice, that smile still on his face.

"Something like that. But we have some more negotiating to do, I believe, before the fuller meeting with your senior partners."

"Nothing would please me more," he said as he strode over to me and leaned down. His mouth went to mine, and one of his hands went to my basket.

"Business negotiation, Hal," I said, pulling away from him—but not fast enough to fool him. He knew I was aching for him in that sense. I opened the briefcase I'd brought in with me, though, and took the photographs out.

"It occurred to me that these photographs work both ways, Hal," I said. "I may not want my family and employers to see these. But I assume you don't want your loved ones and business associates to see them, either. I did my research and know you have a family just as I do. It's fortuitous that your senior partners are here this weekend too, though. This should return us to completely equal grounds in the negotiations. So, perhaps we can start all over again. My people have run all of the numbers and we're confident we can give a much better deal than the French company can."

"You are trying to blackmail me with the photographs I took to blackmail you?" Hal asked. Then, before I could respond, he laughed out loud. "My god, that is cheeky, man. Cheeky and bold. I must say I like your style."

"Then shall we talk the deal again?" I asked, pleased that I had found the key to get the negotiations back on equal, at least, if not necessarily advantageous grounds.

"Come, stand up and come with me. I want to show you something," Hal said.

Warily, I stood. He took me by the hand and walked me out to the grand foyer and then up the side staircase that split half way up. We took the right-hand split and then down a center hallway. The door to one of the rooms was slightly open, and Hal pushed it a bit more open. The overwhelming sensation I got when I looked into the room was the color green. A dark, rich green. The next sensation was the sound of full effort, wheezing sex. Only after that did my visual sense kick in to where I could see the young Frenchman, Sean Dupre, naked and on his back on the top of the bed, with his arms pulled above his head, his wrists tied to the top railing of the ornate headboard of the canopy bed and his legs stretched up and tied to the posters at the opposite corners of foot of the bed. Robert Smythe, equally naked, was standing between Dupre's thighs and fucking him with a great deal of huffing and puffing.

Now I knew what Hal had meant about Dupre being tied up and both Hal and Smythe had meant when they talked of going riding with the young Frenchman.

"As you can see," Hal said in sotto voce as he pulled the door to the Green Room to and pulled me out into the center of the hall, "Robert Smythe is still making up his mind about the bid. If he doesn't fall in love with Sean—and he is a very sweet young man, if not yet a seasoned negotiator—you may have an interview with Bob later this evening to try to win his vote. So, it's fortuitous for you after all that you have come here. And, as you can see, our photographs aren't going to shock Bob one bit. Now, I believe the end of the hall is next. The Blue Room."

I almost gasped when we peeked into a larger bedroom suite at the end of the hallway, decorated in blue, when Hal quietly clicked the door open and I saw that his father was putting his personal gun away inside Hal's wife, Muriel, on another four-poster bed. She was bent over the bed on her belly and he was fucking her from behind doggy style. Her face showed almost a blank, this-is-my-duty neutral expression. His face was florid, but he obviously was enjoying himself.

"My father and I share and share alike, Doug," Hal said when we were back in the hallway. "So, you can see that my family is not likely to be intimidated by these photographs. And if you think that either my wife or my father will be shocked seeing me fuck another man, I must apprise you that I went to the best of English public schools—as did my father—and as did the men in my wife's family. We have quite a tradition of buggery in all of the best schools here, you know. My senior partners expect me to win the negotiations I take on for the firm—any way I can."

I was flabbergasted and couldn't quite manage to say anything.

"Now, I wonder if we'll find the young people in Vicki's or Eddie's rooms?"

"My god, you can't mean? . . . they went off to play tennis."

"Oh, neither one of them plays tennis," Hal said with a little laugh. "They just like to fuck in tennis gear. And don't looked so shocked. They aren't biologically related. Eddie is Muriel's from her first marriage and Vicki is mine from my first marriage. Now, come. Come to the other hallway. That's where my bedroom is. That's where you can give me your best bid—and I can enjoy fucking you again."

I gave him the best blow job I could muster as he lay back on the center of the red brocade-covered four-poster in the suite at the other end of the bedroom hall in what had to be the Red Room. And then I climbed over him and sank my channel on his cock and, my chest plastered to his, and raised my pelvis enough for Hal to do the fucking—because that's how he said he wanted to do it. Before he was finished, he turned me onto my back, pushed his knees under my rump to lift my channel to his cock, and finished me with deep, fast strokes.

"That was nice," he said when he was done. "You have much more experience than Sean does. I also like your initiative in not just leaving the negotiations to us. So, I'll tell you what. Show me the notes where your company registers the very lowest bid they've authorized you to make. We'll add five million to that, and if it's under the French company's open bid, you'll have my vote."

"Thank you," I moaned. "What I mean is thank you for the fuck. If you'll fuck me again, it sounds like it's a good deal."

"I'll be happy to do so tonight—if you still want me to after Bob Smythe and my father are finished with you. Both have said they want a crack at you. We can go on to the Green Room now, and I'll ride the Frenchie again while Smythe has his way with you. If I know my father, he won't be finished with Muriel until dinner time, but he should be able to visit your room in the night. I think you'll be amazed at how well he fucks. I know I am. You will stay for dinner and the night, I hope."

I turned over and moaned—and then cried out—as Hal started to stuff what he could of fingers and fist in my channel. These would possibly be the hardest negotiations I'd ever conducted.

The Refusal

It was a long shot, but Langley said the Station in Mongu had to do something, so quick plans were made and a team from the special section was sent out to Central Africa. A new warlord had risen in the remote province to the east, and, as remote as the province was, it was about the most important region to U.S. interests in the whole of Africa.

The magic word was uranium.

The province was laced with it, providing probably the largest known largely untapped deposits of the most precious element in the world. And now it was controlled by a crazy, upstart warlord who was showing the finger to the central government and picking and choosing among all of the offers for mining the stuff.

General Kirungi of the Banyao was a monster of a man—in both size and temperament. He'd gotten the nickname "the gorilla" because of his size and his lack of sophistication or care for political correctness or diplomatic niceties. He was a law unto himself and had a reputation for simply killing anyone with his bare hands who stood in the way of his voracious appetites. He was said to be seven feet tall—although no one had gotten close enough to him with a tape measure to verify that—and he was a mountain of a man—big bellied and fat assed. But it was all deception; it was all hard muscle. He was a dark chocolate brown, but his body was covered with blue tattooing, reflecting that he had emerged directly from the jungle to push all men aside in his province and had become a virtual king in his little fiefdom.

The United States, naturally, wanted to ensure that they were able to acquire the uranium in his province—or to keep it away from select others if they couldn't have it themselves—although Kirungi had been teasing and holding them off for more than a year—just as he was doing with the Russians and Chinese and Indians and Iranians. The rumor was that he was most amenable to the offers from the North Koreans, although U.S. intelligence analysis had concluded that he had floated this rumor himself to pique the interest of the West. Although Kirungi was called dumb and primitive by many, wily and maverick actually would hit closer to the mark.

The man had propelled himself to center stage in Africa so precipitously and in such a short time that there virtually was nothing known of his background. All that U.S. intelligence had to go on was that he was the first-born son of a local tribal chief, who had sent him to a private school in France, where he had been expelled for sexually assaulting three students. All of the students were males and redheads. This was all the analysts had found in his background other than that he had an assistant who followed closely behind him and made everything happen that Kirungi wanted to happen. Shisa was of the Bamasaaba rather than Kirungi's Banyao, but there was a tie between them. Shisa was married to Kirungi's favorite daughter, who he indulged in every way.

That was it; that was all U.S. intelligence had to work with, and establishing U.S. supremacy in access to the uranium was thus a chancy possibility—but it was something they had to try.

The provincial capital of Kalaibo was overrun with mining engineering teams speaking a cacophony of languages when a two-man team from the Belgian-based international consortium Agorabasse arrived in the city. Eric Scanlon, documented as a Canadian, was a distinctive man. He had blazing red hair and a cocky countenance despite appearing to be a good ten years younger than he was. He was slight of build, which helped explain his in-your-face cockiness, and he moved like a dancer, although this was more because he had been an Olympic gymnast and had maintained the physique of one. He dressed flamboyantly for the dusty plains rimming the jungle forests of Central Africa and exuded more than his share of self-confidence.

His assistant, Brian Townsend, traveled under an Australian passport, and he was as different from his boss as he could be. Tall and hulky, dark and handsome in a square-cut fashion. He was the quiet one, but the one with an open, friendly smile. The one comfortable in wrinkled bush jacket and khaki shorts and combat boots; the one carrying all of the equipment.

General Kirungi's first sighting of Eric Scanlon was in his favorite male bordello on the outskirts of Kalaibo. Kirungi had made his choice for the night and was being led back to the best room in the house when he passed an open door and heard moaning and murmuring that was not in the local dialect.

Eric Scanlon was laying on his back in a black-leather sling suspended from the ceiling by chains, with his alabaster legs spread and lifted in a harness and a large-boned local African stud with a thick cock fucking him in slow strokes.

Kirungi's attention was riveted on the young Westerner's flaming red hair—both the mop of curls on his head and the finer curling at his bush—and by his diminutive size. He was also mesmerized by the sounds of pleasure the man was voicing in the fuck. Kirungi's cock went immediately at attention, and, in short order, he left his choice for the evening barely conscious on the floor of the bordello's best room, unable to close his legs and of no use to the establishment for several more days, and backtracked to get another look at the redhead.

Kirungi couldn't get the redheaded Westerner out of his mind while he was taking his pleasure, but when he returned to the room where he'd seen him, the man was gone.

Three days later, though, Eric Scanlon, with Brian Townsend in tow, was sitting in Kirungi's office, doing what he could to charm the tribal chief—which didn't take much, since Kirungi had spent the three days obsessing over Scanlon's red hair and alabaster skin and his moaning at the fucking of an

African stud. Kirungi had put out feelers on who this man could be, and his assistant, Shisa, who was standing by the door during this meeting, had worked his magic and moved the paperwork for Scanlon's requested meeting with the provincial chief to the top of the pile, moving him past petitioners who had been waiting for their audience for weeks.

Kirungi was cagey in the discussions, speaking of possibilities and mentioning gigantic sums and suggesting that they did need to talk further on it. Then, as the empty-talk negotiations drew to a close, Kirungi suggested that Shisa take Brian Townsend to his own office and offer him a beer and talk about uranium as an element and the mining techniques thereof, topics that Kirungi admitted bored him—that he had some higher-level discussions yet to conduct with Mr. Scanlon.

"Twenty-five or thirty minutes, that's all I'll need," Kirungi said.

When they were alone, Kirungi leaned over the top of his desk, exuding an image of a massive man who made the desk look like children's furniture, although it was well over standard size, and stared directly into Scanlon's eyes.

"And did you enjoy the fuck at the Kojo House, Mr. Scanlon?" he asked, with a smile.

Eric Scanlon looked scandalized and worked his jaw as if he couldn't think of a thing to say at this direct and shocking question.

"No need for games, Mr. Scanlon," Kirungi continued. "I saw you there, and I heard you. You were enjoying being fucked by a big African cock."

"On occasion, yes, I do enjoy it," Scanlon said, and to show Kirungi he had fully recovered his wits, he fished a pack of cigarettes out of his top pocket and lit one up with a lighter from his trouser pocket. He blew a ring of smoke in the air and then lowered his face and gave the African tribal chief a sardonic smile.

"And did you enjoy being fucked at Kojo House, general?"

"I don't get fucked, Mr. Scanlon. I fuck. And I have a bigger cock than anything you can buy at Kojo House. I would like to fuck you."

"Oh really? And would we do that at Kojo House?" Scanlon asked, keeping his voice at bantering level. This was a dangerous part of this game.

"Here. Now. I can split you and have you groveling at my feet in twenty minutes," Kirungi said. "I think you will enjoy it as much as I do." And the way he said it reflected that he totally believed what he had said. "$200 U.S. and all of the cocks you want at Kojo House. How does that sound? I know you asked for the biggest cock they had at Kojo House. My men checked on that. I can give you what you want. And perhaps the second time you will want to pay me for it." He sat back in his chair and gave a hearty laugh. Scanlon wondered if perhaps he had spent all morning devising that joke.

"I'd rather we talked some more on the mining deal my company is offering you. Perhaps you can look that over and we can meet again in a few days. And then, yes, I might like to take your cock. I do love big, black cocks." Scanlon was leveling a confident smile at Kirungi, but he was seething inside. All was not ready yet. He didn't want to take Kirungi's cock any more than was absolutely necessary for the operation.

"You know I could take you right here, don't you, Mr. Scanlon?"

"Yes, probably," Scanlon answered in a light, "who cares" voice, "but has any company or government offered anything close to what Agorabasse has for these mining rights? I think it best that we make a whole evening of it as either a deal celebration or some other accommodation, don't you? Or don't you really have any uranium to sell? How about signing my petition for survey rights out near Lukulu, so I know whether I really want to let you fuck me? I'd like to know that there's really something worth fucking over."

"My cocking is worth all of the uranium in Africa," Kirungi retorted, on the edge between wanting to trade witticisms and wanting to reach across the desk and throttle this arrogant little man. "But I'll sign your survey petition. The uranium is there."

Scanlon had been pushing the buzzer in his pocket in panic for several minutes now—summoning Brian Townsend to somehow get back to this office, and it was at this point that

Townsend did arrive, with a somewhat chagrined-expressioned Shisa behind him.

Kirungi gave Shisa a nasty look as Scanlon stood and made a hasty retreat, but not before Kirungi invited Scanlon to view a tribal dance ceremony with him in three day's time, which Scanlon happily accepted.

They left Kirungi towering over his desk—having worked him up into the frenzy they wanted, although they walked a risky line in dealing with him. Kirungi wanted to fuck the cocky Eric Scanlon now more than ever.

Kirungi tried to entice Scanlon into his Mercedes after the tribal dance ceremony later in the week, but Scanlon managed to somewhat gracefully get out of his grip with nothing more than Kirungi copping a feel of his basket and forcing Scanlon to take the measure of his cock through his regimental blue trousers. The gasp that Scanlon emitted at this feel was genuine.

The U.S. intelligence now had something to work with, and Townsend reported that he'd be able to handle Shisa to keep him away from the operations room for as long as was needed.

It took two days. But when everything was set up, Townsend made the call to Shisa.

"Mr. Scanlon would love to do as the general suggests," Townsend said. "Just tell him that, please. And he is anxious. He doesn't want to wait until he gets back to Kalaibo. We're at the village of Lukulu, where we're doing the surveying you approved. Mr. Scanlon could meet with the general in the governmental office here if he wishes. And oh, by the way, we've been called back to Belgium for consultations, so we'll probably have to go directly back to the capital from here and fly to Belgium. Mr. Scanlon's not sure when we can return."

The tribal chief's Mercedes roared up in a gigantic cloud of dust to the front of the governmental office in the small village of Lukulu in less than three hours. Out stepped a broadly smiling General Kirungi followed by a less-than-smiling Shisa.

Brian Townsend was standing at the door into the one-room office.

"Mr. Scanlon is inside, general," he said. "I suggest that Mr. Shisa might want to walk over to the town's hotel with me for a drink and some technical discussions while you meet with Mr. Scanlon."

"That sounds quite satisfactory," the general said, and he cast an evil eye to Shisa, who walked off somewhat reluctantly with the hulking Brian Townsend.

Kirungi drew in a breath when he opened the door of the office. Eric Scanlon was sitting on the edge of the desk, facing the door, completely nude, legs spread, and rubbing oil on his cock. He had already oiled his passage well.

Kirungi was making the sound of a bull in heat as he turned the lock of the door behind him and was still stripping off his clothes as he reached the desk. He reached out his big mitts for Scanlon, and a laughing Eric Scanlon reached down for the charging general's monstrous cock with oiled hands.

Scanlon wasn't laughing for long, as a bellowing Kirungi grabbed his legs, wishboned them, and then took his cock in one hand and started stuffing it into Scanlon's channel. Once having gained a sure purchase inside Scanlon's canal, Kirungi took hold of Scanlon's hips and jerked the redhead's pelvis down further on his cock. Scanlon screamed out and rose up and pushed his fists against Kirungi's massive chest. Kirungi laughed and backhanded the smaller man across the mouth. Scanlon came back up and was slapped again. Stunned, Scanlon laid back and whimpered and moaned. And then he started to grunt and groan and writhe under the huge African, as Kirungi's cock filled out and sank deeper and he started to piston Scanlon's channel like a jackhammer.

It was all over in fifteen minutes, leaving Scanlon nearly unconscious, collapsed on the desktop right where Kirungi had found him and groaning and holding his legs as spread as he could get them.

"I give you five minutes and then we do it again," Kirungi said.

Scanlon groaned.

"And did you find cocking that good at the Kojo House, Mr. Scanlon?" Kirungi asked.

Scanlon whimpered something unintelligible and Kirungi laughed, a deep-throated, fully self-satisfied guffaw.

That's when the lock in the door turned and it opened and three men incongruously in black, tailored suits entered. Two of the men, noticeably armed, stood by the door after it was closed, and the third man walked over to a nearby chair and sat down.

Kirungi looked at them warily. Scanlon lay where he was, panting lightly.

"Are you all right, Eric?" the man asked in a decidedly American accent.

"I'll survive . . . I think," Scanlon answered in a small voice that merged into a moan.

"Hello, General Kirungi, my name is Sam Winterberry. I'm on a temporary assignment to the American embassy here until we can reach some sort of accommodation with you over the uranium mining rights in your province."

"Why the fuck do I care who you are?" Kirungi bellowed.

"Well, if you'll look up in the corner of the room, you'll see video cameras up there. You have been a star on film, general. And we thought perhaps that rather than showing these films in the capital, you might—"

"What the fuck do I care what you show in the capital?" Kirungi growled. And then he laughed. "They all know I fuck men. My wives know I fuck men. The whole province knows I fuck men. And anyone who doesn't like that I'll just snap in two."

It was quite a tableau. The two black-suited G-men at the door; Sam Winterberry, sitting properly in his chair in a tailored suit that was completely out of place here in the African outback; and the provincial tribal chief, standing tall and bulky and naked, his cock half hard and dripping from his taking of Eric Scanlon. Winterberry had a wary expression, and Kirungi had an expression that covered both belligerence and amusement.

After two full moments of silence, Winterberry stood, sighed, and said, "Ah well, it was worth a try. We'll still be happy to talk to you about price and arrangements. No hard feelings, I hope."

He put his hand out, and Kirungi just stood there, looking incredulous, no doubt wondering if all Americans were this demented.

"And to ensure there are no hard feelings," Winterberry, his hand still extended, "we would be happy to give you thirty more minutes with Mr. Scanlon. Eric?"

"Yes, oh god yes," Scanlon mumbled. "Best fuck I've ever had. If he can just . . . go . . . more slowly."

Kirungi gave a broad grin and reached out his hand and shook with Winterberry.

As Winterberry and his two colleagues clicked the door to the governmental office behind them, Kirungi was between Scanlon's legs again and stuffing himself into Scanlon's channel, and Scanlon was crying out, "Slowly . . . oh, gawwd, slowly . . . Oh yesssss!"

"Now, gentlemen, down the street to the hotel, if you please. We gave that little chance of working, but we have thirty minutes for the backup plan."

At the hotel, in a second floor room that had been previously outfitted with video cameras, Kirungi's assistant and son-in-law, Shisa was shuddering and writhing and crying out in passion as he lay, naked, on his back on a bed and Brian Townsend, his knees wedged under the African's buttocks, his thighs splitting the African's thighs, and his hands on the African's hips, pulled Shisa's channel down and up on his cock and moved a hand to Shisa's cock in time to control the African's ejaculation.

Shisa was still groaning from Townsend's own finish deep inside him, when the door to the corridor opened and the three suited men walked in. When the door closed, two of the men, visibly armed, stood on either side of the door, while the third one walked over and sat down in a nearby straight chair.

"Hello, Mr. Shisa. my name is Sam Winterberry. I'm on a temporary assignment to the American embassy here until we can reach some sort of accommodation with your country over the uranium mining rights in your province."

"What?" Shisa said, trying to shrink away into the wallpaper, but held fast by a still-impaling Brian Townsend.

"I think we have a trade that will please us both, Mr. Shisa," Winterberry said. "You may release him now, Brian, if you will. And go down the hall to the bath and clean yourself up. We should be ready to go in another twenty minutes or so."

And then, as Townsend got up with a grunt, pulled on his bush shorts, and went through the door to the corridor that one of Winterberry's colleagues held open for him, Winterberry turned back to a quaking Shisa, who now was buried in the bed covers.

"If you look up in the corners of the room, Mr. Shisa, you will see small video cameras. I'm sure we have some lovely footage of your encounter with Mr. Townsend. Now we would like to have a friend in the provincial office when it comes to giving out uranium mining rights, and I'm sure that your wife, who we understand is General Kirungi's favorite daughter, would not be pleased to see these videos. Would you like to make an arrangement with us? We would, naturally, be happy to put you on a consultant's stipend—all very private, of course."

Shisa hunched there under his covers, trying to speak but unable to do so.

"It is, of course, an offer of very limited availability, Mr. Shisa." Winterberry made a dramatic gesture of looking at his wrist watch. "Your general is a man who doesn't linger over his pleasures. I calculate that you have ten minutes or less to mull over this offer and be dressed and standing down by his Mercedes unless we want him figuring out what has transpired here. Do you really want him to know that you have broken his favorite daughter's heart?"

Shisa was standing by the Mercedes when General Kirungi emerged, all smiles, from the governmental office.

The U.S. team's SUV was parked behind the hotel. After the Mercedes had roared off in a cloud of smoke, Brian Townsend helped Eric get cleaned up at the hotel, while the two silent colleagues dismounted the video cameras. And then they were off, headed back to Kalaibo in the dust cloud that still lingered in the wake of Kirungi's Mercedes.

"How much longer will we be in Kalaibo?" Scanlon mumbled from the backseat.

"Oh, no more than five days," Winterberry answered. "We have Shisa. Now we have to set up his communications and give him instructions and some guidance in protecting himself. At least four days, maybe five. Why do you ask?"

"The general wants to meet me at Kojo House tomorrow night. Do you mind if I meet him again?"

Winterberry just smiled indulgently. He was in a good mood. One way or the other they had completed their assignment.

The Syrian Rent-Boy

"You'll be doing a great service. You'll be saving lives."

I could see why that might be so, but why did I still feel so used? And why was he forcing me to do this rather than someone in his own service, from his own country? I wondered that so much that I asked him.

"I'm from the American embassy. And all of my colleagues are known and watched. I can't get close to Zahlé, let alone across the border into Syria. You're Canadian and a newsman. You have a good excuse to be in the refugee camp."

And just when did you discover I was a Canadian newsman, I wondered. But then I had to laugh dryly. Of course you knew. You knew, Hal Hessler, if that's even your real name. You knew even before we met in Bardo, in the restaurant's gay-friendly bar, on Hamra Street. Didn't you? I was an easy mark, wasn't I?

Hal had been moving around the living area of the flat, naked, exposing what he had captured me with—one of the main attributes that he still held me with. If it only were the photographs and the video, I would have brazened it out, laughed in his face, walked out of the flat, and dared him to use the photographs. But there also was what he had swinging between his thighs. I couldn't deny that. Couldn't deny I wanted that. Did I shock him how easy I was?

He came up close behind me, where I was sitting, naked under a thin robe on a stool at the kitchen island, all of his documents fanned out in front of me. He had already fucked me on the bed and would do so again. We were just taking a break. Or so I had thought. I'd made coffee, and when I turned around, he'd put those photographs and documents on the kitchen island and switched on the TV across the room, in the living area. A video was showing Hal fucking me on the bed and me begging for it. Then he told me what it meant and what I was going to do for him.

He embraced me from behind where I was sitting on the stool at the kitchen island, his lips going to the hollow of my neck and his hands pulling the front of the robe open and cupping my pecs, his thumbs going to my nipples. I moaned. I could do no more. I was putty in his hands.

"It will be easy for you and simple, you can even get a story out of it. We've arranged for your clearances to cross the border and spend three days in the refugee camp, interviewing the Syrian dissidents there. It will be a great news story."

"And I will contact these twenty-two people, give them these letters from their relatives in Cyprus, and convince them just to walk across the border with me?"

It sounded a bit too pat for me.

"Yes, just like that. That's all. The fix is in at the border. All you do is walk them to a café, the Café Clemenceau in Zahlé, and there will be a bus to bring them to Beirut, and a plane to fly them to safety in Cyprus."

"These twenty-two? These are important to you because they have relatives the CIA is obligated to?"

Hal gave me a hard look, took his hands off my chest—which I felt, guiltily, with a tremor of regret—and started pacing the flat again. He obviously hadn't wanted me to name who was at the bottom of all of this. I, conversely, felt it must be named—who was doing this to me. Who had seduced me into this position.

Seduced. That was the best word for it. He had been sitting at one end of the bar at Bardo when I came in. I was all keyed up from a hard day interviewing Syrians who somehow had made it as far as Beirut. I'd had a day of them trying to convince me that the Syrian regime was using chemical weapons on the dissidents and begging me to tell the world. I took notes, promising them that I would write up something—while knowing there wasn't much to write without some sort of tangible proof. I was depressed. I came into Bardo vulnerable and lonely—oh so lonely.

And, there being no use fooling myself. I came looking for what I got. I felt so guilty not being able to do anything with this Syrian situation that I wanted to be punished.

He had been just what aroused me the most. Hal Hessler. Tall and built big—built really big once his clothes were off. Younger than I was by a good ten years. A blond buzz cut, a twinkle in the blue eyes, laugher lines around the smile. Open, easy going, confident, straightforward. I would have known he was an American. In fact, as squared away as he was, I thought through our first two encounters that he was a Marine guard at the American embassy—before he lowered the boom and let me know he was so much more than that.

We were the only two at the bar. It was early. That I had decided to start drinking early reflected how rough my day had been—how much I needed crutches. Hal Hessler was just one more of those crutches. He raised his beer glass to me and smiled. I smiled back. He called the bartender over, who then informed me that the next round had been paid for by the gentleman at the end of the bar. As we both drank, we stared at each other down the length of the bar. His face was expressive. I wasn't sure what he was offering, if anything, but we were in a gay bar after all, and there was nothing in the gazes I returned that would give him the idea he couldn't have it—any of it; anything he wanted to do to me, as long as I could forget everything else while he was doing it.

Then he made what he was offering in addition to a free drink clear—at least to those of us who knew the traditional handkerchief codes—when, still keeping his eyes piercing mine, he took two handkerchiefs from his left back pocket and laid them on top of the bar. A camouflage-colored one, signaling military discipline, and a mustard-colored one, announcing over eight inches. Having come out of the left side told me he was a top.

I hadn't brought any handkerchiefs. The Lebanese wouldn't know what any of the colors represented. I had assumed that it would be a Lebanese Arab fucking me that night. I liked them.

I swallowed hard, pushed away from the bar, and headed to the men's room. I told myself that I really did need to take a piss. As I was finishing at a urinal and before I zipped up, he slid in at the urinal next to mine and exposed his cock. The mustard-colored handkerchief hadn't lied. I could have swallowed my teeth at seeing how thick and long he was. And hard. He hadn't come in there to piss. He turned to me, put one hand on the back of my neck to pull my face to his and wrapped the other hand around my exposed cock. The camouflage-colored hanky hadn't lied either. He was a take charge guy.

It took no more than that. It was a seduction by him, that was for sure. But I gave no indication that I didn't want it. I couldn't have that day. I did want it. I'd had such a rough day that I didn't even begin to think why he had thought—how he had known—that what he was offering was something I wanted. When we disengaged from the kiss, his other hand still squeezing and slow stroking my cock, my eyes went to the bank of stalls.

But he pushed me to my knees right there, with that hand gripping the back of my neck, and both of the roughness and insistence of his touch and the raw public nature of where we were, in the open in the men's room, sent an electric charge through me. When he'd had enough of me sucking his cock and balls, he pushed my head away. I looked at the stalls again, assuming we'd finish in there, but he had other plans.

"I have a flat nearby," he whispered. "We'll be more comfortable there—safer."

Safer. I could see humor in that now.

I wanted it so bad and, just as he had advertised, it was him inside me. I sometimes took cock, but it usually was me giving it. I wanted it so badly that I lowered to my knees just inside the door of the flat and sucked his cock again. I wanted it so badly that he just lay on his back on the bed the first time and I straddled his hips and rode the cock cowboy style. He let

204

me, but he was a man wanting to be in control. He embraced me close twice after that—muscular enough to move me how and where he wanted me—and fucked me hard. I didn't object. If I was the one being fucked, this was the way I wanted it.

The flat. I should have known even from that. It was conveniently near Bardo, near enough so that I wouldn't have second thoughts going there. And it was just a hotel flat. Nothing personal in it at all. This wasn't where Hal lived. I was a newsman. I should have caught on to that. This was just a flat for assignations. What I now knew to be a CIA safe house—I knew that without Hal ever saying those three letters. And of course we had to do it in this flat. The photographs and the video. This was the place outfitted to obtain those when I thought we were alone.

"Yes, these are all families of assets to U.S. intelligence," Hal answered, returning my attention to the documents in front of me. Even now he couldn't use the three letters. "They do important service for us—and for our allies. For Canada too. You are serving your own country's interests in this. These are important people to us. So getting their relatives out of that refugee camp inside the Syrian border is important to us—and to Canada as well."

But we both know that journalists are supposed to be neutral and that Western intelligence services are not supposed to use us this way, I thought. That's why you've gone to these lengths to suborn me. I didn't say it, though—not least because I couldn't. Hal had returned to stand very close behind me. One hand had cupped my chin and raised my mouth to his. His other hand had glided down my chest and belly and cupped my balls and cock. He held them close and I was getting hard again.

Hard for him—despite all that he was forcing me to do.

He released my mouth, and I leaned forward on the stool, my arms stiff-armed wide on the counter, my face staring down on the pile of documents he was giving me. His lips working the back of my neck. One hand still holding my balls and cock, the other one having pulled the robe up behind me and having snaked down the small of my back and into my crack, two fingers in my hole. Searching for, finding my prostate.

I moaned and groaned for him for several minutes as he worked both my cock and my channel with his hands. With a little cry and a jerk I ejaculated into the base of the kitchen island. I wondered if this had been caught on camera too. I supposed, though, that it didn't matter anymore.

He removed his hands from where they were but not from my body. They were cupping my pecs again and he was leaning his chin on my shoulder and playing with my ear lobes with his teeth.

I looked down at the documents and counted the letters.

"Seven letters. You said there were twenty-two refugees."

"Yes. Seven families. That accounts for twenty-one of them."

"Only twenty-one?"

"Yes. We couldn't get a letter for one of them, Asu Gemal, in time. You will have to talk him in without the letter. But he is very important to us. You'll have to talk him in."

"Why again is this so urgent?"

Hal paused before he answered, gauging, I suppose, how much I should know. "The Syrian regime is going to gas that camp in four days. Probably sarin gas. Extremely deadly. You have to go in tomorrow—and be out in three days."

"Gas the camp? But how do you know this?" My mind was racing now. The newsman in me. This would be the proof I needed—or at least a great on-the-scene story. Or near the scene at least, if I didn't want to be gassed too. I could just stay in Zahlé and then I'd be the reporter on the scene. But, my god, the horror of it. All of those people killed. And we—we in the West—knew about it in the advance. And couldn't—wouldn't be—doing anything about it. But I couldn't do anything about it either. Well, I could do at least a little. I could go into that camp and pull at least twenty-two people to safety. In that, Hal was right about doing some service. Better than nothing.

"I'm going to fuck you again."

"Yes," I murmured. "Go back to the bed. I'll be there in—"

"I'm going to fuck you here, on the floor. Get down on all fours." I watched his hand go to the kitchen counter next to where the documents were strewn and pick up a Golden Ticket condom ring. These were scattered throughout the flat, as there was no telling where he would decide to take me. It was part of the thrill of being fucked by him. I also knew, of course, that he was checking—checking on whether he retained control of me after what I now knew about what this entailed. I wanted the fuck, but he needn't have bothered. I still would do anything he told me to do. Knowing should have changed everything, but it changed nothing. I was a whore for him.

He pulled my robe off me as I stepped away from the stool and went down on all fours on an Oriental prayer rug. He crouched over me, covering me close from above. I howled when he thrust that thick, long, hard cock inside me and almost immediately started pumping me hard and deep. His chest was pressed against my back, his arms embracing my torso closely, his teeth holding the scruff of my neck like a wolf holding a cub steady. We both howled and barked as he took me rough and hard.

After a bit, he pulled out of me and rose off my back. Without losing hold of my waist with his hands, though, he turned me onto my back, putting my weight on my shoulders. He pulled my torso and hips up to him, with his arms under my thighs, and thrust inside me again and resumed pumping. I tried reaching for his chest with my arms, but could only reach as far as his upper, meaty thighs, where I dug my fingernails in, holding him to me.

As he pumped my ass, his eyes were boring into mine, watching me express my ecstasy at what he was doing to me. His eyes were telling me that I was his to do whatever he wanted with. Mine were not contradicting him. As I arched my back, my arms now extended from my sides and my hands clawing at the nubby carpeting under the prayer rug, I ejaculated again. I could tell that he came at nearly the same time.

"Tomorrow, 9:00 a.m. in Zahlé, at the Café Clemenceau," he said in a low, hoarse voice.

"Yes," I answered.

When I left the flat later that afternoon, stumbling from the effects of his cocking, Hal handed me an envelope stuffed with Syrian currency. I gave him a quizzical look.

"Make sure you take that into Syria with you. I think you will need it."

* * * *

Most of the first day in the refugee camp was spent in tracking down the seven families for which I had letters. I couldn't go straight for the families, though. I spent half of my time interviewing generally. I would have to produce a news piece on this visit or there would be questions why I'd done this. I had managed to come up with enough other names of people in the camp—from refugees who had made it to Beirut and had urged me to do something—so that it would not raise suspicion when I asked for these specific seven families also. It broke my heart, though, to interview people who I knew were not going to be leaving the camp before the gas attack—if the intelligence on that was correct.

Despite the reticence of all to leave Syria, most of the seven target families were willing to make the extreme change, conditioned, I'm sure by the truly primitive conditions in the camp. It nearly broke my spirit, though, when I couldn't convince two of the families, both of four, to go with me. They either didn't believe the letter was genuine or they would not attempt the change. I was equally saddened to find that another of the families had recently lost a daughter. They told me she had died and showed me photographs of a lovely young woman of nineteen or so, but the mother just started wailing and the father closed down when I asked what she had died of. Outside their tent, others were willing to tell me that Syrian camp guards had come and dragged the young woman out of the tent and away. I didn't really need to hear more of the specifics on her demise then.

Toward nightfall, having had what success I thought I was going to have, although I'd make another run at the holdout families the next day, I started looking for this Asu Gemal, who Hal had told me to be sure to convince to leave. Finding him wasn't that easy, and I soon realized why.

I went through the camp's bazaar, asking shopkeepers if they knew where I could find a young man named Asu Gemal. Each time I got hard looks, and more than once, the shopkeeper, after giving me a pointed look, spat on the ground and turned away. At last one, obsequious and sweating fat man, though, gave me a licentious look and told me I'd find Asu on his back in the tent of one Sargon. He had no trouble giving me directions. And, since he paired that with a proposition of his own, I had no trouble then either knowing why I'd gotten the reaction I had from the others or why Hal had picked me for this assignment. It also started me to thinking that maybe this Asu Gemal was key to the whole operation.

At the designated tent I paid Sargon for two hours with Asu, and, although he gave me a surprised and then a speculative look, he took my money, told me to wait a moment, pushed aside a carpet hanging, and went into an attached, smaller tent adjacent to the larger one.

The young man was already on all fours, his pert little butt pointed to the entrance of his small tent, when I entered. He was mostly naked, with a small and berry-brown body, which was very well proportioned. His only attire consisted of gold serpentine bracelets on his biceps and flat sandals on his feet, with laces of gold string winding around his well-turned calves nearly up to the knees.

There were condoms on a small ivory-inlaid table at one side of the entrance into the tent and a chair on the other side where I could fold and lay my clothes. Most of the space in the tent was taken up by a large bed with silken sheets on it and a mound of garishly colored pillows in silk cases.

I was hard by the time I'd taken my clothes off and folded them and crowned myself with a condom. There was a bottle of lubricant on the table too, but I could tell by the glistening wetness of the young man's well-opened hole and the slickness of his spread inner thighs that he'd already been prepared.

I knew what I had to do. And now I knew why it had been me who Hal was forcing to be here. And I only had a couple of days.

I approached the young man from the rear; crouched over his hips; pulled his face around to mine with a hand gently cupping his chin; and, to a surprised look on his face, gently took his lips with mine and kissed him deeply. After positioning the bulb of my cock at his channel entrance, where he was stretched enough for me to hold the bulb just inside the entrance, I encircled his waist with my arm. While holding his lips with mine, I slowly and deeply entered him with my cock. He was open, but I am horse hung, so he still was belabored to take me.

He was sighing and moaning as I began to stroke inside him slowly, with long, deep strokes. He writhed a bit in my embrace and purred, obviously not having been treated anything like this by his other customers in the rough and tumble camp, and came for me, having moved one of his hands back to stroke his own cock.

He gave me a dreamy look as I picked him up and laid him on his back on the edge of the bed and, after cleaning his cock with my mouth, kissed all up and down his body. He sighed for me and kept whispering words in Arabic that I recognized as endearments. When I entered him again with my cock, he wrapped his legs around the small of my back, holding me close into him, and pulled my face down to his for a kiss, while I slow-stroked him to my own ejaculation. He was a beautiful young man. A face that was more beautiful than handsome. Almond-shaped eyes with large, brown pupils. Long, dark eyelashes. Rose-bud lips with a shy smile even with the mixed pain and pleasure on his face of taking a big cock. I knew mine was bigger than most he took. That it was a challenge to him.

Not long after that I took him again, with his chest on the surface of the bed, pillows under his belly to lift his buttocks to me, his legs spread wide, and his arms extended, hands clutching at bunched-up sheeting and fists opening and closing to the rhythm of a fuck that was harder and even deeper this time. From the noises he was making and the countermotion of his hips, I didn't think that his response to the cocking was all an act by a talented rent-boy.

It had been my intent to convince him that I wasn't the usual client. To press this home, most of the second hour was spent with us reclining on the bed in an embrace, Asu cuddled into my chest, with me prompting him to tell me all about himself and clucking in sympathy and giving him praise as I could in an effort for him to like me. But I needed him to love me, to be lost to me in the same why I was lost to Hal Hessler—or whoever that American spy really was.

I felt I was close to that near the end of the second hour, when he gently pushed me on my back, crowned my cock with a condom he applied deftly with his teeth, and rode me to another mutual ejaculation.

He asked me as I left if I'd be back, and I told him then that I thought I loved him and would be back the next night.

"How much?" I asked when I was back in the main tent with Sargon.

"You know the hourly rate," Sargon said.

"No, I mean how much to buy him and take him away?"

Sargon gave me a speculative look. "He is very valuable to me. He is my livelihood."

"I see openings to three other tents from here," I said. "I don't think he's your only livelihood. And I don't think you'll have a problem replacing him well enough to satisfy the men in this camp." I didn't want to reveal that I thought that Sargon and his whole stable would be dead within a few days.

"But he is my best. I would . . . no, I must say, I have hoped that there would be a way for Asu."

"A way?"

"He is like a son to me. I had hoped he could get out of the camp and into Lebanon."

I didn't know if he was just jacking up the price, but I asked, "Why do you say that?"

"Asu is here in hiding. The regime is looking for him. He was the catamite of a very important general before he escaped to here. He heard things he should not have heard, including that he was going to have to die for what he knew. So he escaped to here."

I felt the tumblers falling into place—both why, perhaps, that the Syrians were going to gas the camp, an attack on their own people—to be rid of Asu—and why Hal's people wanted him—to wring Syrian state secrets from him. "I can take him to safety. How much?"

I was at least a bit exhilarated the next day when I convinced one of the holdout families to leave with me. But I spent much of the day worrying about what I was going to do about Asu. I couldn't deny it. I was more than a little in love with him myself even after only two hours with him. I had paid an exorbitant amount for him—Hal obviously had known what I needed a big chuck of Syrian money for—and left it to Sargon to explain that he'd been sold and that it was in his best interests to leave with me.

Before I left for Sargon's tent, I called a clerk I trusted completely in the Beirut news office, thankful that cell reception carried to this border area. Then, as I moved through the bazaar toward Sargon's complex of tents, I gathered what was needed for the plan that I had hastily forged.

Asu greeted me with a broad smile on his face, tears in his eyes, and on his back with his thighs spread open and pillows under the small of his back. I nearly couldn't hold myself from firing off as I kept my eyes on him and stripped near the entrance. I reached for a pile of condoms.

"No need for that if you are clean," he called to me in a whispery voice. "Sargon is a doctor. He tests frequently. I am clean. I would like to feel you inside me."

I rushed the bed, barely making it there, between his thighs, my lips plastered to him, and my cock sliding inside him, with both of us moving our hips, when one, two, three strokes I had flooded his insides with my cum.

Asu's eyes went wide as our lips parted. "You really do want me. You really do love me."

"Yes, I really do want you and I really do love you," I murmured, my voice choked with emotion, because I knew it was true and now Asu knew it too. This was the zenith of his decision to make. If he told me he didn't want to go with me, I'd let him go and find some way of dealing with Hal and his CIA operations. But I would let him go inside Lebanon. I owed him that much.

"Sargon told me, but I couldn't be sure . . . not until you were willing to make love to me with no condoms."

"But you were willing to let me bareback you."

"Of course. I love you. And you are my savior."

I had never gone completely soft and felt myself hardening again.

"I must fuck you again. Now. I can't help myself. Hard and deep. Full possession."

"Yes, please. Do whatever you want with me. I'm yours."

No forced backup, as with Hal and me. An unconditional surrender.

"Give me full control," I commanded. And Asu went limp under me.

I raised up on my knees, between his thighs. His knees bent and his feet were flat on the surface of the bed. He let his torso, head, and arms dangle back toward the mattress, and panted and groaned and moaned softly as, my arms encasing his waist, I pounded, pounded, pounded his ass channel hard and deep, making him totally, fully mine. He gave himself to me completely, and I managed a nearly mutual ejaculation.

Laying there, him in my arms, as we cooled down in a postcoital reverie, I told him what must be done the next day and kissed away all fears and concerns he had.

"When must you leave tonight?" he asked.

"I have paid for you and I have paid for this tent for the night. I'm going to be inside you, fucking you, making you mine, all night." He moaned as I started once more doing exactly what I told him I was going to do. Asu never wavered in giving me anything I wanted and in whispering to me of his love and total surrender to me.

* * * *

213

Sargon did a double take the next morning after Asu had prepared himself and we were leaving, but he just smiled and nodded his head.

"Sargon," I asked. "Do you have the contacts to get word into the Syrian military."

"Of course, they are my best customers."

"Then, ask no questions, but get word through channels as quickly and as high up the authority chain that you can that Asu died in the night. That he was knifed to death by a client. You can hint that the Hezbollah got him. And then, however you can manage it, it would be in your interests to get yourself and all your loved ones across the border before morning."

Sargon gave him a hard look, but then nodded his head in acknowledgment of what he was being told.

I didn't know if Asu was the only reason the Syrians would attack the camp with gas, but if so, perhaps I could help stave that off. It was worth a try.

We crossed into Lebanon late in the morning without trouble, the border guards just winking at us as we did so. Six complete families. Seventeen people. Hal had told me that he didn't expect them all to accept the offer, so this would be a good number. He would have been pleased if Asu Gemal had been one of the documented refugees to cross the border. But he wouldn't be pleased, because I would have to tell him that I had been too late. That Asu had been knifed and killed—the rumor being that the Hezbollah had found him and murdered him. The gossip coming out of the camp, spread by Sargon, would confirm that for Hal's people as well as for the Syrian regime. But still Hal would not be pleased at all, I knew.

We had to walk through the bazaar in Zahlé en route to the Café Clemenceau. When I saw Sami, the clerk from my office, strolling in the bazaar, I signaled to him and pulled aside the "daughter" of one of the families.

"Listen to me, Asu," I said to the "daughter" I had created in the night. "See that man over there? His name is Sami. He's a friend of mine. I want you to drift away from our group and go in his direction. I have pointed you out to him. He will take you to Tyre."

214

"I can't go with you to Beirut?" Asu, dressed and documented as a beautiful young Syrian maiden, asked plaintively. "You told me—"

"Yes, we will be together for much of the time. Sami has arranged a flat for us in Tyre. I can't say more than that you are in as much danger here in Lebanon as in Syria. I will take care of you. I will take you to Canada when it is safe to do so. Just trust me."

As I watched Asu waft away and meet up with Sami, I looked around for CIA surveillance. I was sure there would be some even before we got the Café Clemenceau. But Sami made it obvious that he was tempting the young maiden away, showing her necklaces of gold from a vendor's booth and buying her one. I hoped and trusted that any surveillance would be seeing a young woman, a woman of little import to them—at least until it was too late to find Asu—being seduced away by a good-looking, smooth-talking Lebanese man.

We counted noses at the Café Clemenceau, Hal Hessler and I, as the families boarded the bus. Other men appeared from where they had been watching the group move from the border and through the bazaar, to help explain why the count was off, and Hal just shrugged his shoulders. He wasn't, after all, all that interested in saving refugees, certainly not young women. His operation had been to intercept a young man who had access to Syrian military plans and could be interrogated to pull those out of him. And that part of the plan had gone south when he'd received intell that told him Asu Gemal had been gotten to by the Hezbollah allies of the Syrian regime. He wasn't half surprised.

"You did well, John," he said, turning to me, obviously seeing no need for me to ever know what the real operation was. "Come back to the flat with me now."

"Yes," I replied.

"I'm going to fuck you silly."

"Yes." As much as I loved Asu—and I did love Asu—I would never give up what Hal had to offer me until I had to.

Two weeks later, I was happy to note that the refugee camp on the Syrian side of the border at Zahlé had not yet been gassed. I didn't care whether it was because Hal had received bad intell on that or whether my message about Asu had reached the upper levels of the Syrian military and they no longer felt such an attack was needed. I was just happy that it hadn't happened yet. It helped me accept the service that had been forced on me. I could assuage my guilt with the belief that many people's lives had been saved by my taking on the assignment.

And after two weeks I was settling into an acceptable pattern. Twice a week Hal fucked me silly in the Beirut flat and twice a week I made love to Asu in the Tyre flat. I would keep going back to Hal as long as he wanted me, knowing, though, that his wanting me rested on whether he could make operational use of me. I went to Asu because I couldn't stay away. I rested and did my job on the other three days. I don't think Hal ever was careful enough to check on the missing daughter. There certainly was no evidence he'd bothered to find out that the daughter of the family had been killed in the refugee camp.

Only one glitch arose—near the end of the second week after the Syria extraction—that caused me pause in gloating over having put one over on the CIA. We were on the bed in the Beirut flat. Hal was on his back, palming my pecs and thumbing my nipples, while I was spread-eagled on top of him, holding myself suspended over him, facing the ceiling, supported on my bent arms positioned on either side of his shoulders and on my bent-knees legs, feet planted on either side of his thighs. I was using the leverage of my feet to rise and fall on Hal's cock.

"The money, John. What happened to the Syrian money I gave you?"

"Oh," I answered between pants. Of course. The money. He'd given it to me to pay for Asu's freedom. He had known at the time that I would need it. I hadn't known that.

I gave a little cry as he gathered my body into his, pulling me down on top of him close, his legs lacing through my thighs to entrap my legs, his cock sinking deep inside me, one strong arm embracing my chest, the hand of the other one gripping my balls. He squeezed the balls and I whimpered.

"The money, John. Tell me about the money or I'll crush your nuts."

I teared up. He already was crushing my nuts.

"I'll . . . I'll give it all back to you, Hal."

He laughed and released my balls. "See, Mr. High and Mighty, not much difference between us, is there?"

"Sorry," I murmured. "Can't blame a guy for trying. I'll have it all back to you the next time we meet here."

"No, you can keep it," Hal answered in an offhand voice. "It's just money. It's worth it to know that you're no better than me."

He deftly turned us, putting me on my belly and him covering me from on top. "Present," he commanded, his fist grasping the back of my neck, holding my chest to the surface of the bed. I drew my knees up and raised my ass to him, giving a little cry as he thrust inside me and started to pump me hard.

Jehovah forgive me, but I loved this. And would keep coming back to it as long as Hal wanted me. But he'd get his money back. I had made a gaff there, but I didn't want Asu's life to have been paid for by the CIA anyway. I'd give them their blood money back.

The Trouble with Dirk

Karl pulled himself up to a sitting position against the headboard of the bed, pulled the used condom off his cock, tossed it in the vicinity of the wastebasket, and reached for the pack of cigarettes on the nightstand. Lighting up and blowing smoke at the ceiling, he watched as the rent-boy came out of the bathroom and padded, unselfconsciously around the sparsely furnished room of the Axelhaus fleabag on Lietzenburger Strasse in the center of Berlin's Schöneberg gay district.

Dirk's body was slight, thin, but not emaciated, more lithe, Karl guessed, and short. More boyish than masculine. The balls were tight to his body, round, distinct, and the cock was small, what some would call pert. He was a platinum blond, which probably came from a bottle, but he had done the pubes as well, which were trimmed to a close-cropped V. He had piercings—a ball in his tongue and small rings, one in his left nipple, one in his navel, and one Karl had found under Dirk's balls that had elicited a very interesting Energizer Bunny effect in Dirk when Karl had gently pulled it with his teeth. There was, as far as Karl had determined, only the one tattoo, on the young man's lower right belly: the word, "baby," which, when he'd asked, Dirk had said, "As in your."

And that was pretty much what Karl saw in Dirk that would turn a lot of men on. Someone willing to be their baby.

Boyish, without being underage, compliant, experienced, and with a hole you could drive a truck into but that closed up tight to closely fit any cock inside it. He'd be quite an asset if he could be trained.

Karl sat and puffed as he watched Dirk dress, standing near the bed, not the least bit shy. He was dressing in leathers, as Karl had requested, in consideration for the operation at hand. And he had managed a sexy and vulnerable look with it. Black leather, form-fitting pants, with zipper down the butt crack as well as in front and also down the calves, and a half-length black leather vest that was held together, not fully covering his chest, though, with black lacings. The vest exposed his navel and that "baby" tattoo. Cute little black boots.

As Dirk was zipping up in all directions, Karl repeated the directions for the third time. "You remember where to pick it up—the Hengst Club on Kleistrasse in forty-five minutes. He'll proposition you and give you an envelope, and then you'll deliver it to the man stopping at the park bench in Volkspark and propositioning you. Then you're to be back here at 5:00 p.m. to report to me. Are you sure you have that?"

"Yes, yes."

Karl reached for his wallet on the nightstand and took out a wad of euros. "This should cover it all. Don't ask either of the men for money. Do the switch and move on afterward. Got that?"

"Yes," Dirk said. He hesitated, not knowing if the man would want a kiss or a compliment on his prowess before he left. This wasn't a usual trick. He hadn't even been told Karl would fuck him. He thought he'd just be getting the instructions. No matter, though. He decided a kiss wasn't needed and turned and left the room. Karl didn't call after him. He was busy looking for his cell phone.

"Lars," he said into the phone after he'd punched the numbers, "OK, it's all set up."

"I still just don't know," the man at the other end of the line said. "I'm still not sure of this. The trouble with this young man of yours—"

"It will work fine, Lars."

"You remembered to tell him the man passing on the envelope would be Middle Eastern, didn't you?—but not specifically Iranian."

"Yes, of course," Karl answered. But he'd given a quick assurance on that that he wasn't sure about. Had he actually told Dirk that? He couldn't remember.

"And there's something off with your whole scenario. A rent-boy and the gay district."

"We discussed this. It's the perfect cover."

"But you didn't tell him to actually have sex with his contacts, did you?"

"No, of course not." And this Karl was certain of. He hadn't said anything at all to Dirk about having sex with either the pick up or the drop off. He'd just said the men would proposition him, not actually demand to carry through with the sex. It was just so they'd fit in with the surroundings.

He had a little twinge about that, though. He'd been told to give Dirk instructions; he hadn't been told to fuck him. But Dirk was such a sweet little piece. Karl hadn't been able to resist. The young man had been so eager to please. And he *had* pleased Karl. Such a soft mouth.

Down at the entrance to the hotel, a beefy hand reached out and roughly pulled Dirk into the manager's office. The heavy-set man gathered Dirk in close to his body and glared down into the young man's face.

"You can't just do tricks here and not give me a cut," he said. "What kind of a hotel do you think this is?"

Both of them knew what kind of hotel this was. "It wasn't really a trick—well, not completely a trick. The man upstairs should have taken care of you."

"I don't work with 'the men upstairs,'" the man growled. Dirk turned his head away from the assault of the beer breath. "I work with the rent-boys. So, are you going to work with me?"

Dirk didn't have time to haggle and he was a bit upset that he'd said that it hadn't been the usual trick upstairs. He'd been told in no uncertain terms that this all was hush hush and in service to the country. He docilely let the man bend him over the desk, chuckle at finding there was a convenient zipper down his butt crack, and take his cut out in a quick butt fuck.

* * * *

The club named Hengst, German for "Stallion," on Kleistrasse, was just about as raunchy, all-out-there gay leather as you could find in Berlin. No doubt Karl chose it with the idea that the thoughts and attention of any men there would be as far away from espionage as one could possibly get. To Dirk, though, it was eye-popping opportunity.

Dirk felt suddenly sexy and as if he'd fallen into a candy store as soon as he had entered Hengst. He'd never been here before. He'd never realized that the gay scene could be so open and hedonist even in Berlin. The place was dimly lit and smoke filled. It wasn't crowded, but those who were here were really into the atmosphere—and into what was happening on the small stage at the other end of the room from the bar and down the shallow-stepped tiers.

Dirk backed up to the bar as he looked out over the crowd for his possible connection and was getting an overhead view of the stage action. And what was happening there was riveting. A young man, pretty much of the same type as Dirk himself, was playing a pole, Roman motif. He was wearing a short skirt and laced up gold sandals and had gold bands around his biceps and his forehead. Standing on either side of him as he worked on the pole were two bulky gladiators. In short order, as Dirk's time at the bar spun out, the three men were on a couch down there, with the pole dancer in the middle taking the cocks of the two gladiators in a shared hole.

The clientele was already pretty much ahead of the entertainment when Dirk arrived. Most of the tables on the tiers banking down to the stage were occupied by shadowy figures in various stages of copulation. The only table with only a single occupant was taken by a swarthy-looking, thin man, whose eyes lighted on Dirk as soon as the young man entered the room.

The swarthy stranger was half rising and beckoning to Dirk, but Dirk had backed into two strong arms at the bar, which gathered his small body into the barstool, where a massive leatherman was perched. He was a muscle-bound biker type, wearing a black leather vest over a hairy barrel chest; leather pants open at the crotch, with his privates covered by a leather codpiece. His costume was completed by black leather boots and a black leather beret-type hat.

The bruiser had taken possession of Dirk straightaway with no preliminaries. Dirk whispered, "Are you the man?"

"I'm the man for you, sweet cheeks," the hulk growled. Even while he answered he was unzipping Dirk's butt crack. It didn't take him long to release the pouch holding in his cock and balls, either, or to go to town by putting Dirk on the cock.

Must be my contact, Dirk, thought. He'll slip me the envelope while everyone thinks we're hot and heavy doing something else.

What the leatherman was slipping Dirk, though, was a massive cock. Remaining perched on the bar stool, he held the much smaller rent boy in front of him, encasing him in beefy, tattooed arms, a hand cupping Dirk's chin. Dirk moved his legs back on either side of the stool and leveraged off the front panel of the bar with his feet, fucking himself on the cock, at first waiting for the exchange to happen, but quite soon concentrating on the rough fuck and on the DP performance down on the stage.

This spying thing could be a lot of fun, he thought.

Another biker type cozied up to the bar next to the fucking pair in mid fuck and started participating to the extent the first big bruiser would let him. Stroking Dirk's body, kissing Dirk. Even kissing the other biker.

When the first biker had fired off, he released Dirk, who immediately found himself in the embrace of the second biker. The first one snapped up his crotch pouch and started to move off.

"Hey," Dirk called after him, "Don't you have something to—?"

"If you wanted to be paid, blondie, you should have said something off the top," the leatherman said, as he turned and kept on walking.

"Not money. Don't you have—?"

"I've got what you want, sweetie," The second biker said, holding Dirk tight to him and using his other hand to explore.

"Oh, good," Dirk said.

The biker threw Dirk over his shoulder and moved across the bar front to a doorway covered with a beaded curtain. He fucked Dirk against the wall in the dark hallway beyond, with Dirk's legs hooked on his hips and Dirk's arms around his neck.

He too, though, just zipped up and disappeared back through the beaded curtain after he was finished.

Dirk stumbled out into the main room, only then seeing the swarthy-looking man at a table a couple of tiers down toward the stage waving frantically at him.

As Karl had told Dirk the exchange would happen, the man unzipped Dirk's leather pants at the slit in the calf of the right leg, inserted an envelope, and then zipped the leg back up. The man had seemed a little nonplused when Dirk sat in his lap, facing him, and on his cock as he was making the exchange—but he didn't complain about the unexpected attention.

If his control had, in fact, told Dirk not to fuck his contacts, Dirk hadn't been listening.

* * * *

The man was already sitting on the designated bench in the Volkspark when Dirk sashayed up to him. Dirk smiled at the man, who gave a big smile back.

What a sweet little piece, the man thought. Just what he'd come into the park to pick up.

"You want me to give it to you here or over in those bushes there, where it will be more private?"

Although surprised at how direct Dirk was about it, the man naturally chose the bushes. Dirk knelt in front of him, giving him a blow job, which the man managed to interrupt before he erupted. He put Dirk on all fours and rode him hard. That butt crack zipper of Dirk's was getting a real workout today.

After they were done, Dirk unzipped the leg of his calf and extracted the envelope. "Here, this is for you."

"For me?" The man asked, bewildered. He knew they hadn't set on a price, but he'd naturally expected that he'd be the one to be paying.

"I don't think—"

"Here. Take it. This is for you."

"Well, OK." The man took the envelope, flattered that the little honey had taken him for a male prostitute—one that he wanted to fuck with. He stuffed it in his pocket without looking inside, zipped up his fly, and left Dirk there to zip himself up in various places and to relace his vest. The man had gotten to feel up the little honey real well. Dirk had rather enjoyed that. He had an hour and a half to kill and he already was in the park, which was a good pickup spot.

Might as well make some more money while he was waiting to hook up with Karl again in the hotel.

Another man was sitting at the same bench when Dirk came out of the bushes.

Dirk was going to pass him by, though, because the man was glowering as he looked at his watch. Obviously something was late in working out for him. He looked up and saw Dirk and motioned him over.

"Got something for me?" he asked when Dirk came over.

"Maybe, but it'll cost you," Dirk answered.

Little bastard, the man thought. Just like someone new to this to try to shake him down. Lars had told him this one was wet behind the ears. But a real honey he was. Would sure like to dip into that, the man thought. "How much?" he asked, curious on how big the shakedown would be.

Dirk named a price. It didn't seem like much.

"OK. So, give."

"How about in those bushes over there?"

"Sure, if that's what you want."

Dirk had dropped down in front of the man and had his cock fished out and was swallowing it before the man knew what was happening. The thought of Dirk being a really nice little piece swam up to blot out whatever else the man was thinking of, so that, twenty minutes later he was just finishing up fucking Dirk in the missionary position under the bushes.

"OK, so now, where's the envelope you were supposed to give me?" the man said as he was standing over Dirk, pulling his trousers up, zipping up, and buckling his belt.

"The envelope?" Dirk said, a frown crossing his face.

* * * *

Karl was lying on the bed in the Axelhaus hotel room, smoking a cigarette and fingering a condom packet when his cell phone buzzed. He turned and looked at his watch that he'd placed on the nightstand next to the phone. Dirk should be along in a few minutes. Karl was ready for him. In for a penny, in for a pound, he thought. He'd fucked the young man before sending him off; there'd be no reason not to fuck when he came back, as well. Different controllers handled their assets in different ways. It was just the sort of discipline the rent-boy understood. Or so Karl rationalized his desire to dip his stick again.

"Hello."

"Karl, you dumb shit. Do you know where your asset for this operation is right now?"

"He should be along in a few minutes," Karl answered, stung a bit by what Lars had called him. But they'd never been what you could call friends. Lars never had given him full credit for his contribution to the intell operations.

"No, he's not going to be along in a few minutes, Karl. He's right here . . . hey, you two stop that stuff." The last phrase sounded dimmer, like it was directed away from the telephone.

"Excuse me?"

"He fucked it up, Karl. He gave the envelope to the wrong man. And he bumbled the handoff in the club too. Whose idea was it to send a little honeypot into a leatherman fuck club and expect him to be inconspicuous?"

"Shit."

"Hey, I said to knock it off over there. Shit!"

"What's that, Lars? Who are you talking to?"

226

"The agent who brought the rent-boy in is spiking him over in the corner. Your Dirk is in his lap, fucking himself on the man's dick. Neither one of them listening to me. What sort of pants are those, anyway, with a zipper up the butt?"

"Listen, Lars, how was I to know—?"

"You fucked him before sending him off on the operation, didn't you? You're there naked now, waiting for him to check back in and lay down and open his legs for you, aren't you? You picked a randy rent-boy just to get your rocks off at government expense, didn't you?"

Karl, flooded with guilt, dropped the condom packet he was fingering and pulled the bedspread up to cover his nakedness—like the phone had a camera or something. "No, of course not," he answered indignantly. "But the envelope. How much damage—?"

"No damage except to our budget and time, Karl. And you know why there's no intell damage? I told you your operation plan was off the wall. Do you think I'd just let this little fucker . . . I said knock that off you two . . . waltz out there on a real operation without a trial? It was just an exercise, Karl. Nothing important was being passed. But the very next time you want to let your dick plan an operation, think back on this one."

"I think it was a good idea, Lars. Using a rent-boy is a good operational plan."

"But picking one who is so randy he has a zipper up his butt isn't a good plan, Karl. You were thinking with your dick. And then throwing him into sex pits. . . . You know what the trouble with your Dirk is, don't you?"

"I have a notion you're going to tell me."

"The trouble with Dirk is that you picked someone who would open his legs for any man, any time, and lose track of the operation . . . and . . . and who has a zipper up his butt."

"You gonna spike him too?" Karl asked.

"No comment," was the reply.

Thorodian Horse

Old King Severmist of the Orgas stood on a rock outcropping on the sea side of the pass through the Golden Mountains down into the rich plains of Thorodia and shook his fists in frustration and despair. For the third time in as many days the frontal assault on the High Castle of King Kleemus had failed.

"How much longer will you hold against my might?" the old king roared. "Two long years. See this beard? It nigh reaches the ground and is as gray as the skies over your winter land."

"Perhaps it is time to suggest just going around the castle and down into the valley, sire," one of the king's advisers said timidly, cowering at the king's side. Unfortunately, he had come too close, though, and, with one swipe of his mail-encased hand, the king slapped him across the path, from whence he did not rise.

The king knew they could not continue this siege for two more years. His own health would not permit it. He would not live to enter Thorodia then, and all would be lost without him at the helm.

"The high castle remains the key," he growled. "It is the strongest point in Thorodia. If we take the castle, all of the rest in the valley will open their doors to us. If not, it is a fight on every doorstep and a lance at our backs, between us and the

229

sea. We must have the castle. Must I do the thinking for us all? Is there no one here with the wit to follow on from me?"

"Father," a small voice spoke up from the shadows, "Might I—?"

"Why be you here?" the king cried out, almost in anguish. "You belong in the train with the women and the other women in men's clothes. How dare you attend and speak out. Better yet, get you to the High Castle. From what is reported to me, those within are sodomites all."

"We have Raum in the castle. Perhaps we—"

"Be damned and be gone with you, pup. It is because of you that Raum is there. I'll have no more words from you, boy."

And then all was silent as the shadows of night descended on the pass from the sea through the Golden Mountains and down into Thorodia, and the lights in the High Castle yet burned, telling of comfort and safety.

* * * *

The Grand Marshal of Thorodia, the man closest to King Kleemus and his principal military adviser, the man who had devised and carried out the successful defense of Thorodia against the invading barbarian from the sea in close consort with his king for the past two years, was galloping through the forest at the valley base of the High Castle with his small band of hunters, bringing home venison. The Grand Marshal distained the forces of the Orgas and went out on these forays on purpose to show those under siege in the High Castle how safe they were in his hands. Few raiding parties ventured beyond the castle and down into the valley, and the Grand Marshal's spies knew when they were afoot.

But on the road to the castle, the Grand Marshal pulled his horse up and his lip curled up. Here was something he had not been apprised of. Heads would roll for overlooking this.

Off on the side of the trail he spied a gypsy wagon, turned on its side, its contents strewn out around it and obviously the subject of pillage.

The Grand Marshal trotted over to the wagon, its scarlet and yellow wheels still spinning, and reached down and jerked an arrow out of the undercarriage and lifted it up for all to see.

"Double-edged point," said one minion.

"Red feather," said another.

"An arrow of the Orga," chimed in a third.

The Grand Marshal nodded his head in grim agreement. The Orga were becoming bolder. They were foraying too far into the valley. And his spies had missed this intrusion.

All of the riders were startled by the sound of a groan—coming from under the upturned wagon. Quick as a dart, two of the minions dismounted and, with all of their strength, lifted the wagon, and a third pulled out the body of a young man.

The rescuer turned him over on his back, and the Grand Marshal's heart leapt in his chest and his cock stood at immediate attention.

The young man was beautifully built and provocatively displayed. He was blond, and slight and lithe—a dancer's body, with every part perfectly formed. An achingly beautiful face, with full, rosy lips and tussled golden curls cascading down to his shoulders. He was nearly naked, stripped to the waist, gold belted, and wearing diaphanous, billowing pantaloons of some white material shot through with threads of gold. He had gold snake bracelets encircling his biceps and gold rings in his nipples, and, as could clearly be seen, a gold ring in the bulb of his cock as well.

"Does he live?" The Grand Marshal asked in a strained voice, and upon hearing an assent, he dismounted and moved in one graceful, fluid motion to where the young man lay.

"Lay him on the carriage body," he commanded, and the young man was lifted and laid on his back on the edge of the carriage.

The Grand Marshal withdrew his dirk knife and gathered up the flimsy material of the young man's pantaloons at the crotch in one fist and slit through the material with the knife he held in the other hand. Sheathing his knife, he spread the young man's legs with hands fisting his ankles.

With the first strong thrust of his engorged cock in the young man's channel, the youth's watery-blue eyes opened in shock and he cried out in the taking. "Oh, oh, Lord. Nay, please I beg you. I have never . . . Oh, no, I am undone." His cries turned to moans and groans, as the Grand Marshal's minions just stood about, looking at the ground—when they weren't stealing furtive looks at the taking of the young man. No one raised a hand to stay the Grand Marshal. He was the second-most powerful man in the land, his blood and lust ran hot, and—save for deference to King Kleemus himself—he took his pleasures when and with whom he would.

The young golden god's cries of undoing changed in short order to cries for the fuck. He arched his back and raised his pelvis and started meeting the Grand Marshal's relentless thrustings with counterthrusts of his own. He cried out of the Grand Marshal's artistry and mastery of the cocking and of how he'd never known it could be like this and how much he loved the movement of the Grand Marshal's superior member deep inside him. He writhed and trembled and shuddered beneath the onslaught of the old warrior, and his small hands reached out and caressed the thick matting of hair on the Grand Marshal's chest. He reached up and palmed the back of the old warrior's neck, brought his face down to his, and opened his sweet lips to the invasion of the Grand Marshal's tongue.

Not long before the Grand Marshal experienced the longest and strongest ejaculation of his recent memory, the young god had given up his own seed with the rubbing of his gold-ringed cock head on the old man's still-hard belly.

By the time the climax ensued, an objective observer would be hard pressed to suppose just who had fucked who—and the Grand Marshal was hopelessly smitten.

The young man, Cleus by name, and a wandering musician and dancer by claimed trade, was taken up to the castle and installed in the Grand Marshal's apartments, where the Grand Marshal became besotted with watching him dance and then fucking him day and night until it became clear to

King Kleemus that he was not being as fully attended as he once had been by his principal adviser. This did not necessarily set well with the king.

The king was not the only one who had taken notice of this change in circumstance. His young attendant and sometimes lover, the barbarian Raum, had also heard rumors of the young, enticing god living in the Grand Marshal's apartments, a handsome young dancer with watery blue eyes, full rosy lips, and golden rings at the nipples and cock head. Raum knew of only one person in the world who met this description. He therefore availed himself of the first opportunity to seek the now-infamous youth out. That opportunity came with the first hunting foray the Grand Marshal made—now reluctantly made—out of the castle since he had happened upon the young lover who had melted years off his felt age and made his penis a strong sword upon demand once more.

Cleus was gliding along the corridor in the Grand Marshal's apartments that afternoon, when a strong hand reached out from behind a hanging tapestry and pulled the young man into the darkness behind. Raum devoured Cleus' lips with fervent kisses. Cleus, in turn, climbed Raum's pelvis with his thighs, and Raum fucked him deeply and long, pushing Cleus against the wall of the castle behind the shimmering tapestry and bouncing the shoulder blades of his prey mercilessly against the hard stone.

Thus were reunited the lovers—the son of King Severmist, who had discovered his only son in the embrace of one of his foremost warriors, Raum, who had been banished to the almost certain death of spying inside the besieged High Castle of the Thorodians as long as his wits could keep him alive.

Afterward the two slithered off to Raum's own humble room, and Raum gave Cleus a proper and prolonged fucking, Cleus on his back, legs akimbo and pelvis thrust up to received Raum's young, strong cocking, being ridden hard and for a great distance in contrast to the old Grand Marshal's almost pitiful pokings, and Raum stroking Cleus to multiple comings with thumb rubbing piss slit through the center of the golden cock ring.

"What are you doing here?" Raum asked through heavy breathing after they had spent themselves and were embracing, each part of them held as closely together as possible. "It would be the death of you if you were discovered. Did the Grand Marshal capture you without realizing who he had?"

"Nay, the Grand Marshal captured me because I meant him to," Cleus answered. And then he laughed. He became immediately more serious, though. "We are getting nowhere with this siege, and the time of King Severmist's passing is close at hand. I am the rightful heir, and I mean to step into my rightful place, unopposed, by delivering Thorodia to the Orgas at long last."

"A heavy task," Raum whispered, his voice displaying his fear for his young lover. "You have seen how it is with the Thorodians. How strong Thorodia is."

"But not as strong as it was before I came," Cleus said.

"What do you mean? What are you planning? What can I do to help?"

"Many questions, and I love you all the more, Raum, master of my seed, for your last question, couching within it your pledge of loyalty to me and my kingship. What we must do is divide King Kleemus and the Grand Marshal. The strength of Thorodia has been their strong union. I have already started weakening that. And then I must be put within striking distance of the king at the right moment. There are, indeed, actions you can take to serve those ends."

"Command my hand, my liege," Raum said.

"Fuck my hole; mingle your seed with mine" Cleus countered, and then both young men laughed, as Raum proceeded to do just that.

* * * *

From that point began the campaign of Cleus and Raum to divide the Thorodians' strength.

The king was already irritated at the Grand Marshal's unaccustomed absences, and while Cleus made sure that the

Grand Marshal was abed fucking him as much of the time as possible, Raum was working on the king, asking him if he knew of the new, young, mesmerizing dancer the Grand Marshal had acquired. Asking the king if the Grand Marshal had ever offered to share the delights of watching Cleus perform.

The king had not been so invited. Indeed, before Raum started mentioning the possibility, he'd never thought of this being a slight at all. But the king was already just a bit unhappy with the Grand Marshal, and now he wanted to assert his kingship.

He commanded the Grand Marshal to bring the dancer Cleus before him in a private audience of just the three of them. And the Grand Marshal, seeing nothing amiss afoot, quickly brought the young Cleus, perfumed, fluffed up, and sensuously costumed, forth to the king's private chambers.

Cleus danced a dance of passion and provocative display for the king, a dance that wound up with Cleus only in a golden belt, his gold snake bicep bracelets, his nipple and cock rings, and a warm smile on his face and a fluttering of his long eyelashes over watery blue eyes, his face turned toward the king, but his channel lowered into the lap of the overcome-with-lust Grand Marshal.

Three days later, at the king's strong suggestion, the Grand Marshal ventured out on another one of his hunting trips into the forests on the valley side of the High Castle. When he returned, however, he found the gates of the castle closed to him and a large force of the Orga coming over the hill.

The king was not seen out of his apartments for two weeks after that, busy as he was in discovering the charms of his new lover, the dancer Cleus.

Toward the end of that period, the king found Cleus lying on his couch, naked and despondent one afternoon. The king dropped his own robes and came in beside Cleus and lifted his young lover's leg and thrust a cock that hadn't been this hard for anyone in years into the young god's passage. Although Cleus returned his kisses and murmured his love and devotion and praised the masterful cocking of the king, though, the king sensed a continued despondency.

"What is wrong, little one? I sense you are sad."

"It is only thinking of the future, sire. I want nothing more than for this to go on forever—your magnificent strong cock showing me new avenues to paradise daily. But where is it going? What is to become of us? The barbarians are at the gate. I fear for our lives. I could not bear our lives to change from what we have become."

"Never fear, my love," the king said. "I have a secret."

"A secret?" Cleus asked, his eyes full of innocence. He turned his face to the king's and nibbled on his ear, while his hand went to the king's rouged nipples.

"Yes, a secret. A secret passageway. We can escape into the mountains whenever we need to. And I have another, hidden castle in the mountains, not far from here, and stronger than this one. We are safe. We will always be safe."

"A secret passageway?" Cleus repeated.

"Yes, I will show it to you. A passageway to a water gate coming out in a cave by a mountain stream."

And, after Cleus had fucked the king to heaven once more, the king, indeed, showed Cleus the passageway to safety. And Cleus showed Raum the passageway that could be used in either direction. And Raum, on a clear night within the week, when he was standing duty on the castle walls at the sea side, shot off the fire arrow with message attached that was a prearranged one-way communications means between the forces of King Severmist's Orgas and their spy within the High Castle.

And on the night that the army of King Severmist crept into the cave beside the mountain stream and under the castle walls and into the very center of the castle keep, Cleus was abed with the king of the Thorodians.

Cleus was on his back with King Kleemus knelt between his legs, sheathing his sword inside Cleus' channel. And at the first hint of the sounds Cleus was waiting to hear, he unsheathed his own dirk knife from under one of the pillows and sheathed it again up through the underbelly of the king of the Thorodians. He was standing, in robes of gold, beside the bed of the dead king, taking on a kingly stance as the

236

forces of the Orgas—his forces—rushed in the room to celebrate the victory of Prince Cleus—soon to be King Cleus—over the Thorodians, undeniably won by wit and cleverness where brute force could not prevail.

~

About the Author

Habu is one of the pen names of a former supersonic spy jet pilot, intelligence agent, male model, movie actor, and diplomat. A wild youth in South East Asia was spent enjoying whatever sexual opportunities came his way, and much of his gay male writing is about recalling incidents from those days and inventing ones he'd perhaps have liked to experience. He now leads a very quiet and ordinary happily married family life.

An American, he is a published mainstream novelist and short story writer under another name and in another dimension of his life. He has written or cowritten (with Sabb) approaching 1,000 published short stories and over 100 published erotica e-books, primarily of gay fiction but also memoir, straight fiction and ménage fiction. His hand and creative writing can be seen in stories and books by habu, sr71plt, Dirk Hessian, Shabbu, and Stephen Kessel—among unrevealed others that might surprise readers. The fictionalized GM memoir *Flying High, Diving Deep* is loosely based on his life experiences. He can be found at the adults only gay male site BarbarianSpy, which he shares with Sabb and Dirk Hessian.

You can send feedback about this e-book directly to habu, or send general feedback on this e-book to BarbarianSpy.

Our authors always like to receive feedback, and appreciate it when readers post reviews at distributors and other sites.

BarbarianSpy

FOR LITERARY HEAT

Not all books listed below may currently be on release.
* indicates the book is available in paperback and e-book.

BOOKS BY DIRK HESSIAN
Xtreme Erotica
The King's Men
Shores of Tripoli
Prophecy of Noto
Pretender's Fate
General Erotica/Romance
Fire Down the Valley*
Constantinople*
The Beautiful Way*
Blue and Gray
Colonel's Treasure
Beginning of Time
Labyrinth

BOOKS BY HABU
Gay Erotica
Memoir Faction
Flying High, Diving Deep*
Xtreme Erotica
Apyko: The Greek Pimp
Visits of the Schlange
Second Coming: Emile La Cour Unleashed
Vortex: Sacrificed by Curiosity*
Dark Angel Sounding *(in e-book & included in Sounding:Ultimate Control Paperback)**
Sounding: Ultimate Control (*Print Only*)*
Sounding Five *(in e-book & included in Sounding:Ultimate Control paperback)**

General Erotica
Romance
Trading Partners (Valentines Day)
Friday Nights with Lenny (Christmas Romance)
Snowy, Snowy Nights (Christmas Romance)
Four Coins
Lower Than the Heart (Valentines Day)
Brambleton
Gotta Keep Trying
Finding Amnad
Platres Conclave
Other Novels/Novellas
Cruising Gigolo (bisexual)
Prepared in Cape Verdi
Gilded Cage
House on Park
Anything for Ambition
Dance of the Ravishers
Hard Knocks U*
My Neighbor's Spa*
Man's Man: Tales of a High Priced Gay Hooker*
Trip Money
Clint Folsom Mysteries Compendium Volume 1*
Death to Blonds - Stolen Judgment (Clint Folsom
Mystery)*
Clint Folsom Mysteries Compendium Volume 2*
The Indian Doctor
Sailorboy
Home to Fire Island
Choke Hold
Gay Erotica Anthologies
Spy Tails 001*
Spy Tails 002*
Doubled*
Doubled Again*
Tails in the Tropics*
Tails in the Med*

Tails in the West*
Rough Riders*
Grab Bag 1*
Grab Bag 2*
Grab Bag 3*
Grab Bag 4*
Grab Bag 5*
Beyond the Beaded Curtain*
Habu's Christmas Balls
The Sporting Life*
Fetish Galore!*
Literary Gay Erotica
Cairo Surrender*
The Handyman*
Homeward Bound
Journey to Mirage*
Menage Erotica
Cruising Gigolo
13 Ways for Halloween
Luther*
The Indian Prince
Literary GLBT Fiction
Summer of Denial
BOOKS BY SHABBU
Velvet Interrogation
Finding Jason
Dirty Pool
Operation Black Jade
Cigars!*
Angel in the Barn
Gayly Complicated*
Despoiling David
The Tree of Idleness*
I Met a Man
Rough Road to Happiness
BOOKS BY SABB
Hiring in Hollywood
The Legend of Holleystone Grange

Surprise Encounters
She is He
Wrong Man
Loyal to his King
Barbarian Tales - Book One - Traveler's Tales*
Barbarian Tales - Book Two - Journeys Begin*
Barbarian Tales - Book Three - The Inheritance*
Barbarian Tales - Book Four - Road to Persepolis*